The Pirate

THE PIRATE

The City of Dreams
Book Two

The Scottish novelist Joan Fallon, currently lives and works in the south of Spain. She writes both contemporary and historical fiction, and almost all her books have a strong female protagonist. **She is the author of:**

FICTION:
Spanish Lavender
The House on the Beach
Loving Harry
Santiago Tales
The Only Blue Door
Palette of Secrets
The Thread That Binds Us
Love Is All

The al-Andalus series:
The Shining City (Book 1)
The Eye of the Falcon (Book 2)
The Ring of Flames (Book 3)

The City of Dreams series
The Apothecary (Book 1)

NON-FICTION:
Daughters of Spain

(all are available in paperback and as ebooks)

www.joanfallon.co.uk

JOAN FALLON

THE PIRATE

SCOTT PUBLISHING
(ESPAÑA)

ACKNOWLEDGMENTS

My sincere thanks to my editor Sara Starbuck for helping me to create an exciting novel out of a turbulent period in history, to Angela Hagenow for her excellent proof reading and to Lawston Designs for the cover. Their advice and support have been invaluable.

HISTORICAL CHARACTERS

Ali ibn Hammud al-Nasir Khalifa of Qurtubah 1016 -1018

His eldest son:

Yahya ibn Ali ibn Hammud al-Mutali, Khalifa of Qurtuba 1021-1023 and 1025-1026 and Khalifa of Malaqah 1026-1035 (Yahya 1)

His second son:

Idris ibn Ali al-Mutaayyad Khalifa of Malaqah 1035-1039 (Idris 1)

Eldest son of Yahya I and Fatima:

Hasan ibn Yahya ibn Ali Khalifa of Malaqah 1040-1042

Second son of Yahya I and Fatima:

Idris ibn Yahya ibn Ali (Ben Yahya) Khalifa of Malaqah 1042 -47 (Idris II)

Sons of Idris I:

Muhammad ibn Idris ibn Ali ruler of al-Jazira

Yahya ibn Idris (Yahya II)

Abu al-Qasim Muhammad ibn Abbad, Abbad I ruler of Isbiliya

Badis ben Habus sultan of Garnata

Samuel ibn Nagrilla was a Jewish scholar, poet and politician, grand vizier to rulers of Garnata

Naja al-Siqlabi an ex-slave who became tutor to the sons of Yahya I

Ibn Baqanna grand vizier to Idris I

Mujahid al-Amiri, Sultan of Dénia

Abd Allah ibn Aglab, governor of the Balearic Islands

Zuhair, sultan of Álmeria

MAIN FICTIONAL CHARACTERS
Makoud ibn Qasim
Abal and Basma (his wives)
Umar ibn Makoud
Ibrahim ibn Makoud
Dirar ibn Makoud
his daughter Aisha bint Makoud
his son-in-law Bakr ibn Assam
General Rashad
Admiral al-Maraghi
Avi, Jewish merchant and friend of Makoud
Captain Mustafa Bey

PLACE NAMES

Al-Andalus the Islamic name given to Moorish Spain

Alboran Sea the part of the Mediterranean near Málaga

Al-Jazira the city of Algeciras

Garnata the city of Granada

Isbiliya the city of Seville

Écija, a town between Córdoba and Seville

Jebel al-Tarik Gibraltar

Maghreb the region of North West Africa bordering the Mediterranean Sea

Malaqah the city of Málaga

Mayurqa, the island of Mallorca

Medina Mayurqa Palma Mallorca

Middle Sea one name for the Mediterranean

Mursiya, the taifa of Murcia

Qadis the city of Cádiz

Qarmuña the city of Carmona

Qartayannat al-Halfa the city of Cartagena

Qurtubah the city of Córdoba

Sea of Darkness one name for the Atlantic Ocean

Sebta the town of Ceuta in North Africa

For Ray,
without whose love and support none of these
books would have been written.

At times of distress, strengthen your heart,
Even if you stand at death's door.
The lamp has light before it is extinguished.
Wounded lions still know how to roar.

Samuel ibn Naghrila (11th century Jewish poet)

MALAQAH

1039 - 1040 AD

CHAPTER 1

Bakr opened his eyes to total blackness, not the darkness of a starless night but that of a pitch-black hole, with no chink of light to alleviate it. Where the hell was he? His head was pounding and when he tried to sit up he realised that he was bound hand and foot, face down in the slimy hold of a ship. Gradually, as his senses returned to him, he became aware of the gentle roll of the sea; they were anchored in sheltered water.

A low groan came from somewhere on his right. He wasn't alone.

'Who's there?' he whispered.

'Bakr? Is that you. Thanks be to Allah. I thought you were dead and I was alone in this infernal place.'

'Asim? What happened? Where are we?' Asim was the yard's foreman.

'Don't you remember anything? The pirate ship? Nothing?'

'No, my mind is a blank and my head is pounding as if all the devils in hell were hammering in it.'

'Not surprised. Gave you a pretty heavy blow, they did. Wonder they didn't kill you. I thought they had by the way you went down. Like a poleaxed bull.'

'So it was pirates?'

'Looked like that to me. To be honest it was all over so fast I didn't take much in. Too busy fighting them off. Then the next thing I knew there was a sack over my head and some big bugger had me over his shoulder.'

Despite the situation Bakr had to smile; Asim was as round as he was tall. It would have had to have been a strong man to lift him.

'How many did they take?' he asked.

'As far as I know, just you, me and Kamil; he's in here somewhere. Probably still unconscious. Or dead.'

Bakr needed a moment to process all this news. Pirate raids were nothing new along the coast; in fact they were a regular and costly occurrence. Thieves and cutthroats by another name, that's all they were. No-one was safe from them and the khalifa's navy were useless at controlling them.

But why them? Pirates usually attacked merchant ships, or kidnapped women and children to sell as slaves in North Africa. Sometimes the less successful ones raided the coastal villages for food and anything else worth taking, but to attack a shipbuilding yard; this seemed odd. And during the day, too. At night the yard was securely locked and Bakr paid a couple of ex-soldiers to patrol the area in case anyone tried to break in. He had never expected an attack first thing in the morning.

He pulled at his bonds but only succeeded in making them bite deeper into his flesh. A stream of oaths flew off his lips as he struggled to get free.

'There's no point trying to get loose, sayyad. I've been trying for the last hour and almost cut my hands off in the attempt. It's impossible.'

'So you've been awake the whole time?' asked Bakr.

'Yes, more's the pity. I've envied you and Kamil, lying there snoring away in peaceful oblivion.'

'Well man, what have you learnt about where we are?'

'I have a good idea. If you remember the wind was coming from the west this morning. When they set sail they had the wind behind them, so I reckon they're heading east.'

'And then where?'

'Well, they will want to keep close to the shore so they will either turn south and head for North Africa or go north.'

'The Balearic Islands?'

'That would be my guess. If they were headed for North Africa they would have sailed south when they left Malaqah.'

'But where are we now? How long have we been sailing?' asked Bakr.

'Well, it's hard to tell when you're shut in this filthy hold, with no glimpse of the sky, but the fact that my stomach is empty and my body thinks it's time to go to sleep, I'd guess that we've been sailing all day and it's now night-time.'

'And how far is it to the Balearic Islands, with a fair wind behind us?' Bakr paused, calculating the maximum speed of a boat such as this. He had a fair idea of what kind of vessel it was and its top speed would be five or six Arab miles an hour; he hadn't spent all his life building ships not to be able to identify those favoured by the pirates. For them speed and manoeuvrability were important for survival. Without a doubt this would have a shallow draught so it could make its way inland, rowing up river to attack local villages. It would need to be fast and light, with one or maybe two sails and a couple of defensive towers on the deck. There would be little accommodation for the pirates, all the space was required for the oars. In fact they were probably being held in the only storage space available on board ship.

'Four hundred Arab miles? Maybe a bit more. Can't tell how long it will take to get there. Depends if we're making any more stops. This is the first one so far and I guess we're here for the night.'

'So according to you we were captured early morning?' Bakr tried to remember what he'd been doing when they struck. The last image he could bring to mind was that of his wife as he kissed her goodbye after breakfast. It was all a blank after that.

'Yes. You were checking the hull of the new ship we're building for the khalifa. Kamil and I were finishing the caulking. We wanted to get it done early so it had plenty of time to dry.'

'And that's when they attacked?'

'Yes. There was a thick mist rolling in from the sea; that's why we never saw them. The next thing I knew you were lying on your back and Kamil was screeching like a wounded parrot.'

'So that must have been about six o'clock. And your stomach estimates that it's twelve hours or more since it's had any food?'

'At least.'

'And how long have we been anchored here?'

'Maybe an hour. It's hard to say. Time has little meaning when you're in the dark like this.'

'Very well. So we've travelled about sixty nautical miles?'

'And all the time with the wind in our favour.'

'So maybe a bit further, but still heading for the Balearic Islands.'

The sound of sniffling and grunting came from the darkness; Kamil was waking up. 'Is that you, Asim? Are you all right?' he asked, his voice shaking a little.

'He's fine, but like the rest of us he's tied hand and foot,' said Bakr. 'What about you, lad? Can you loosen your ropes at all?'

'Sayyad. You're not dead.' It sounded as though the young apprentice was going to break into sobs of relief.

'I certainly hope not. I'm planning on going to paradise when I die, not a smelly hell hole like this.'

'Someone's coming,' said Asim.

They heard the creak of bolts as the heavy door was lifted. Bakr blinked, momentarily blinded as someone thrust a lighted torch in and peered down at them.

'So you're awake,' the pirate said and slid down a short ladder into the hold. He stuck the torch into a rickety holder on the side of the ship and looked at them. 'Which of you is the boss?' he barked. He was an enormous man, wearing only loose pantaloons fastened with a scarlet sash and an embroidered waistcoat which revealed a body built for strength. His muscular arms gleamed in the torchlight; this must have been the man who carried Asim onto the ship.

'That's me,' said Bakr, wondering what was coming next.

'Right.'

The pirate pulled a curved blade out of his belt and leant over him. Bakr could feel his stomach churning. Was this it? Was he going to die lying there with his face in bilge water? Was this to be his ignominious end? Never to see his beautiful Aisha again? He felt the man grab his hands and pull them backwards. Next thing he knew he'd been cut loose. He rolled over and pulled himself into a sitting position, unable to believe that he was still alive. The pirate was doing the same to the other two. Asim sat staring at him and rubbing his wrists. None of them spoke.

'Eat,' said the pirate and threw them a loaf of flat bread and some dried fish. Then he passed a flagon of water to Bakr and said, 'Drink.'

The water was slightly salty but it tasted as good as any he'd ever drunk before. He passed it to Asim. 'What's wrong?' he whispered, concerned because his foreman continued to stare at him.

'It's your face,' he said. 'It's covered in blood.'

Bakr put his hand to his face and felt the dried blood. Then he touched his head; the sharp pain made him cry out. There was a wound as long as a hand's span stretching from his forehead and back through his hair. Blood continued to seep out of it and stain his turban.

The pirate took no more notice of them; he picked up the torch and within seconds they were once again in the dark.

'What are we going to do?' asked Kamil.

'Not much we can do, lad. Not at the moment,' said Asim.

'The question is, why did they take us? What do they want us for? They might get something for you two in a slave market, but me? I'm too old to fetch a good price. So why us?' said Bakr.

'Can't we try to escape?' asked Kamil, his voice decidedly shaky.

'Where would we go, that's if we could get out of this locked hold and past thirty armed pirates? No, lad, there's no chance of escape until we reach our destination,' said Asim.

'If we're right and we're heading for the Balearic Islands, it's going to take the best part of a week to get there. Maybe longer if we stop every night,' said Bakr. The thought of a week sitting in the cold and the dark was not good. The next time the pirate came down with their food he'd demand to see the captain. There was a reason that they were here and still alive. Pirates were infamous for taking no prisoners for the very simple reason that space on board was limited. So why were they using up valuable storage space with three men of no obvious value to them?

CHAPTER 2

Aisha was bathing the baby when she heard someone calling her name.

'Aisha. Aisha, where are you? Something terrible has happened.' It was Hala, the wife of one of the men who worked for Bakr.

'Just a moment.' She picked the chubby child out of the bath water and patted his body dry. Then she quickly smeared a little oil on his skin and wrapped him in his blanket.

By the time she got to the door, her mother-in-law and her sisters-in-law were already there.

'Pirates,' screamed her mother-in-law. 'Pirates.'

'What about pirates?' Aisha asked, turning cold at the thought that something awful had happened to Bakr.

'Oh, Aisha, the pirates have kidnapped the sayyad and two of his men. They've gone. Disappeared,' said Hala

'Dead. He'll be dead. Oh my darling boy,' cried her mother-in-law, beating her chest in anguish and letting the tears run down her cheeks unheeded. Rayya and Rudaba just stared at her in silence, uncomprehending. The baby, sensing everyone's distress, began to howl.

'Come in, Hala. Now sit down and tell me everything,' Aisha said with all the serenity she could muster. She turned to Rayya and said, 'Please bring some tea for Hala.' Her sister-in-law moved away to do as she was asked, but not before scowling at Aisha. Although nothing was said openly, the two sisters who still lived at home resented Bakr's new wife and did little to hide it.

'This morning it happened. Sadan saw it all. They came out of the mist and headed for the new boat, where the men were working. There were four of them. Pirates, he said. Armed to the teeth. They took Bakr, his foreman and the young apprentice. It all happened so fast that nobody could do anything,' Hala blurted out, tears running down her cheeks.

Aisha's mother-in-law let out a long moan.

'Nobody else? They took nobody else?' Aisha asked, rocking the baby gently in her arms. 'Why them? What will they do with them?' She knew little of pirates except that they were cruel, vicious men. Why would they want Bakr and two of his workers? It didn't make sense. Her eyes filled with tears and it was all she could do to stop herself breaking down and sobbing. She loved her husband and the thought that he might be dead terrified her. But this wasn't the time to lose control. There would be time enough for that when she was alone in her room. Now she had to remain strong if she was to do anything to help Bakr and his family.

She took a deep breath. 'Well, Hala?'

Hala shook her head. 'I don't know, Aisha,' she whispered, wiping her eyes.

'What about the yard? Are the men still working,' she asked.

'No, of course not. They've gone home. Why would they work when they won't get paid?' asked Hala, obviously surprised at the question.

'But the new ship. Bakr promised the khalifa that it would be ready by the new moon.'

'Well I can't see that happening now, without Bakr,' said Rudaba. 'How can you worry about the business at a time like this? Your husband's been kidnapped. It's no time to be talking about new ships and delivery times.'

'It's for that very reason. It is Bakr's business. It's what pays for us all to live here, you, his mother, his children. He has given his life to building that business. I'm not going to let it collapse now. When he comes home I want him to see that we have looked after it, that we never gave up hope that he would return. Now you can lock yourself in your room and cry for him as though he were dead, but don't expect me to join you. My husband will be back and when he is I want him to see that we have cared for what is his.'

Rudaba didn't reply, but flounced out of the room and slammed the door to show her anger. Aisha was mistress of the house and in Bakr's absence her word was law.

'Is Sadan at home? Maybe I should speak to him?' she asked Hala.

'Oh, no. You mustn't get involved at the yard. The men won't like it.'

Aisha remembered the day she had shown an interest in Bakr's business; as tactfully as he could he'd made it clear that women were not allowed in the shipyard because the men saw it as bad luck. So Hala was right; it would do no good to go there herself. But that didn't mean that someone else couldn't go on her behalf.

'Mama, can you look after the baby for me; he's due for his morning sleep. I must go and speak to my father right away.'

'I will, Aisha, but you must heed what your friend says; women mustn't get involved in business that is not theirs,' said her mother-in-law, wiping her eyes and taking the baby from Aisha.

That child was the one thing that bound her to Aisha. She loved her new grandchild and considered it a blessing that she was a grandmother again after believing that Bakr would never remarry.

'I won't be long,' said Aisha, picking up her djellaba and wrapping it around her shoulders.

As she walked through the narrow streets that led to her father's apothecary shop, she thought back to the day she had first met Bakr. Her father had asked her to help him treat one of his customers who had a bad cut on his leg. She had barely given Bakr a second glance at the time, so engrossed was she in stitching his wound, but he told her, many months later, that that was the moment when he knew he could love her. Before the year was out they had married. He was a good husband, loving and caring, and above all respectful of her and her needs, and she had grown very fond of him. Now she realised just how much she loved him. There was an empty space in her heart when she thought that she might never see him again, a hole that only he could fill. She couldn't let that happen. She had lost one husband to fate; she was not going to lose another one. She would do everything in her power to find him and bring him back to her.

*

When Aisha arrived at her parents' home, Makoud was in the back of the shop making up some medicine for one of his customers, whilst her brother Ibrahim was wrapping up some herbs in a vine leaf for a woman with an infected eye.

'As-salama alaykum, princess. This is a surprise,' her father said the moment he set eyes on her.

'Wa alaykum e-salam, Baba. I've come with bad news,' she said immediately.

'The children? Are they all right?' he asked, putting down the pestle and mortar he'd been using and coming across to hug her.

'The children are fine, Baba. The older ones are in school and I've left the baby with my mother-in-law. No, this has nothing to do with the children. Can we go upstairs and talk for a minute, please?'

'Of course, my dearest girl. Ibrahim, mind the shop for a moment,' he called through to his son.

Once they were sitting down on the patio, Aisha couldn't hold back her tears any longer.

'What is it, child? What ails you?' Makoud asked, taking her hand in his.

'Aisha? I thought I heard your voice. What's happened? Is that husband of yours being cruel to you?' asked her mother. 'Why the tears?'

'Bakr has been kidnapped,' she sobbed. 'He and two of his men have been taken by the pirates. We don't know where he is.'

'Oh, my dear child, that's terrible,' said her mother, gathering her into her arms as she did when she was a small child. 'So you want to come home?'

Aisha pulled away from her. 'No, Mama. I want to find him and bring him back.'

'But how will you do that?' asked Makoud.

'I don't know yet. But there is something else I need your help with first,' she said, wiping the tears from her face with her scarf.

'Of course, whatever I can do for you,' he said.

'All the men at the shipyard have gone home. They say they won't work anymore because there's no-one to pay them.'

'I can understand that. Nobody wants to work for free.'

'But if they don't work there will be no money to pay anyone. I need you to be my representative. They won't allow me to go into the yard. Some superstitious rubbish about it being unlucky for a woman to enter the shipyard. So I can't tell them what to do. You must do it for me.'

'But I don't know anything about building ships. I'm an apothecary.'

'You don't need to. You just need to talk to some of them and find out whom we can put in charge until Bakr comes back.'

'But it's unlikely that he will ever come back. You do realise that don't you?' said Makoud. 'The pirates could have taken him anywhere. They could have sold him to someone in North Africa or even further afield.'

'Who, apart from me, would want Bakr? He's not young anymore. People want slaves for a reason and it's usually to do with hard work. I don't believe that's the reason they took him. I've been thinking about it and it sounds as though they came especially for those three men. But why?'

'Because they can repair ships,' said Ibrahim, who was standing on the stairs listening to them.

'I thought you were watching the shop,' said his father.

'I've locked the door. It's not as though we've been rushed off our feet this morning.'

'You're right, Ibrahim. It's his skill they want,' said Aisha. 'Why else raid a shipyard?'

'Very well, I'll help you sort out the business, but I don't see how you're going to pay the men. They won't come and work for nothing. Loyalty only goes so far,' said Makoud. 'It doesn't feed your family.'

'I can find the money to pay them until we sell the khalifa's new ship. Don't worry about that. Bakr used to tell me all about his business,' said Aisha, struggling not to break down again. She would be strong; she owed this to her husband.

'So what do you suggest we do?' asked her father.

'I want you to go to the house of Sadan and Hala. I'll go with you. You must tell him that it is important to get the men back to work and to finish the khalifa's new ship. Ask Sadan who is the best man to take the place of the foreman.'

'They kidnapped the foreman as well?'

'Yes, and a young apprentice who is the son of the chief librarian. I have to let him know what has happened,' she added. 'We can go there, later.'

'Will you stay and have something to eat with us, Aisha?' her mother asked, stroking her daughter's hair.

'No, Mama. I haven't time. I must get the yard working again as soon as possible. I'll bring the children over tomorrow, instead.'

'I hope you know what you're doing, child,' she said. 'This is not women's work.'

'It's my husband's work and I must help him,' said Aisha sharply. Why weren't people taking her seriously?

'Give me a few minutes to finish making up the cough mixture for one of my customers and I'll be right with you,' said Makoud.

'Thank you, Baba. We'll go straight to Sadan's house.'

*

It didn't take long to reach Hala's home. Makoud knocked at the door and waited. He wasn't sure exactly what Aisha expected him to achieve, but he knew he had to do something to help her and this seemed the most likely to succeed. Finding Bakr would be a much more difficult task; how she expected them to rescue him was anybody's guess.

'As-salama alaykum, Aisha,' said Hala when she opened the door. She stared at Makoud with a look of puzzlement on her face.

'This is my father, Makoud ibn Ahmad, the apothecary,' replied Aisha. 'He is Bakr's father-in-law and, as his nearest male relative, he will be taking charge of the business. He would like to speak to your husband, if that is convenient.'

'Ahlan, sayyad,' said Hala. 'Please come in.'

'Ahlan wa sahlan,' said Makoud, removing his shoes and entering the narrow house. It was in a row of homes that Bakr had built for his workmen, and was very close to the shipyard.

'Please be seated and I will fetch Sadan. He is on the roof terrace, feeding his pigeons.'

Makoud looked across at his daughter. There were no signs of tears on her face now. She looked calm and in control. Maybe he'd underestimated her. Perhaps she would be able to run Bakr's business in his absence. She was right to try. How else would she be able to keep that big house of theirs running and feed all Bakr's dependents?

A ruddy faced man came into the room. He was wearing a grubby tunic and turban. 'As-salama alaykum,' he said. 'Sayeda.'

'Wa alaykum e-salam, Sadan. May I introduce my father, Makoud ibn Ahmad. He would like to speak with you,' said Aisha.

The man nodded, a little reluctantly, Makoud thought. 'What do you want?' he asked.

'I understand you work at the shipyard?' said Makoud.

'Did. I did work at the shipyard. I'll have to look for another job now.'

'Not necessarily. That's why I have come to talk to you. We need your help,' said Makoud.

Sadan looked at Aisha suspiciously. 'What sort of help? I can't take her into the yard, you know. It would be unlucky.'

Makoud bit back the inclination to say that things couldn't be much unluckier than they already were, and instead replied, 'No, we don't want that. I am going to be running the business from now on, at least until Bakr returns. But I know nothing about building ships. I'm not a carpenter; I'm an apothecary. So I need you to advise me on who's the best man to take over the job of foreman.'

He waited while Sadan thought for a moment. Then Sadan said, 'Wife, bring our friends some tea. There is a lot for us to talk about.'

While Hala poured out cup after cup of piping hot fruit tea, the men talked about the problems of finding a suitable man for the job. Hala suggested that Aisha might like to leave the men to talk business on their own, but Aisha declined, just as Makoud knew she would; she sat there sipping her tea, watching and listening to all that was said.

'There is a man,' said Sada at last. 'His name is al-Najjar, the carpenter; he's retired now. He worked for Bakr for twenty years but last year he had a bad accident. As you know, Bakr owns a small part of the oak forest up in the mountains and employs men to manage the logging. When we have orders for new ships, they float the timber down the Guadalmedina river, right up to the shipyard. It was Najjar's job that day to get the wood ashore before it reached the sea. He was trying to pull one of the oak logs on land when he slipped into the river and was caught underneath a floating tree trunk. He'd have been crushed to death if it hadn't been for Bakr's swiftness; he pulled him out from under the logs and dragged him up the bank but not before Najjar had received a heavy blow on his back from one of the oaks. Now he walks with a stick and is unable to do any physical work, but he knows all there is to know about shipbuilding.'

'Well Sadan, it sounds as though he could be our man. From what you've said he would make an excellent foreman. And it sounds as though he has a debt to repay to Bakr. So where do we find him?'

'He still lives in one of the shipbuilder's houses; Bakr said he deserved it after all his years' service. He's just three houses down the hill.'

'Will you take us to him?' Makoud asked.

'I will, but I have one question first.'

'Yes?'

'How will we get paid?'

Makoud turned to Aisha. 'Maybe you'd like to answer that, Aisha.'

'Yes. There's no need to worry about your pay. If we finish the khalifa's ship we will receive immediate payment and that will be enough to keep the yard going for at least a twelvemonth. Until then I have enough money to continue paying the men as before. My husband confided in me about all aspects of his business. You and the others have no need to worry; I know exactly how much money the business has and how much he paid in wages each month.'

'What about the foreman's family? He has a wife and six children. How will they live now that he has been kidnapped?' asked Hala, returning with a fresh jug of tea.

'I will speak to her,' said Aisha. 'Now, can we go and meet al-Najjar?'

'Of course,' said Sadan, finishing the last drop of his tea in his glass. 'Please give me a few moments to change out of my dirty clothes.'

Aisha sipped the fresh tea. Was Sadan just humouring her? Or did he really believe they could run the shipyard without Bakr? Maybe she was taking on more than she could really cope with.

CHAPTER 3

The next time their captor brought their food, Bakr dragged himself towards him and said, 'I demand to see your captain.'

'Well he doesn't want to see you,' the man snarled and thrust a bowl of food into his hands.

'He will when he hears what I have to say,' said Bakr and threw the food on the ground. 'Tell him the owner of the shipyard wants to speak to him now.'

The man glared at him. He lifted his foot as though he was about to kick him but then thought better of it. Instead he turned to the others and said, 'Looks as though you're going hungry today,' and climbed up the ladder and shut the door with an ominous clang.

'What have you done, sayyad?' said the foreman. He bent across to try and salvage some of the bread, but it had landed in a puddle of filthy bilge water and none of them were so hungry that they could eat it.

'If we stay in this rat infested hole until we reach our destination, we're going to die. We need to get up on deck. If we're really important to him, then he'll want to keep us healthy.'

'And if we're not?' asked Kamil.

'Then he'll leave us down here to rot or he'll throw us overboard. But I don't think either of those will happen. Pirates are only interested in making money. They do nothing unless they can see a profit in it; they will sell us into slavery, put us to work on their ship or, if they think we're rich enough, they will ransom us. I don't know why they took us, but they took us for a reason and they're not going to let us die, not yet anyway.'

Before he could say anything else, the hold door opened again and the pirate returned. 'Right you are. The captain says you can come on deck, but don't even think of trying to escape. The nearest land is miles away,' he said, drawing his dagger and slicing through the ropes that still bound Bakr's ankles.

As he tried to stand up he felt his legs buckle beneath him; he was weaker than he had realised.

'Lean on me, sayyad,' said Asim. Between them, he and Kamil pushed Bakr through the hatchway and into the daylight.

At first Bakr was blinded by the glare of the sun reflecting off the sea but gradually his eyes adjusted to the outside world and he saw for the first time the ship that had taken him away from his home. It was as he'd expected, a long wooden galley with about thirty pairs of oars, set in two banks, one above decks and one below, and with two men at each oar; there had to be a crew of between one hundred and fifty and two hundred men. In the prow was an elevated forecastle where one of the pirates stood on lookout. Besides the rowers, the ship was propelled by a triangular lateen sail, which with the following wind was increasing their speed to about seven nautical miles an hour. He breathed in deeply, desperate to get the foul stench of the hold out of his lungs.

'Right, come with me,' said the burly pirate, closing the hatch on the anxious faces of Kamil and Asim.

'Aren't you going to let them out?' Bakr asked.

'Nobody said anything about them. They can stay where they are.'

They were about five Arab miles away from the shore; a coastline that looked so lush and green, so inviting that, if he'd had the strength, he would have jumped overboard then and there and swum towards it.

'Get a move on,' the pirate said, pushing him so hard that he almost fell.

The captain's quarters were simple, a berth in the stern covered by a cotton tent; he was seated cross-legged on a goatskin rug. As Bakr approached he made no motion for him to sit down.

Instead he asked, 'What is it?' He looked at Bakr, examining him carefully. 'What makes you think you are in any position to demand to see me? What do you want?'

'Then why have you agreed to speak to me?' asked Bakr. He had met men like the captain before; he was the lowest of the low, a thief, probably a murderer, but he had more intelligence than the regular pirate so the others held him in high esteem. Intelligence or ruthlessness, whichever it was, it was enough for them to respect and obey him. Bakr prayed that it was for his intelligence, if not, he'd be swimming for his life very soon.

'What is your name?' The captain spoke softly. Without doubt a Berber, his skin was further darkened by the sun. A jagged white scar ran from his right eye—which was covered with a black eye-patch—down to his chin where it disappeared behind his thin, straggly beard; the injury was surely the result of some long-ago fight. A gold earring hung from his right ear, a superstitious habit which was said to improve the eyesight.

'Bakr ibn Assam.'

'You own a shipyard?'

'You know I do. It was in that shipyard that your men attacked us and kidnapped us,' he said, his anger making his voice rise.

'Indeed. So what can I do for you, Bakr ibn Assam?' There was a touch of sarcasm in the way he said his name.

'You can tell me why you have kidnapped us. Are you planning on selling us in the slave market? You won't get much for me, I can assure you. I'm far too old to be a valuable slave.'

'Now that's where you are wrong, Bakr ibn Assam, because you are a very valuable man, to the right person.'

Bakr looked at him in astonishment. What in the name of Allah was this all about?

'And who would that person be?' he asked, moderating his tone a little this time.

'Is that all you wanted to know, Bakr ibn Assam?' asked the captain, his voice now as slippery as a snake. He adjusted his dark robes so that Bakr caught a flash of a red tunic underneath.

'I have seen your ship and I know that its top speed is probably only seven or eight nautical miles. It will take days to get to the Balearic Islands. If I and my men have to stay locked up in that filthy hold the whole time, you will have dead men on your hands by the time you arrive. Then how valuable will we be to you?'

'So you propose I let you come on deck?'

'Yes. And give us some water to wash. How can we pray to Allah if we are unclean?'

'I do not care if you pray to Allah or anyone else. The only person you need to pray to now, is me. I am the only one who can help you, not Allah, not Jehovah, not Jesus.

Just me. Remember that,' he shouted. For a minute or two he glared at Bakr.

Was that it? Was he going to throw him back in the hold? Bakr held his breath and waited until at last the captain said, 'However I will allow you to come up on deck for a while each day; you will eat your food here with the crew.'

'Thank you. And my men?'

'Yes.' He paused. 'And what makes you think we're headed for the Balearic Islands?' the captain asked.

'It's the obvious place. Far enough from the mainland, but not too far. Clean water and safe harbours. Also I have heard talk that the islands are a favourite place for ships such as yours to rest up. Anyway,' Bakr said, looking at the sky, 'You've been travelling east-north-east since we left Malaqah, which will take you straight past the Balearic Islands.'

'Are you a carpenter or a seaman?' asked the captain. 'You appear to know a lot about handling a ship. Maybe we'll get you to work your passage instead.'

'I'm a carpenter, but my life has been spent designing and building ships. I couldn't fail to learn something of seamanship on the way.'

The captain seemed to have tired of their conversation. He turned away and called to the pirate who'd escorted Bakr on deck. 'Get this man clean. He stinks. And get the other two out of the hold and clean them up as well. They are allowed to be on deck during the day but throw them back in the hold at night.'

The burly pirate grabbed Bakr's arm and pulled him towards a large butt of seawater. 'Right, clean yourself up,' he said, handing him a ladle. 'I'll get the other two.'

As Bakr ducked his head in the bucket of seawater, he felt the pain start again in his head. The salt stung the open wound but the bleeding appeared to have stopped. How he wished Aisha was there to look at it for him, to rub on some of that soothing salve which she used on the children's cuts and grazes. He thought back to the day he'd first met her, when she had stitched a wound in his leg; how soft her hands, how gentle her touch. He sighed. What was she doing right now? He imagined her feeding the baby, or maybe making some lunch for the children when they arrived home from school. Was she missing him? Did she think he was dead? His poor darling, how upset she must be, not knowing what had become of him.

He knew he would be able to love her from that first moment, but he never thought he could love her as much as he did. Standing there, dripping with sea water, his head throbbing, he could still feel the warmth of that happiness which had coloured his life since the day she agreed to marry him. Whenever he thought of her he began to smile, no matter where he was; he couldn't help it. His eyes would glow with the delight of her and then the men in the shipyard would nudge one another and whisper 'The daft bastard's in love.'

The hatch door opened and Asim and Kamil staggered into the bright sunlight, blinking like a pair of bedraggled owls.

'Clean yourselves up,' snarled the burly pirate.

The ship was pitching slightly and the prisoners had problems keeping their balance; Kamil lurched towards the water butt and clung to it.

'Do you know where we're going?' he whispered to Bakr as he sluiced himself down with the cold water.

Bakr shook his head. 'Not for sure, but I think our guess about the Balearics was right.' Then as Asim joined them in their ablutions, he added, 'We can stay on deck until nightfall. Then it's back into the hold. Sorry that's the best I could get him to agree to.'

He should have argued a bit more, but until he had a better idea of the captain's temperament, he didn't want to risk pushing him too far. If they were to escape, whether from the ship or after they'd landed, they needed to make the captain trust them. He looked around him; there was nowhere on the ship to store food and the water barrels they had were few. They already knew that the pirates stopped each night to rest; it was likely that some of them went ashore just before dawn to get food and water. That was the best time to raid small farms and fishing villages along the coast; they'd take what they needed and make a quick escape. By the time the local people realised what had happened they would have rowed back to the ship and set sail. Apart from these nocturnal breaks the pirates stayed on board; they would cook, eat, drink, wash—although it didn't look as though they did much of that— and sleep on deck. This was their world when they were at sea.

A man on the top deck began to sing and beat out a rhythm on a small drum; the ship picked up speed as the rowers matched their strokes to the music.

'You two can follow me,' said their burly captor. 'You don't think we're going to feed you for nothing.'

Asim and Kamil dried themselves quickly with their dirty djellabas and followed him.

'Where are you taking them?' asked Bakr.

'To pump out the hold. You want to join them?'

He said nothing but watched as his men, now stripped to the waist, lowered themselves back into the darkness. He still had no idea exactly what the captain had in mind for them, nor where they were going. And what was going to happen to them when the pirates finished with them? It was not likely that the captain would let them go home.

CHAPTER 4

Aisha had just finished talking to al-Najjar about how the new ship was progressing when her sister-in-law came in and said, 'There's someone to see you, Aisha. It's Kamil's father.'

'Show him in here, please, Rayya.'

'I'll be getting back to the yard, then,' said al-Najjar, getting up.

She placed her hand on his arm and said, 'No, please wait. I expect he'd like to speak to you as well. You know Kamil, don't you?'

'I did briefly but… Very well, I'll stay and speak to him.'

Aisha had been dreading seeing Kamil's family again; they'd been devastated when she'd told them what had happened to their son. She knew from Bakr that his father had been unhappy when the boy had refused to continue with his studies and told him he wanted to build boats instead. His father, the chief librarian at the university had probably wanted an academic life for his only son, not that of a carpenter.

'As-salama alaykum, sayeda,' a tall, but rather bent man said, as Rayya showed him into the room. 'Thank you for taking the time to see me. I hope you are well, sayeda.'

'Wa alaykum e-salam, Yusuf al-Basir, and welcome to my home. Yes, I am well enough, in the circumstances.' Aisha gave a slight bow and then stretched out her arm to include al-Najjar. 'This is the foreman for the shipyard, al-Najjar,' she said. 'He knows your son.'

At this news the librarian's eyes lit up. 'Indeed? You know my Kamil?'

'I do, but only a little. I retired at almost the same time he started work as an apprentice.'

'Retired?'

'Yes, al-Najjar is kindly working as our foreman until the others return.' She couldn't bring herself to say Bakr's name in front of them in case she began to cry.

'I see. Well, as I'm sure you realise, I've come to ask if you have any news of my son and your husband,' he said, his eyes imploring her to give him a positive answer.

'No, I'm sorry we've heard nothing,' said al-Najjar. 'We have people asking for any sightings of them all along the coast. As soon as we hear something we will let you know.'

Aisha knew he didn't intend to sound unfeeling, but what else could he say? They had heard nothing at all. It was if the three men had vanished off the face of the earth.

'I see.' The librarian looked defeated. 'He is my only son,' he said. 'I have seven daughters and I'd begun to think that Allah would never bless me with a son, when to our great surprise, Kamil was born. He is everything to me and his mother.'

'Stay and have some tea,' Aisha said.

'No, thank you, sayeda; I must get back to my work. It was kind of you to talk to me. Ma'a salama.'

'Alla ysalmak, al-Basir. I hope we have some good news the next time we meet,' she said. 'Don't give up hope.'

He smiled, tears shining in his eyes, and pressed her hand between his own.

Once he'd left, she turned to al-Najjar and said, 'We have to do something to find them. I can't believe even pirates would kidnap three able-bodied men just to kill them. They must be alive. We just need to find out where they are.'

'Oh, sayeda. Do you realise the enormity of the task? There are many pirate ships that sail in these waters. They come here to raid and pillage the coastal villages and then they return to where they feel safe from retribution. That could be anywhere around the Middle Sea: the coast of North Africa, Tunis, Algiers or further north in Italy, France, Crete, the Balearic Islands. Where would we start? And how? Our only hope is that your husband and the others escape and manage to send us word of where they are.'

'But I can't stand this waiting and not knowing if they're alive or dead,' she said, for the first time realising how much worse the uncertainty was; hard though it would be, it would be easier to come to terms with his death.

'Take heart, sayeda. You have the children to care for. If Bakr is alive, I am certain he will make it back to you eventually.'

'Thank you al-Najjar.'

'I really must get back to the yard, sayeda. There is still a lot to do to finish the last order.'

'Of course. I'll see you tomorrow.'

*

Aisha opened the door to her father's shop. As usual he was in his workshop preparing his lotions and creams; fragrant smells drifted across to her, roses, hypericum, rosemary and cumin.

'Daughter, what a nice surprise,' Makoud said, putting down a pot of cream and wiping his hands on his djubbah; it was already stained a medley of grey, blue, orange and green. She smiled; her father was always so careless about his appearance. 'Do you have any news?'

'No, Baba. Nothing at all. That's why I have come to see you. We must do something to try to find them,' she said, and this time she didn't try to hold back the tears. 'It's been more than a week since they disappeared. I'm worried if we don't do something soon we will never find them.'

'Come, sit down, sweet child. You know that you're asking the impossible. How can we find someone when we don't have any idea where they have gone?' he said.

'But we have to try,' she said, sobbing uncontrollably. 'We have to try.'

'Very well. Tonight I'll talk to Avi and I'll take Ibrahim with me. We'll see what we can come up with. Here, dry your eyes, my child.' He took out a handkerchief and tried to mop up her tears.

'And Umar? He might be able to help,' she blubbered, taking the handkerchief from him.

'No, I've already been in touch with him; Umar is preparing for a new campaign. They will be leaving very soon for Écija. It is unlikely but if he hears anything he will get word to us.'

At this Aisha began to cry even more; Umar was the one who got things done in her family. She'd been relying on him to help her.

A noise made her look up and she saw her brother, Ibrahim, standing in the doorway. 'Take Dirar along as well, Baba. He's the one who knows the sea better than any of us,' he said.

'Yes, good idea,' said her father. 'Now, come along, Aisha, crying won't help. You have to be strong for the sake of the children.'

She could see he was not used to her being so helpless, so she blew her nose and nodded at him. But he was wrong. Crying did help. She'd been 'being strong' ever since Bakr had been kidnapped and she'd begun to feel that she was at breaking point, that at any moment she would snap like a stalk of dried corn in the wind. Now she felt better. Not happier but stronger. Keeping all that grief, fear and uncertainty inside her had undermined her strength.

'I'll come as well,' she said. 'What time will you leave?'

'As soon as we close the shop, just before sunset,' he said.

'Very well. I'll be here by then.'

'Go up and see your mother, before you go. She'll give me hell if she knows you came around and didn't go to see her.'

'I will.' She kissed her father on the cheek then went up to see Abal.

*

Her mother-in-law was not pleased when Aisha announced that she was going out that evening and that she would leave the children with her.

'What do you mean going out tonight? On your own? Without a chaperone? No, Aisha I forbid it,' she said, turning puce with anger. 'You are a married woman with children. You cannot go out alone.'

'Don't get so upset, hama. I will be with my father and my brothers. No harm will come to me,' she said. This was just the reaction she had expected from Bakr's mother, but she wasn't going to let it deter her.

'I'm not concerned about you,' she snapped. 'It's your husband's reputation that concerns me, and that of our family. You would never have attempted to do anything so outrageous if Bakr was still here.'

'I wouldn't have to be doing this if Bakr was here. Can't you see I'm trying to find him? The only people who can help us are my father and my brothers. Who is there is in your family that is willing to look for him? Your sons-in-law? Your brothers?' She knew this would quieten her; one son-in-law never came near the house and had forbidden his wife to do so either, the other was a rather ineffectual youth who spent most of his days playing the lute. As for Bakr's uncles, one was dead and the other lived in Qurtubah and was not inclined to travel.

'Well, Rayya will go with you,' she said, clamping her lips together in a way she had of indicating that there was no more to be said on the matter.

'Very well. Tell her to be ready to leave in an hour or I shall go without her.' Her sister-in-law was notorious for the amount of time she spent bathing, dressing her hair and putting kohl around her eyes. Aisha had no intention of wasting time waiting for her to beautify herself.

She picked the baby out of his crib and went in search of the children. The girls were playing on the patio with their dolls, and the boys had invented some game which they played with round pebbles, collected from the beach.

'Mama, look at what we found,' Maryam cried excitedly. She held up a piece of broken pottery; it looked like an old tile but there was a tiny painting of a lion on it. Aisha had never seen anything like it before.

'Where did you find it?' she asked.

'Outside, in the garden. It was covered in mud but we washed it and we're going to put it in the house we're making for our dolls.'

Aisha turned the piece of pottery over but there was nothing to say what it had been or where it had come from. 'I think this must be part of a Roman floor tile. I have heard that many years ago an ancient people called Romans lived in Malaqah, long before we Muslims arrived. They were infidels and so they would decorate their pots and dishes with paintings of animals and people.'

'So where are they now, Mama?' asked little Naila. She was only a couple of years older than the baby. She and her brother, Sandi were Bakr's children by his first wife, now dead. Now they were hers.

'I don't know, darling. They just vanished, many years ago.'

'Just like Baba,' the child said, looking at Aisha with such sad eyes that she wanted to hug her and say that no, her father hadn't vanished; he would be home any day soon.

'Yes, darling, like Baba.'

'I heard the pirates got him,' said Sandi. He was almost ten-years-old now and felt himself to be the man of the house in his father's absence.

Aisha would have preferred that the children didn't know about the pirates, that they remained innocent of what had happened to their father, but it was impossible to keep anything from them in this house. If it wasn't Rayya gossiping about what she'd heard in the market then it was their grandmother.

'We don't know that for sure,' Aisha said gently. 'But what we do know is that if your father is able to escape he

will come straight back here to be with his lovely family.'
She pulled the two girls towards her and gave them a big
hug. She knew better than to try to hug Sandi, although her
own little Imran often sneaked into her bed for a cuddle
when he was alone.

She moved the baby onto her breast for his evening feed
and once he was settled, she sat there watching her children
play. What went on in their little minds? Did they really
understand what had happened to their father? The boys
had abandoned the game with the stones and were now in
the garden playing at pirates, and waving short planks of
wood about as though they were swords. Was this how
children came to terms with the evil in life? Turned it into a
game? If only it was as simple for adults, for her.

*

Makoud was surprised to see that Aisha had arrived with
her sister-in-law in tow, but he greeted her with courtesy
and they immediately set off for Avi's house.

'Where are we going?' she asked. 'I thought we were
going to your father's house, Aisha.'

'That was my father's house; they live above the shop.
Now we are going to talk to Avi, an old friend of my
father's. He's a merchant and has a lot of contacts along the
coast. We hope he can help us.'

'Avi? Is that a Jewish name?' Rayya asked, as they
turned into the Jewish part of the city.

'Yes. My father knew him when they both lived in
Qurtubah.'

'Do you have any objection to going to the house of a
Jew?' Makoud asked.

'No, no. Of course not,' said Rayya, blushing.

'Good, because I think he is the only one who can help us track down your brother.' He didn't have a lot of time for Bakr's sisters, especially this one, the youngest who he guessed had made life difficult for Aisha in her first few months of marriage.

He rang the bell and waited for Avi's servant to let them in.

'As-salama alaykum, Musif. Is your master at home?'

'Wa alaykum e-salam, sayad. Yes, I will let him know you are here.' He looked at the group of them rather curiously; standing behind Makoud were Ibrahim, Dirar, then Aisha and Rayya. 'You have the family with you, sayyad?'

'Yes, indeed.'

As usual, Avi was very happy to see his old friend. 'Makoud, what a pleasant surprise, and you have not come alone. Aisha, how lovely to see you, my dear. Did you want to talk to Rebekah?' He ushered them into his house, calling his wife to come and see them. 'You will take some tea?' he asked. 'Tea, Rebekah. Lots of mint tea. And here is Aisha to see you.'

Makoud smiled at his friend and said, 'That would be lovely, Avi, but we have come to ask for your help. I think Aisha would prefer to remain with the men although I'm sure Rayya would be delighted to take some tea with your wife.'

Rayya scowled at him, but obediently followed Rebekah through to the kitchen.

'So, what can I do to help? Is this about your husband, Aisha?' Avi asked as they all sat down round a low table.

'Yes,' she said. 'It's been a while now and I'm scared that if we don't find him soon we never will.'

'Of course, I understand. But what can I do?'

'We have been wondering about why Bakr and two of his employees were kidnapped. It doesn't seem to have been one of the usual pirate raids; those are more violent and the pirates always take items of value: food, clothes, money, animals. This time it was as if they had come especially for those men. So what do they want with them? Ibrahim thinks they wanted skilled men to either repair a ship or build a new one. If that is true, then we may have a clue to where the pirates have taken them,' said Makoud.

'So, instead of selling the men, they want them to work for them?' said Avi.

'Yes, that's our guess. But if they are repairing their ship, then we need to know where that might be. We know it's hard to find these pirates, so where do they go? Where are their hiding places?'

'It would have to be somewhere very secluded and easy to defend. Remember pirates usually only have one ship. If it was in need of repair they would be very vulnerable while their ship was out of action,' said Dirar.

'Yes. They're not used to fighting on land and most of the crew are oarsmen, not fighters. Their manner of attack is to make sudden, surprise raids and be gone before any soldiers arrive,' added Ibrahim.

'And you think I can help you find where they're hiding?' asked Avi. He was stroking his beard as he often did when he was thinking hard about something.

'You know a lot of people, Avi. I've heard you talk of merchants who live in Álmeria and come to Malaqah to trade, and others along the coast of North Africa. One of them must know which islands the pirates use as a safe haven.'

'Yes, I have many contacts, it's true. As you know, I've already put the word out about the kidnapping but no-one has seen or heard anything. What else can I do?'

'You could ask if anyone knows where the pirates anchor to do their repairs. It will be some remote island, or a cove along the coast, far from any towns and villages,' said Dirar. 'In the meantime I will ask the fishermen. We often get fishing boats from further south in our waters; they might know something.'

'Why don't you speak to the admiral, Baba?' suggested Aisha. 'He knows Bakr well. It was Bakr who helped him convince the khalifa that he should buy stronger ships for the navy. He might know more about where the pirates have their hideout.'

'That's an excellent idea. I'll arrange to see him as soon as I can.'

'But what if we're wrong?' asked Ibrahim. 'What if it's nothing to do with repairing boats? What if they just needed extra crew members? Or if they have sold them in the slave market? What do we do then?'

Makoud looked at his daughter. This was in all their minds. 'Then I'm afraid there is little we can do, except pray that they can escape and return home to us.'

'But we mustn't look on the black side,' said Avi. 'This sounds like a reasonable plan to me so let's keep optimistic and see what we can find out.'

Makoud saw Aisha try to smile, but it was hard for her. Poor child, she'd lost one husband to the plague and now another had been kidnapped.

'Yes, I agree with Avi,' she said. 'Someone must know something about where they've gone. I know we'll find them if we look hard enough.'

'Well I think we have a plan, for now. Aisha why don't you go along and see Rebekah before you go. I know she's dying to talk to you. She'll want to tell you all about Sara and the new baby,' said Avi.

Makoud waited until Aisha had left to join the women and then asked, 'How is your son doing in Garnata?'

'Gideon is well and the business is making lots of money, I'm pleased to say. His wife is a delightful girl and I think he is happy with her. They have two children now, twins.'

'Already? Congratulations. So you have three grandchildren now?'

'Yes, it is good to see the family growing.'

'You don't look very happy. Is something wrong?' asked Makoud. It wasn't normal for his friend to have such a solemn face.

'Gideon is concerned about things in Garnata.'

'What sort of things?' asked Makoud.

'Do you know the history of Garnata al-Yahud?'

Makoud shook his head.

'Well, it was a small Jewish settlement originally, but when the nearby city of Elvira was destroyed in the civil war, the chief of one of the Berber armies, Zawi ben Ziri evacuated the city and founded the taifa and capital city of Garnata. That was about twenty-five years ago now. Since then the Jewish influence in Garnata has increased and, as you probably know, even their grand vizier and the head of their army, Samuel ibn Nagrilla, is a Jew. The city has grown into an important centre of Jewish culture and scholarship. It has always been a happy city. There is no dhimmi status; Jews and Muslims are treated equally and live side by side with no problem. Until just recently, that is.'

'What's happened?' Makoud asked. There were about two hundred Jews living in Malaqah and there had never been any trouble; many of them, including Avi and his family, had fled to the city after the fall of Qurtubah.

'There is a new poet, Abu Ishaq. He's a very strict Muslim and he's been writing poetry to stir up hatred against the Jews; he thinks they have too much power and have pushed the Muslims into an inferior role. Luckily, the sultan, Badis ben Habus doesn't agree; he trusts his grand vizier and ignores this man's inflammatory writing.'

'So why is Gideon worried?'

'The poet has a growing band of followers and Gideon worries that one day they will turn against their Jewish neighbours. He'd like to come back to Malaqah, but the business is doing so well that it would be a shame to abandon it when nothing has actually happened yet. I've suggested he gives it a few more years and then we'll decide.'

'Yes, I can see why you're worried. It's a difficult decision to make.'

'And Aisha? She has made an excellent marriage, I see,' said Avi, looking towards the door to check that she wasn't about to come in.

'She was very happy until this happened,' said Makoud. 'Bakr is a fine man and he treats her with great respect. She is running the business in his absence. Officially I am in charge, but she makes all the decisions. I've always known she was a beauty but I never realised she was so clever.'

'That's good to hear. So she will keep the business running whether Bakr comes back or not?'

'I think she has no option. Bakr's household needs to be fed and there isn't anyone else capable of doing it.'

'Baba, I think we should go. We'll be late for dinner,' said Ibrahim. 'The girls can make their own way home.'

'Yes, and I'd like some sleep before I go to work,' said Dirar, stifling a yawn.

'Of course. Well, keep me informed Avi if you hear anything,' said Makoud. 'My regards to your family. Ma'a salama, my friend.'

'Aleichem shalom, Makoud. I will be in touch.'

As Makoud walked back to the shop, he went over the conversation in his head. If one of these new avenues of enquiry gave them anything, then at least they'd know where to start their search. At the moment they didn't know whether to go north or south, east or west; it would take them years to search the whole length of the coastline, never mind the dozens of tiny islands that were in the Middle Sea. Surely someone knew something that would help them. For Aisha's sake he wanted to remain positive but at the moment it looked an impossible task. But how could he convince her of that?

CHAPTER 5

Idris ibn Ali al-Mutaayyad, Khalifa of Malaqah sat astride his sturdy Arab mare and viewed his army. How splendid they looked in their uniforms with their red cloaks and his own colours, green and white chequered squares, on their shields. The standard bearer lifted the khalifa's shatrang aloft—the new addition of a gold crown on the banner, clear for all to see—and the infantry, clad in their thick leather armour, began to march past. Soon they would be ready to take on the might of Isbiliya and when it was beaten, Malaqah would become the strongest taifa in al-Andalus.

The magnificent jinettes were next, their Arab horses tightly reined to control their excitement, tails held high and heads even higher. The horsemen, with the sun glinting on their chainmail hauberks, pulled out their swords and raised them in salute as they passed their Supreme Commander. He smiled to himself; he was confident that his army would be stronger than that of Isbiliya; they were disciplined and well trained, and many of them were regular soldiers, experienced and loyal to the caliphate. He had bolstered the numbers of his troops with mercenaries and even some militia men from the surrounding countryside, but even these he had put under the command of seasoned officers.

Now it was the turn of the bowmen, first the foot archers unencumbered by much armour and behind them the light cavalry, equipped with scimitars and short bows. Since becoming Khalifa, Idris had been building up both his army and its weaponry. The forges had been turning out swords, daggers, lances, long-handled maces, arrow heads and even javelins, by the thousands. He was determined to prove to the world that Malaqah was stronger than Isbiliya and that he, Idris ibn Ali al-Mutaayyad, was the one who'd made it so. Also, unlike his brother, Yahya, he wasn't going to rush into an attack on Isbiliya without making sure he had plenty of support from his allies. They too were tired of Abbad's hunger for power; it was time to stop him swallowing up the smaller taifas. It was time to go on the offensive. Idris had already sent emissaries to Garnata, Álmeria and Badajoz eliciting their support; he eagerly awaited their replies. His heart quickened as he thought of the enormous army they could muster if they were all on the same side; together they would be invincible.

Still his troops marched past; now it was the engineers and the heavy war machines. How impressive they looked; they would put fear into the hearts of any enemy. It was imperative that they defeated Isbiliya and it wasn't just a matter of pride on his part; he needed a victory to convince the people of Malaqah that he was a worthy khalifa. Just before his brother had died in strange circumstances—even Idris had found his illness inexplicable— Yahya had divided his kingdom into two parts and left one to each of his sons who were still only children at the time. His untimely death meant that the country was left without a strong leader, so the grand vizier had stepped in, arranged for the boys to be sent to Sebta and offered Idris the throne. Then he had sent Idris's eldest son, Muhammad, to al-Jazira to govern there. That had been four years before and now

Hasan, the true heir to the kingdom, was almost of age. He would soon be wanting his throne back. In the meantime Idris wanted to keep the kingdom strong, which was why he needed to prove his strength in battle against their old adversary, Abbad I of Isbiliya. There was a lot to gain if they were victorious and a lot to lose if not.

*

When Idris had finished reviewing the troops, he found his grand vizier, ibn Baqanna, waiting for him in the alcázar. An old man now, he was still a shrewd and cunning negotiator. He had just returned from Álmeria, where he'd been trying to enlist their support for the campaign.

'So what news from our old friend, Zuhair?' Idris asked, throwing himself down on the sofa and signalling for his servant to bring him some water.

Zuhair was the sultan of the taifa of Álmeria and a hard man who, in the past, had repelled the armies of Isbiliya and Valencia on many occasions; Álmeria, with its prosperous textile industry and strategic location was a prize that many coveted. Their ruler certainly had no love for Abbad I.

'He is happy to join forces with Malaqah to defeat Isbiliya, Your Majesty. He will bring a large army, which he himself will lead. Zuhair wants Abbad defeated as much as you do,' said ibn Baqanna.

'How many men?'

'He wouldn't be specific.'

'And what did you offer him in return?' asked Idris. He knew the wily ways of his grand vizier.

'A share of the booty, of course.'

'And?' The spoils of war were always shared between the victors. Had ibn Baqanna promised him anything else? Anything that Idris would not approve of?

'And nothing. What else could I promise him, Your Majesty?'

'Part of the taifa of Isbiliya, perhaps?'

'No, Your majesty. It's too far from Álmeria to be of any use to him. If you must know, I promised nothing but I did allow him to think that we would rally to his aid if there were any more attacks on Álmeria by either the Valencians or…' He hesitated. 'Garnata.'

'But Garnata is our close ally.'

'He knows that. That's why I told him that you could persuade the Zirids to leave Álmeria alone.'

'You know that won't work.'

The grand vizier smiled. 'What else could I say, Your Majesty?'

Ibn Baqanna made a show of being obsequious but Idris knew he couldn't fully trust him; he felt that behind his smooth words and ready smile was a man with a hidden agenda. One which always put ibn Baqanna's needs first.

'I'm glad you're here, Grand Vizier. I want to talk to you about my nephews, Hasan and Ben Yahya. I think it's time they returned to Malaqah. They cannot remain in Sebta all their lives; that would breed resentment and lead to rebellion. Once I have defeated Abbad, I would like them here, where I can see them. They are my brother's sons, after all.'

'That's not a good idea, Your Majesty. Not a good idea at all. They might rally the people against you. After all it was their father who held the throne before you and their inheritance that you took.'

The man was overstepping the mark now. 'Indeed, ibn Baqanna. I am perfectly aware of that. And on whose advice did I become Khalifa?' he asked, his tone as cold as the winter snow on the Sierra de Nieves.

The grand vizier bowed and said, 'On mine, your Majesty. It was the most sensible thing to do at the time. But I ask you to consider. They are still boys and have no experience of running a prosperous country like Malaqah; they would undo all the good work you have done in the last four years.'

'Nevertheless, as soon as I return from the battle at Écija, I shall send for them. It is my duty to my brother and our family.'

'Very well, Your Majesty. Was there anything else you required?'

'Yes, find out if General Rashad has returned from Garnata, and if there is any news from Badajoz. I want to leave for Écija before autumn sets in.'

He watched his grand vizier bow and back his way out of the room. Maybe it was time to look for a new advisor; ibn Baqanna was becoming too confident and far too powerful.

He beckoned his servant, who was standing patiently by the window. 'Send for the chief librarian. I need some diversion from all this talk of politics and war.'

*

Idris liked the chief librarian; he was a cultured man who wasn't afraid to speak to Idris as an equal. Admittedly he never spoke of politics, but they often had interesting exchanges about poetry and philosophy. Yusuf al-Basir had worked in the library for many years and before that he'd been a librarian in Qurtubah, in the days before all the universities and libraries were destroyed. He had managed to save many of the books and manuscripts by smuggling them out one at a time, and when he eventually fled from the city he'd taken as many as he could with him. Idris's father had welcomed Yusuf to Malaqah and given him the job of taking over the existing, rather poor collection of books that they had. Since then the city's library had grown in size and in popularity; each year they had numerous visitors from other lands who came to read and copy the books they held. Al-Basir had been promoted to Chief Librarian during Yahya's rule, and now had a staff of scribes, librarians, translators, copyists and clerks who worked for him.

Idris liked to consider himself a patron of the arts; like his brother, he was eager to continue the work of the Omayyads who, in the tenth century, had earned al-Andalus the reputation of being the cultural heart of Europe. To this end he bought books from all parts of the civilised world, and supported poets and musicians, scribes, philosophers, scientists and astrologers, encouraging them to make their home in Malaqah. He built universities and schools and took a great interest in creating for himself a palace that was not only strongly fortified but beautiful.

'Al-Basir, as-salama alaykum. Come in and show me what delights you have for me today. My soul is heavy from thoughts of warfare and I need to lift my spirits,' he said, as the thin, white-haired librarian was led into his private rooms by his servant.

'Wa alaykum e-salam, Your Majesty. I was delighted to receive your summons. I have brought you a most special book, which I have acquired from a Greek scholar.' He held up a slim volume of beautifully decorated paper, covered in

Arabic script. 'It is a little known work of the Greek poet Homer. At the moment we have only translated the first few chapters but they are so delightful that I think they will revive your spirits.'

Idris smiled in pleasure; he could always rely on Yusuf to bring him something to gladden his heart. He turned to his servant and said, 'Bring some tea for our guest. That mixture of herbs that we know he enjoys.'

The servant bowed and once he'd left, Idris said, 'Come Yusuf. Don't keep me in suspense. Read me what you have.'

For the next hour, Yusuf and Idris discussed the merits and demerits of Greek poetry over Arabic, reading from the new book and quoting from memory many of the more modern poems that both knew by heart.

Idris held the book in his hands, turning the pages one by one, marvelling at the beautiful script and geometric designs that the copyist had used to illustrate it. 'Excellent paper,' he said. 'Very fine.'

'Yes, we received a batch of the best quality from China, only a few weeks ago.'

'Mmm. I wonder will it last as long as papyrus?' said Idris, rubbing the paper between his fingers. 'Although it does have a very smooth finish.'

'I have wondered that too. But it seems to me that it could actually be stronger in certain conditions. It is not so easily affected by the damp, for example,' said the chief librarian, pulling on his beard thoughtfully.

'Yesterday, when I sent my servant to look for you, he couldn't find you and nobody in the library knew where you were,' said Idris, trying not to make it sound like a rebuke.

'I am sorry, Your Majesty. I didn't know you wanted to talk to me.'

'It is of no matter, but where were you?'

The chief librarian looked down at his feet for a while, then he said, 'It was a family matter, Your Majesty. Nothing that should concern you.'

Idris looked at him and said, 'Yusuf, when I ask you a question, I expect an answer. And look at me when I'm talking to you.'

Yusuf looked up immediately; his eyes were full of tears. 'Of course, Your Majesty. My apologies. I did not mean to appear rude. I was looking for my son, Kamil. He is our only male child and almost two weeks ago when he was working in the shipyard, he was taken by pirates. I was hoping for some news of him.'

'And was there any?'

'No, Your Majesty. No-one has heard anything.'

Pirates again. They were a blasted nuisance, constantly disrupting shipping and raiding the villages. The people were terrified of them. Now they had taken the librarian's son. Well there was nothing that could be done. The boy could be anywhere by now; probably sold to the harem of some minor sheikh.

'I am very sorry to hear that. I know it's time we took a harder line with the pirates but they're like a swarm of bees; they fly in and take what they want and then they're gone,' said the khalifa.

'Even bees go back to the hive when they have what they want,' said the chief librarian.

'Indeed.' The man was right; pirates like everyone else needed a base, a place to go back to for rest and repairs. The librarian was a shrewd man; in his own subtle way he was suggesting that Idris send men to seek out the pirates' headquarters. Maybe it wasn't such a bad idea. Find the pirates, destroy their base and capture their ships while they were in harbour. But not now. Now he had to concentrate all his resources on the campaign to Écija. 'I will talk to the admiral of my fleet and tell him of the problem, but don't expect too much. The best I can offer at the moment is that we locate the place where they're hiding and when I return from the campaign, I will look into it,' he said.

'Thank you, Your Majesty.'

He looked disappointed, but surely he knew that the chances of finding his son again were like a grain of sand in the ocean. It would be better to think of him as dead, but he didn't say that to him. His friendship for the librarian wouldn't allow him to destroy his hope.

'The clouds have lifted, now, Yusuf. Why don't we walk in the gardens and you can read some more poetry from Homer to me?'

The chief librarian picked up the book and together they walked along the paved paths of the royal gardens, past bushes of sweet smelling roses, red, pink, yellow and a delicate white. A pair of collared doves sat on a branch of a myrtle tree, cooing to each other. Here, in his beautiful garden all was at peace; the world of war, of pirates and intrigue was a thousand miles away.

CHAPTER 6

The sun was beginning to set over the distant mountains and for a short time the horizon was a blaze of crimson. Now, as the ship pulled into the sheltered harbour the darkness crept closer and made it difficult for Bakr to get a clear idea of their new home. They had arrived at an island; that he could make out from the approach. It appeared to be a long, narrow strip of land, with a range of hills running along the length of it; from the distance it looked like a giant lizard. The harbour in which they were now weighing anchor had been formed by wind and tides into the shape of a horseshoe and was guarded at its entrance by a fortified tower. This was the pirates' secret hideaway.

The shallow draft of the pirate ship meant that it could anchor close to the beach and some of the men were already leaping over the side and wading ashore. A great shout went up from the foreshore where a huge fire was burning on the sand—as much to act as a beacon for the pirates to head for, as to warm those sitting around it—and the waiting people began to run down the beach to greet the pirates.

'Where are we?' whispered Kamil.

'This must be one of the smaller Balearic Islands,' said Asim. 'One of the uninhabited ones, I would guess.'

'So this is their home,' said Kamil, whose face, despite the hardships of the voyage, was flushed with excitement.

'What do we do?' asked Asim.

'Don't worry; I'm sure our big friend will give us our orders any time now. But don't even think of making a break for it; from what I've seen so far there's no way we can get off this island. We need to be patient and see what they have in mind for us,' said Bakr. He was worried that if Asim or Kamil caused any trouble the pirates would kill them. Asim was a good foreman but he could be impulsive and Kamil was ready for some adventure after the long, tedious journey.

'So we're stuck here for ever?' asked Kamil, sounding disappointed.

'I didn't say that. I just think we shouldn't take any chances; we need to learn a bit more about where we are and whether an escape is possible. This isn't the time to take risks. Let's find out why we're here first. It might not be necessary to escape. If we co-operate with the captain and build him the ship he wants, then he'll probably let us go home.'

Asim stared at him. 'Do you really think so, sayyad? And then, what if he did, how would we be received by the khalifa? We would have helped his enemy. As I see it, the pirates will just get rid of us when they're finished with us, and if they don't the khalifa will throw us in goal as soon as we set foot in Malaqah. We're doomed either way.'

'Come on, you three. Over you go,' said the burly pirate who seemed to have been appointed both as their bodyguard and gaoler; roles he performed in much the same way. He gave Kamil such a shove that the boy tumbled over the side and into the water. Seconds later he came to the surface, gasping for air.

'Any more of that and I'll report you to the captain,' said Bakr but the pirate just laughed, flashing his rotten teeth at them.

'And what do you think the captain will say to you? There're plenty more like that little scrap of a lad. He's only still alive because we want your co-operation,' he said. 'So get a move on.'

Bakr lowered himself into the cold water and began to wade towards the beach; his legs were still weak from lack of exercise and the wet sand made it difficult to walk. Once on the beach the warmth of the fire stretched out its arms to him and he trudged towards it and threw himself down as close as he could to the flames. As he looked about he could see everyone looking at him with interest. They were a motley collection, old men and young men, a few women and numerous children; there were also a couple of mangy dogs and about a dozen cats. He had expected hostility but there was no sign of that, only curiosity. One of the old men passed him a pewter flagon—booty from a raid on a rich merchant's ship, no doubt—and signalled for him to drink. He put it to his lips and drank deeply; it was a sweet wine, rich and delicious. It wasn't the first time he'd drunk wine, even though it was frowned upon by the imams, but he was not a habitual drinker. He felt the effects of the alcohol almost immediately and began to relax. If the captain was going to kill him, he'd have done it by now.

Those that had wives and sweethearts on the island had disappeared with them in the direction of a number of rough wooden shacks, the rest of the crew joined those by the fire and began to drink. Sitting side by side, two of the younger pirates placed a strange instrument across their knees and began to play it; while one of the men turned a handle operating the crank which caused the strings to vibrate, the other played a simple melody on the keys. Its sound was not unpleasant but different from anything Bakr had ever heard before and when they finished the pirates clapped their hands in pleasure and shouted for more.

'What strange instrument is that?' Bakr asked the old man who'd given him the wine.

The pirate beamed in pride and replied, 'That, stranger, is an organistrum. A fine instrument, indeed. We stole it from a Christian church.'

'Thank you,' said Bakr as the man refilled his flagon with wine. 'Yes, it is indeed a fine instrument.' He leant back on a piece of driftwood and sipped his wine while he listened to the music. Asim and Kamil were also drinking wine; like him they didn't want to upset their captors by refusing their hospitality. Bakr was already aware of the volatile nature of their captain; he'd witnessed him flog a man who'd displeased him only a few days before. Maybe Asim was right to be so pessimistic. Either way it wouldn't bode well if they upset the captain on their first night on the island.

He now had a clearer idea of how many men made up the crew of the ship; his first estimate had been correct. There were no more than one hundred and sixty, and only a quarter of them were armed as fighting men. The rest, the oarsmen, were not slaves; there were no signs of chains or any form of shackles and they all carried knives in their belts. They were pirates as much as the rest of them, and were likely to be just as handy in a fight.

'Sayyad,' Kamil said, moving closer to Bakr. 'What are we going to do?' His voice was slurred.

'Nothing, lad. We're going to listen to the music and enjoy being on dry land again. I'm sure tomorrow will come soon enough and then we'll know why they have brought us four hundred Arab miles.'

He pulled his cloak around him and settled down in the sand to sleep, lulled by the wine and the music.

*

When Bakr awoke, the fire was a pile of smouldering ashes and his companions of the previous night had all gone. He stood up and stretched his cold, stiff limbs. Kamil and Asim were still asleep beside him. He kicked them gently to rouse them and said, 'Wake up. It's dawn. Everyone else seems to have disappeared.'

Kamil sat up, rubbing the sleep from his eyes. Half awake, he looked like the child he still was. 'I need to piss,' he said plaintively and looked around him for a suitable place. In that moment he reminded Bakr of his own son, one moment so independent and the next so innocent.

'You'll have to go in the sand,' said Asim.

Bakr stripped off his outer clothes and made his way down to the sea. The water was bracingly cold and soon any traces of sleep had disappeared along with the dirt and grime from their voyage. He rubbed his skin vigorously with sand until he could feel it tingling. How wonderful it had been to sleep under the stars last night, instead of inside that awful bilge, with the stench of foul water pervading everything. He dived under the water for one last time, luxuriating in his salt water bath, and then headed for the shore, just in time to see the captain striding towards the dying fire. Their bodyguard was with them.

'Planning to swim back to Malaqah?' the captain asked. 'Do you have a compass? I'd hate to see you swimming in the wrong direction.' He grinned at him, but there was little humour in his words.

'Just getting clean.'

The captain turned to the pirate and said, 'My, my, these Muslims are so fastidious. He'll be washing his clothes next.'

Bakr was puzzled. Most of the pirates he'd seen looked like Muslims; not many Arabs it was true, but there were a great number of Berbers. The rest were made up of a mixture of races, many from northern Europe, some Turks and Greeks, and almost all of them were infidels. Now that he was clean he wanted to find a quiet corner to say his morning prayers but it was looking impossible. He said the first lines of the Fajr silently in his head and hoped that Allah would understand.

'Right. You wanted to know why I've brought you here, well now you will,' said the captain. 'Come with me. All of you.'

They followed him to the far end of the harbour, where a narrow stream wound its way through the trees and down into the sea. Beside the stream was a large makeshift building, half constructed of wooden planks and half covered with old sails. As he soon discovered, this was to be their workshop.

'Here you are. This is where you will work,' said the captain.

'What do you want us to do?' asked Bakr, still not wanting to believe that which was gradually becoming very clear to him.

'Build a ship, of course. You're a shipbuilder, aren't you? Well I need another ship and you and your mates are going to build it.'

'Why don't you steal one?' asked Kamil, saying aloud what they were all thinking. 'Isn't that how pirates get their ships?'

The captain glared at him. 'If I didn't need your master, boy, I'd have your tongue cut out for that impudence.' He looked at Bakr and added, 'I need a ship built to a specific design. I know you build ships for the khalifa of Malaqah's navy; you know how fast they can go and the best design to use to outsmart them. That's what I want. A ship that is both fast and robust, and will be sure to outstrip them.'

'That will take time, Captain,' said Bakr.

'You're not going anywhere are you?' He grinned, revealing a row of gold teeth that gleamed in the sunlight. 'Have to be home in time for dinner, do you?'

'And then what, Captain? Will we be released?'

'Released? Where do you think you are, man? No, get used to it; this is your home now. All of you.'

So Asim was right. The captain would keep them here until they were of no more use to him and then...? He didn't want to contemplate the plans that Captain al-Awar had in mind for them, but now he was pretty sure that they didn't include a trip back to Malaqah.

The captain was getting angry; he didn't like being questioned, so Bakr decided to humour him. 'I will need a lot of wood to build your ship, good, seasoned wood.'

'What do you think that is?' the captain said, pointing to a small mountain covered with more old sails; he pulled back the canvas to reveal an enormous stack of felled trees. 'First class oak. Cut down last year. Will that be good enough for you?'

He'd obviously been planning this for a long time. Bakr began to feel some respect for this man; he was no ordinary pirate, living from one raid to the next. This man was clever and he had ambition; he was looking to the future. The question was, did that make him less dangerous or more so?

'Tools?' asked Bakr.

The captain threw back his head and laughed, 'You will be able to use your own,' he said and pointed inside the building. There, on the sand lay a sack of Bakr's own tools, taken at the time they were kidnapped. The pirates had forgotten nothing.

Bakr couldn't refrain from asking one more question, 'But why me? There are many shipbuilders closer to your base. You didn't need to go all the way to Malaqah to find one.'

'How modest is the Muslim,' he said to the pirate, standing behind him.

'Well, why me?' asked Bakr again, he was feeling manipulated and didn't like it.

'Because you come highly recommended and I only want the best.' The captain twisted a large pearl ring around his finger, as if to emphasise the point. 'If you must know, last year we captured an excellent ship off the coast of Tangiers. Before we threw the captain overboard I managed to get him to tell me who had made it for him. He gave me your name.'

'But how many ships do you need?' asked Kamil. 'After all you can only sail one at a time.'

The captain spun round and hit the boy across the face, knocking him to the ground. 'If I want your opinion, lad, I'll ask for it. How many times do you have to be told to hold your tongue? Now get up,' he shouted.

Kamil staggered to his feet and stood there shaking. Bakr would have to speak to him later; if he didn't learn to curb his tongue he could end up with his throat cut. After all, he was only an apprentice and the captain would soon find one of his own men to replace him.

'Is there anything else you need?' the captain asked, his voice once again as oily as tar-sand.

'Before we can begin, I must work on the design and for that I need to talk to you in more detail about the ship you want.'

'Very well.'

'Leave us now to get started on preparing the wood and then I will come and find you,' Bakr said.

He could see the captain didn't enjoy being given orders, especially in front of the burly pirate, but he grunted his assent and then said to the bodyguard, 'Keep an eye on them.'

So this was why they had been kidnapped; that at least was clear. And what was becoming clearer was what al-Awar would do with them when the ship was finished, when they were of no more use to him. If they were ever going to see their families again it was up to him; he had to get them off this island.

CHAPTER 7

Hasan paced up and down the paths that criss-crossed the palace gardens. It was one of those mornings when the sky was cloudless, and the air was still and as clear as a mountain stream; from the walls of the alcázar he could scan the land and sea around him for mile after Arab mile. He gazed at the giant rock, Jebel al-Tarik, the other Pillar of Hercules which lay across the narrow stretch of water that separated Sebta from al-Andalus. He fancied he could see the apes that roamed freely around its wooded peak and the boats anchored off shore. How he longed to be back home. Al-Andalus was where he belonged; it was where he was born and his birthright. It was only four years since Baba had died, but he still missed him intensely; he had been a good father to all his children, but especially to him. Hasan was his heir and Baba had made a point of walking with him in the grounds of the alcázar most days, talking to him about his early life and how he had become khalifa. Sometimes he quoted poetry to him or told him about the golden days of al-Andalus when there had been greater peace and prosperity. He always said it was important for a ruler to learn about the history of his country, both the good things and the bad; then he would make less mistakes in the future. What would Baba say now, if he knew that Hasan and Ben Yahya had been exiled to Sebta? His uncle never called it exile; he said they would be safe there until Hasan was old enough to rule. Well, in a few weeks he would be fifteen but still no word had come from Malaqah telling him to return. He climbed up the steps and walked along the ramparts, feeling the early sun, warm on his back. Sebta was too small, too confined. He felt like a caged lion here; able to see the place he wanted to be but unable to go there. Below him lay the harbour, as usual crowded with merchant ships from all along the Maghreb, and some from further afield, Greece and Byzantium.

'Prince Hasan, I need to talk to you,' said his tutor, coming out into the garden. 'Come down from there. We must speak.'

Hasan felt a surge of excitement. Had the khalifa summoned him? Was he to return to Malaqah? Would he at last become what his father had promised him?

'What is it, Naja? Has word come from Malaqah? I haven't seen any ship arrive,' he asked, running down the steps towards the man whom he knew as well as his father.

'No, there has been no word.'

'So, what's so urgent?' he asked, peevishly.

'We must meet with the Barghawata. The governor wants to see you; he's heard that you are soon to become a man and I think he wants to know what will happen when you are fifteen.'

'But we don't know what will happen,' said Hasan. 'Until somebody comes from Malaqah to take me home, I'm stuck here with my babysitter.' He knew he shouldn't have said that—Naja was as much a friend as his tutor and guardian—but he was getting frustrated with everyone telling him what to do. It was time he began to assert his authority.

'Don't be so impatient, my Prince. Your time will come very soon. I have heard that your uncle is about to go to war with Isbiliya; he thinks he can achieve what his brother failed to do.'

'He is going to fight Abbad I? Why hasn't he sent for me to help him? Does he think I am still a child? My father was younger than me when he went on his first campaign. How am I supposed to learn how to become Supreme Commander of the army if I don't go into battle?'

'Maybe he has no intention of letting you become Supreme Commander,' said his mother, who had come up behind them.

'What do you mean, Mama?'

Fatima looked at Naja and said, 'Well, Naja, what is your opinion? Will that evil, conniving man allow my sons to return and claim what is theirs?'

'I'm sorry, Sayidda, to whom do you refer?'

'To that weasel, ibn Baqanna, of course. He has my brother-in-law under his thumb. I'm sure Idris would have invited Hasan back by now; it was never his idea to send them here in the first place. We would still be in our home in Malaqah if that interfering vizier hadn't intervened. My husband would turn in his grave if he knew that I and my sons were living in this tiny enclave on the edge of the Maghreb, where we are governed by the Barghawata, and they only tolerate us being here because they are too busy fighting their neighbours to do anything about us. My brother-in-law is an idiot; he thinks the Barghawata are ruling Sebta on his behalf but they are using him. As long as it looks as though Sebta is part of the taifa of Malaqah, it keeps their enemies at bay.'

Hasan looked at his mother in surprise. He had never heard her talk like that before; she too was beginning to show her frustration.

'I'm sorry, Sayyida, but I can't comment on that. I have never been privy to the discussions between the khalifa and his grand vizier,' said Naja, also surprised by Fatima's outburst.

'Hmph. You're as bad as the rest of them. What am I supposed to do, sit here in this forsaken city and wait for someone to murder my sons? Because that's what will happen if they are perceived as a threat to the crown. All it would take is for ibn Baqanna to send word to the governor. He would slit their throats as soon as look at them.'

Naja looked down at his feet. At last he said, 'Please forgive me, Sayidda, but I must take Prince Hasan to speak with Abu Mansur.' He bowed and then beckoned for Hasan to follow him.

'Ma'a salama, Mama. I'll come and see you later in the zenana,' Hasan said, kissing his mother on the cheek.

He followed Naja out of the alcazaba. Behind them walked six members of the Palace Guard; he went nowhere without his bodyguards. Normally he resented their presence, but his mother's words had worried him; maybe their lives really were in danger.

*

Abu Mansur lived within the alcazaba, just a short distance away from Hasan and his mother, in a modest stone house with a white facade. He was a very old man and had ruled the Barghawata and Sebta for over fifty years, but although he was old, he was shrewd and just as ambitious as he'd been in his youth. Naja had warned Hasan never to trust him and on no account to take him for a fool because that he certainly was not.

The Barghawata were a mixture of different Berber tribes, united in their strange version of Islam and their rebellious past. Hasan's mother hated them all. She hated the way they preached equality and frowned upon the traditional hierarchy of the Hammudid dynasty; she hated the way they had corrupted the words of the Quran and produced their own version, but above all she hated the fact that she, the widow of a Hammudid khalifa now had to bow before this disgusting old man, whose family a few generations previously had been herding goats on the slopes of the Atlas mountains. All this went through Hasan's mind as he waited to be called into the presence of the governor of Sebta.

'Do you know why he wants to see me?' he asked Naja for the third time.

The ex-slave shook his head. 'All I can say is that there will be a reason behind this courtesy and it might not be to our advantage.'

The heavy studded door swung open and two dark-skinned guards with bare chests and feet stood aside to let Hasan enter, but when Naja tried to follow him they barred his way with their lances.

'But I am the Prince's guardian,' he protested. 'I must accompany him everywhere.'

The guards didn't speak but neither did they move.

'Don't worry, Naja. I'll be all right,' said Hasan, sounding braver than he felt.

He had been into the governor's house only once before, the day they arrived in Sebta. Since then Abu Mansur had made no attempt to contact him or his mother, speaking only to Naja.

'As-salama alaykum, Prince Hasan,' said Abu Mansur. 'Please come in and be seated.'

'Wa alaykum e-salam, sayyad.'

Hasan sat down on a low sofa covered in goat's skin, the type of seating that could be found in bars and taverns in Malaqah. He looked around the room surreptitiously, not wanting to appear critical. There were none of the rich wall hangings and Persian carpets that were in the royal palace, no velvet cushions, no silk covers. There was just a low table by the wall, with a large copy of the Quran resting on it, and another wooden table next to the sofa with plates of dates and figs. The lighting, what there was of it, came from simple oil lamps which were still lit even though it was well past dawn.

'It is a while since I last saw you, Prince Hasan,' said the old man, his chest wheezing as he spoke. 'You have grown into a man, I see.'

Hasan had no idea what to reply so he said nothing. That had always been Baba's advice, 'When in doubt, say nothing.'

'I am sure you know why I have sent for you,' he continued.

Hasan shook his head. The governor must think he was a complete fool or a mute.

'You will come of age next week, I believe. That is a momentous time for a young man. The moment when you cease to be a child and become an adult.'

He picked up the plate of dates and handed it to Hasan, who took one gratefully, not because he was hungry but because at last here was something he could respond to.

'They come from the grounds of the alcazaba,' the old man said, helping himself to one as well. 'The best dates in Sebta.'

'They are very nice,' said Hasan, wishing that Naja was there.

'And when you are a man, what are you going to do? Stay here playing chess all day with that friend of yours? Or plan for your future?'

Hasan swallowed the rest of the date and said, 'I haven't decided yet.' His voice sounded decidedly squeaky.

'Has Naja not advised you what is best for your future? He is your guardian; surely he has some plans for you?'

Hasan realised that it was time to take control of the conversation before Abu Mansur put words into his mouth. 'Naja al-Siqlabi is my tutor and my guardian, but my uncle will decide what is best for me to do, not him.'

'Your uncle? Idris I you mean? The man who usurped your throne? What advice will he give you I wonder?' The old man stared at him, his beady eyes barely visible beneath their drooping eyelids.

Hasan thought it best not to answer.

'Well, as no-one else is advising you, then I will,' Abu Mansur said after a moment's pause. He pulled at his white beard. 'Go back to Malaqah boy and claim your birthright. That's my advice to you. There is no future for you here in Sebta.' Then he leaned back and closed his eyes. Their conversation was over.

Hasan stood up and a servant, almost as old as the governor, appeared from out of the gloom and opened the door for him.

'Well?' asked Naja, as soon as he saw him.

'Nothing. Nothing at all,' said Hasan.

*

His mother was in the zenana with her maidservant, when he returned. The visit to Abu Mansur had been strange; he couldn't quite work out what the man wanted from him. Was it a warning? Or was he suggesting that he would help him get back his throne? And what would happen if he didn't take his advice?

'So, what did he say?' Fatima asked, the moment she set eyes on him. She was wearing a long gold djubbah and a scarf of the same colour covered her greying hair. Around her neck were ropes of gleaming pearls and large rubies glowed on her hands. She was still beautiful and looked every bit a queen, except for the smudged kohl around her eyes; she'd been crying again.

Fatima spent most of her days crying or praying; they were her main activities. He remembered how lively she had been in Malaqah and how she'd loved to play with her sons. As the wife of the khalifa, she had reigned supreme in the harem, surrounded by hundreds of servants. Not now. The manner in which she and her sons had been ripped from their home had changed all their lives. He remembered that awful day; they had been allowed no time to say goodbye to their relatives and friends. One of ibn Baqanna's servants had come and instructed them to pack only what they could carry and would only allow Fatima's personal maid and Naja to accompany them. It was as if they had committed a crime.

'Tell me. What did the old goat want?' she repeated.

'He was very friendly, Mama, and said he just wanted to see how I was and that we should have a special celebration to honour my coming of age.'

'Ridiculous. That's an occasion just for the family. Why would you want a big celebration? Nobody else does that. What's he after, I wonder?'

'I don't know, Mama. But he did ask me if I wanted to return to Malaqah.'

'And what did you say?'

'I told him that I did, when my uncle sent for me.'

'Good boy. Don't let that Barghawata upstart know what you're thinking. I'm sure he wants rid of us.'

'But it's true, Mama. I do want to return home but how can I if my uncle is against it?'

'I do not believe he is against his nephews returning to Malaqah; he is just a weak man who cannot stand up to his counsellors. Once you are of age, and Idris has returned from fighting the Abbadites, then we will speak to him,' Fatima said. 'In the meantime be careful of Abu Mansur. It would suit him very well if you were no longer here.'

'Do you mean if I lived in Malaqah?' He hesitated. Should he tell her what else he'd said?

'Yes, that or dead. You must be careful Hasan. Do not leave the alcazaba unless you have to, and then only with your guards. Do you understand me?'

'Yes Mama.'

'Where is your brother?'

'I expect he is where he always is, hunting with his friends,' he grumbled.

Ben Yahya irritated him. One minute he behaved as though all he wanted to do was hunt and chat to his friends, but whenever Hasan said anything about becoming khalifa, his attitude changed and he would remind Hasan that he wasn't the only one who had been deprived of his inheritance, that he also had rights. Inevitably they ended up fighting about who would make the best khalifa; it had been fun when they were younger, but now was the time to take it seriously. Not that either of them were in a position to do anything about it at the moment.

'Well I don't want him wandering too far at the moment, either. Send him to see me when he gets back. You boys have to realise that now you are of an age to rule, there will be people out there that will try to stop you.'

'I understand, Mama.'

'Yes, but does your brother?'

It was well into the morning by now and Ben Yahya must surely have returned from the hunt. Hasan walked across to the stables to see if his horse was there.

'Where are you off to?' called his friend Aqbal. 'Do you want a game of chess?'

'I'm looking for my brother. Have you seen him?'

'Yes, just now. He looked as though he was heading for the cook house; he had a brace of hares in his hand,' he replied. 'Come on, you've got time for a quick game.'

'There's no such thing as a quick game of chess, and you know it. Maybe later. How about this evening?'

'Sounds all right with me.' He waved and then headed back the way he'd come.

So Ben Yahya had been successful on the hunt. Lately his younger brother had become obsessed with exercising his birds. He had a goshawk, a gyr falcon and two peregrine falcons and almost every day he took them out hunting. Naja had spoken to him a few times about not spending enough time on his studies but it was like talking to a stone; he would always agree and then the next day he'd be missing from his class. You couldn't rely on him. If Baba were still alive Ben Yahya would never have dared to miss a single lesson; Baba would have impressed on him the importance of a good education for any prospective ruler. He would have made it clear that his sons needed to show they were worthy of the prize. Hasan understood that and had always worked hard, trying to live up to his father's name. Ben Yahya cared more about his birds than studying, and yet he still thought he had as much right to his father's throne as Hasan.

A flock of white storks were circling above him, waiting for the thermals which would help them cross the Narrow Straits. He stopped and watched them for a moment; there must have been two hundred at least, all preparing themselves to return to their summer breeding grounds.

'Hasan. What are you doing?' called Ben Yahya. He had a small falcon on his wrist, its jesses held tightly in his hand.

'Looking for you. Mama wants to talk to you.'

'Later. I just want to spend some time training this little bird. Isn't she a beauty?'

'No, Mama said she wanted to see you right away. And Naja's annoyed that you missed your mathematics lesson.' All exaggerations, Naja hadn't said anything about Ben Yahya, but Hasan was still annoyed with his younger brother. Him and his damned birds. He knew that their uncle had deprived them of their inheritance but he was happy to leave it all to Hasan to sort out.

'Oh very well. There's no need to be so grumpy. You should be happy; you'll be fifteen next week and then nobody will be able to boss you about.'

'Just take that bird back to the falcon house and go to see Mama; she's worried about you.'

Reluctantly his brother retraced his steps; he knew his mother would never allow him to take a bird into the zenana.

Once again Hasan was overcome with the desire to escape from this tiny promontory, to get on the first ship and sail away. The destination was unimportant; he just wanted to get away from everything: his mother, his lazy brother, Abu Mansur, and most of all Naja, who seemed to be watching his every move. He looked up again at the storks which continued to wheel above him in a giant circle. Like him they too were frightened to make the move; the conditions had to be just right to cross safely. So when would they be right for him? Suddenly the storks were off and, like a white cloud they floated across to al-Andalus.

CHAPTER 8

Idris I stood on the ramparts of the alcazaba looking at his new ship in the harbour below; it was a beauty and just what was needed to strengthen his navy.

'You're sure it's fast enough?' he asked the admiral, who stood at his side. 'And will carry all the troops I specified?'

'It is, Your Majesty. It's the fastest ship in the fleet. And because of the extra sails there is room for many more soldiers.'

'Excellent. Then we must order some more.'

'I'm not sure if we will ever get another as good as that one, Your Majesty,' said the admiral.

'Why ever not?'

'Have you not heard? The builder of that ship, Bakr ibn Assam has been kidnapped by pirates. This happened back in the spring.'

'So how did they manage to get the ship finished in time, with no master shipwright?'

'I don't know, Your Majesty. There's talk that his father-in-law took over the business.'

'He's a shipwright too?'

'No, Your Majesty, he's an apothecary.'

'What?'

Idris paused. What had the chief librarian said about his son being kidnapped when he was working in the shipyard? Could this have been at the same time? He'd promised the man that he'd try to find what had happened to the boy, but with the preparations for the forthcoming campaign he'd forgotten all about it. He'd let his friend down.

'When was this exactly?' he asked.

'It must have been four months ago now. They took two other men from the yard as well.'

'Was one of them a young lad?'

'An apprentice, yes, Your Majesty.'

'And we have no idea where they've taken them?'

'No, Your Majesty. The pirates could have taken them anywhere; they have bases dotted all around the Middle Sea. Our main concern is to stop them raiding the coast of Malaqah and attacking our merchant ships. That in itself is a difficult task; the pirates come and go so swiftly that by the time we hear of the attack they have vanished and taken their booty with them.'

'I don't want excuses. These pirate attacks are a menace; they frighten our people and they disrupt trade. It's time we did more to deter them.'

'Yes, Your Majesty,' said the admiral, looking distinctly uncomfortable.

'I want Bakr ibn Assam and his men found and returned to Malaqah. Is that clear?'

'Yes, Your Majesty. I will do what I can, but it won't be easy. They may not even be still alive.'

'Of course they're alive. Why would pirates kidnap three skilled men and then kill them? Find them and bring them to me. That's an order.'

'Yes, Your Majesty. I will see to it right away.'

Idris knew he'd given the man an impossible task, but it was important to find out where the men were and if they really were still alive. Bakr was an excellent shipwright and

Idris needed more ships of that quality, but more importantly, he didn't want Bakr building ships for the pirates that were capable of outrunning his own navy.

'Wait. You must have some idea where the pirates have their bases. Every ship needs repairs from time to time. Where do they go to do them?' asked Idris.

'There are places that are renowned as havens for pirates. Those closest to Malaqah lie along the coast of the Maghreb, but there are others near Álmeria and Dénia.'

'So that's where you should look. I will speak to the grand vizier and get him to send messages to the rulers of these areas. I am sure if there were pirates using one of their bays as a haven, they would know of it. Someone has to know something.'

'Indeed, Your Majesty, but there are scores of pirate ships; how will we know if it is the one who took the shipwright?'

Idris looked proudly down at his new ship. 'If they are building ships like that one, I don't think they will be easy to hide. And the next time pirates sail into Malaqah and attack our merchant ships, I don't want to discover that they have faster ships than us. I want to know the strength of our enemy beforehand.'

'Yes, Your Majesty. I will do what I can,' said Admiral al-Maraghi, bowing rather quickly and hurrying down from the ramparts.

*

It was almost the middle of summer by the time the grand vizier brought Idris any news.

'Your Majesty, I have word from Álmeria. The sultan Zuhair says that the most likely place to look for the pirates is in the Balearic Islands. He suggests that we speak to

Mujahid al-Amiri, the sultan of Dénia; the islands are part of his taifa.'

'I know Mujahid; he is a cultured man. But I thought you'd already sent a message to him?'

'Yes, but he said that he could do nothing to help.'

'Is that all? I know for a fact that he has a powerful navy, which is how he conquered the Balearic Islands in the first place. Surely there is something he could do? The khalifa of Malaqah requests his help and all he says is that he can do nothing?'

'I'm sorry, Your Majesty. According to Zuhair, Mujahid al-Amari is worried there will be an uprising from the Balearic Islanders; their governor has made an agreement with the pirates. He wants independence from Denía and the pirates are giving him their support in return for being allowed to live on their island. That is probably the reason for his reluctance.'

'Which island is it?'

'Dragonera. It is a deserted island on the outskirts of the archipelago; its only inhabitants are a large species of lizard. Nothing much grows there. No use to anyone really.'

'Except the pirates. Well at least you have gained some useful information. It is possible that Bakr is being held there.'

'Yes, Your Majesty, but we cannot be sure—there are many other pirate havens—and we cannot send naval ships to investigate without upsetting the governor, Abid Allah ibn Aglab,' said ibn Baqanna.

'Mmm. I don't want to alienate Mujahid. You never know when he could be a useful ally against Isbiliya,' said Idris, tugging on his beard in frustration.

'Maybe you could agree to support him against this ibn Aglab in return for his help,' suggested ibn Baqanna.

'That could be a costly ransom for three kidnapped men. I'm not sure the shipwright is that valuable to me. Let me think about it. Have you spoken to Admiral al-Maraghi about this?'

'I am going to see him now.'

'Very well. See what he advises and let me know. No, better still, send him to me at once.'

'Yes, Your Majesty,' said ibn Baqanna, bowing hastily before he left.

*

The admiral bowed low before the khalifa and waited for him to speak. He was a good man, loyal and trustworthy. Maybe he should have sent him to negotiate with Mujahid al-Amiri instead of ibn Baqanna. But the admiral was no politician; the sultan of Dénia would have him wrapped around his little finger within a few minutes.

'Well, what do you have to say for yourself, Admiral? Almost two moons have passed and I am still waiting for news of this shipwright.'

'Your Majesty, I have not been to see you because I have had nothing to report. The shipbuilder and his men seem to have disappeared from the face of the earth.'

'Is that so? And have you explored all the corners of the earth? I think not. I didn't ask you to. I asked you to search the places where the pirates are most likely to have taken the shipwright. I have now heard of one possible place, the island of Dragonera, a minute piece of rock in the Middle Sea. According to my sources this is the most likely place to find these men.'

'Your Majesty, the grand vizier told me about this island but it isn't possible to land there. He says he cannot get permission for your ships to search Dragonera. What can I do?' He bowed again.

'Stand up straight, man. What do you think? Is it right that one of our allies would refuse to help us find someone we hold in high regard? Someone stolen from us by pirates?'

'No, Your Majesty.'

'No, neither do I. I will send General Rashad to speak to the sultan of Dénia. If Mujahid knows what's good for him, he will co-operate with us on this matter.'

General Rashad was his most experienced general and, unlike the admiral who was an excellent tactician when it came to a sea battle, he was a man who knew his way around the negotiating table.

'This matter has to be resolved. You will dispatch your fastest ship and your best captain to Dénia with the general on board. I want those men found as soon as possible,' continued Idris. 'Send a message to General Rashad telling him I must speak to him at once. I will wait for him in the throne room.'

'Yes, Your Majesty,' the admiral said, bowing once more and backing out of the room.

Idris sighed. This business was beginning to irritate him. He should be concentrating on the forthcoming campaign, not worrying about a shipbuilder and his men, but he couldn't leave until it was resolved. The truth was that he couldn't look Yusuf in the eye until he could assure him that he'd done everything he could to find his son. He thought of his own children, in particular his sons, one of whom was ruling the taifa of al-Jazira, and another two still at home with their mother. He had felt blessed when they had been born. How would he feel if one day pirates came and stole them from him?

He walked over to the window and gazed down at the busy harbour below the walls of the alcazaba. Malaqah relied on its maritime trade; that's where most of the city's wealth came from. It was about time someone did something to curb this scourge of pirates that threatened both lives and livelihoods. If they found the pirates' haven and destroyed their ships it would send a signal to other pirates that it was dangerous to attack Malaqah, that their khalifa was a force to be reckoned with and there was nowhere they could hide from him. He smiled. It would do his reputation no harm. The merchants, in particular, would support his actions. It was always good to have the support of the businessmen of the city.

'Your Majesty, General Rashad is waiting for you in the throne room,' said one of his guards.

Good. The general would know how to handle Mujahid. 'As-salama alaykum, General,' he said, walking up to his throne and sitting down. He spread his robes around him and waited for the general to approach.

'Wa alaykum e-salam, Your Majesty. You wanted to see me?'

'Yes, General. I want you to go immediately to Dénia and speak with our dear friend and ally, Mujahid al-Amiri. I want you to impress on him the importance of allowing my men to search the island of Dragonera for the pirates who kidnapped three of our citizens a few months ago. Is that clear?'

'Are you referring to the shipbuilder, Your Majesty?'

'I am indeed. The admiral will provide you with a fast ship and his most trustworthy captain. You are to leave right away.'

'With respect, Your Majesty, what about the campaign? I need to oversee the arrangements for my troops.'

'Of course. Don't worry. You will be back in two weeks. Plenty of time before we march. I plan to leave for Écija in six weeks.'

'It won't be easy to persuade Mujahid. He doesn't want to stir up trouble with the governor.'

'He's the sultan of Dénia, a large and prosperous taifa. The governor of the Balearic Islands is under his command. If Mujahid is our friend then he will grant us access to that island and the governor will do as he is told.'

'I will do my best, Your Majesty.'

Idris stood up, catching his long robe in his right hand and looping it over his left arm. 'Good. I know I can rely on you, General. And send me a message as soon as you have any news.'

General Rashad bowed and backed out of the room. He didn't look very happy but Idris knew he would do all in his power to complete his mission; that was the sort of man he was.

In the meantime he must make some plans regarding his nephews. If anything happened to him in the battle, Idris wanted to be sure that he had done right by his brother. He couldn't trust ibn Baqanna to honour his wishes; he'd seen how duplicitous he'd been when Yahya had died, encouraging Idris to take the throne despite the fact that Yahya had specifically named his sons as his heirs. He regretted it now, even though his nephews had been far too young to rule at the time. But this year Hasan would come of age and Idris was going to make sure that in the eventuality of his death in battle, his nephew would inherit what was rightfully his. He needed to put it all down in writing, so that there was no discrepancy. But who could he trust to record his wishes?

He motioned for his servant to approach. 'Bring the Chief Librarian to me, right away. I will wait for him in the Throne Room,' he ordered.

CHAPTER 9

Makoud was surprised to see Avi standing in the shop talking to Ibrahim.

'As-salama alaykum, dear friend. What brings you here?'

'Aleichem shalom, Makoud. I was just congratulating Ibrahim on passing his exams. So we have two qualified apothecaries in the family now.'

'Yes, he did very well,' said Makoud, putting his arm around his son. He had been delighted when Ibrahim came home and told him. Now he could be sure that the business he was working so hard to build up would stay in the family. 'Do you have some news for us?'

'I do. Nothing concrete but at least I think I have identified some of the pirates' retreats.'

'Excellent. Come upstairs and we can talk. You'll look after the shop, Ibrahim?' he asked.

'Of course, Baba. We're due to close soon, anyway. It's too hot for anyone to be out.'

It was a scorching day, and even in their normally cool house the heat was unbearable, so Makoud took his guest up onto the roof terrace, which his wives had cleared of all the jumble that had cluttered it previously and furnished it with two low divans and a couple of tables. A few pots containing sweet smelling herbs and scarlet geraniums completed the transformation.

'You have a fine view,' said Avi, appreciatively taking a seat under the canvas awning that had been stretched across the terrace to shield it from the full force of the sun. 'I can see my own ships down there.' He pointed to two merchant ships anchored in the harbour.

'Those are yours? I have often wondered which were your ships. It has become one of my favourite pastimes, sitting here, watching the shipping,' said Makoud. 'Just a moment and I'll ask Abal to make us some cold lemonade.'

'Is Dirar home?' asked Avi. 'I think it would be useful if he joined us.'

'He's probably sleeping but it's time he was up, anyway. I'll give him a call. What about Aisha?'

'No, there's no need to send for her. Why raise her hopes when we have nothing definite to tell her?'

Once they were all settled, and sipping the cold lemonade, Avi began, 'My captains have made enquiries at every port they have entered. So far, it is not good news because there are a number of pirate havens, especially along the coast of the Maghreb. There are numerous small inlets which pirates frequent and there is no way of finding out which is the one where they're holding Bakr. Besides which, no-one has heard of anyone building a new ship, or even doing the sort of repairs that would require a shipwright.'

Makoud felt his heart sink. The Maghreb coast was long and treacherous, stretching from the Narrow Straits along the full length of the Atlas Mountains and beyond. It was a thriving trading area, frequented by merchants from across the Middle Sea and camel trains from the interior. Anyone could buy the men and take them back with them to the Sahara, or Egypt, or anywhere else where they would never be heard of again. There would be no way of ever finding them once they were sold. They would vanish forever.

'But they tell me that there are other places where the pirates hole up to do their repairs, further east. One place in particular is notorious for pirates. The island of Crete.'

'But that's miles away,' said Dirar. 'That's almost in Greece, the other end of the Middle Sea. Surely pirates that raid along this coast aren't going to travel all the way to Crete to careen their ships.'

'So you think they're somewhere closer to Malaqah?' Ibrahim asked.

'Yes, why would they waste time and energy travelling further than they need to? The Maghreb seems the most sensible to me,' said Dirar. 'I think we should concentrate our search there.'

'Have you found out anything from the other fishermen?' asked Avi.

'Sometimes fishing boats from further north come into our waters, looking for the tuna. There are a number of them here at the moment; now is the best time for catching tuna, because they have just finished spawning,' Dirar added. 'I'll ask around.'

'Good. What about you, Makoud? Have you spoken to the admiral?' asked Avi.

'No, but we have just delivered the new boat, so it is a good time to speak to him. I'll go there tomorrow. He has to pay for the boat, anyway. I can ask him what he knows at the same time.' Makoud felt a little ashamed that he hadn't done anything sooner, but he was embarrassed to approach the admiral of the fleet on a personal matter. Still it had to be done; they had to explore all avenues and the others were expecting him to do his part.

'That's good. Very well. Can you all come to my house, tomorrow evening and we'll see if we are able to come up with a plan for rescuing them,' said Avi. He was a good man to have on your side in a crisis. Normally so jovial and relaxed, when he had business to do, he was different, organised and decisive.

'Will you stay and eat with us, friend?' Makoud asked.

'Thank you, but no. I must get back to my family. I'll see you all tomorrow at sunset. Aleichem shalom, my friends.'

Makoud's sons stood and wished Avi a safe journey home, while Makoud accompanied him to the door. 'Do you think we will ever find them?' he asked. 'Do you think they're even still alive?'

'We must pray to our gods that they are. Surely with the help of both Allah and Jehovah we will find them,' he said with his familiar smile. 'Until tomorrow, dear friend. Aleichem shalom.'

'Alla ysalmak, Avi.'

*

After they had left, Makoud sat there a while longer, looking at the ships below him in the harbour. There was a great deal of activity going on; it seemed as if the fleet was getting ready to leave. He leapt up. There was no time to lose; if they left now they might not be back for months. He had to speak to the admiral right away.

He rushed through the shop, leaving a surprised Ibrahim staring after him as he ran down the road towards the harbour, his dubbah flapping behind him.

A large merchant ship was being unloaded and a stream of porters were ferrying goods from the ship to the waiting mules that were patiently lined up alongside the quay. He pushed his way through until he found the harbour master.

'As-salama alaykum, my good man,' he said. 'Can you tell me if the admiral is aboard his ship?'

'Wa alaykum e-salam, Apothecary. You look agitated.'

'I am indeed. I need to speak to Admiral al-Maraghi. It's a very important matter.'

'Well he's not here. He doesn't usually board until just before his ship is ready to leave. And that won't be until dawn tomorrow. I expect you'll find him in the alcazaba.'

Makoud heaved a huge sigh of relief. So there was still time.

'Thank you.'

He would have stayed and chatted to the harbour master, who often came into his shop, but a dispute had broken out among the porters and the man hurried away to intervene.

As he wandered back up the path to the city he spotted Dirar in the distance, talking to some fishermen, not the men his son usually fished with, but strangers. He waved.

'Baba, wait a minute,' called Dirar and ran across to greet him. 'I have some news.'

'Well, what is it?' he asked.

'Those men, they're here fishing for tuna. They've been fishing all along the coast of north Africa and not seen nor heard anything about Bakr but one of them said he'd heard a rumour that a pirate called Captain al-Awar has been boasting that he will soon have a fleet of ships that will outstrip the khalifa's.'

'Do they know where this man is?'

'No, but they don't think he rests up in the Maghreb. They know the name but no-one remembers having seen him or his men in that area.'

'So we're no further forward.'

'Yes we are, Baba. We can stop looking at north Africa and concentrate on the rest of the coast of the Middle Sea. Focus more to the north.'

'I suppose so.' How many hundreds of miles of coast did that leave them?

'Have you spoken to the admiral?' asked Dirar.

'No. I'm on my way to see him now,' Makoud admitted, a little embarrassed at his lack of effort.

'Tell him what I've told you. Remember they said his name was al-Awar.'

'Very well, son. I will. Good work,' he added.

'I must get back to my boat now,' Dirar said. 'Ma'a salama, Baba.'

'Alla ysalmak, my son.'

Makoud smiled; truly Allah had blessed him with three good sons.

*

The guard at the gate to the alcazaba recognised him at once and said, 'As-salama alaykum, Apothecary. Where are you off to this lovely morning?'

'I need to speak to the admiral of the fleet,' he said, a little tersely.

'About those new boats you're building for him, I suppose.' Makoud must have looked surprised at his words because the guard continued, 'Oh we all know that you're in charge of the shipyard now that Bakr is gone.'

There was little that people didn't know in this city, and the guards, who were always on sentry duty, seemed to know more than most.

'Of course. I need to keep the admiral advised on how the work is progressing,' he said, not wanting to gossip with the guard.

'Well you go along, then,' he said, stepping to one side to let Makoud through the archway and into the outer courtyard. 'Do you know the way?'

Makoud stopped. He had no idea which way to go. The truth was he hated going into the alcazaba ever since his oldest son, Umar had been arrested for something he didn't do and thrown in the dungeons. That had been a frightening time but eventually they had managed to prove Umar's innocence and he'd been released. Just recently his son had been promoted to nazir and was now in charge of a troop of sixteen men. He had felt very proud when Umar had come home to give them the news.

'No, actually I don't.'

'It's not far. His office is just up that path, through the archway and along there on the right hand side. You can't miss it,' said the guard. He turned away from the apothecary to hold his lance across the entrance and block the path of a man on horseback. Makoud heard him demand to know who he was.

He made his way up the cobbled path, past the guard at the next gate and through the archway as directed. The sentry at the entrance to the alcazaba had obviously allowed the stranger to enter because now the man galloped past him, causing Makoud to step quickly out of his way. Rude bastard. Where was he going in such a hurry? On the right hand side, close to the walls of the alcazaba were a number of stone buildings. One of these had to be the admiral's office, and he decided it was probably the one with a guard standing to attention outside the door.

'I'd like to speak to Admiral al-Maraghi,' he said to the sentry, who was regarding him a little suspiciously.

'Who are you? What's your name and what is your business with the admiral?' he asked.

'Please tell Admiral al-Maraghi that Makoud, the new manager of the shipyard would like to speak to him as a matter of urgency.'

'Shipyard?' The guard looked surprised at this, but knocked on the door and when it opened, he stood aside to allow Makoud to enter.

One of the admiral's servants led Makoud into a light and airy room which overlooked the harbour. The admiral was seated on a low divan, drinking fruit juice.

'Makoud, how nice to see you,' he said. 'Come, sit down and have some of this delicious juice. It's made from a mixture of lime, lemons and peaches. Quite refreshing in this hot weather.'

He wiped his face with a small cotton cloth.

'As-salama alaykum, sayyad. Thank you for seeing me,' said Makoud.

'So, why are you here? And why the urgency? I hope nothing has happened with the new ship. The khalifa is very anxious to receive it.'

Makoud waited while the servant poured some juice into a glass for him then said, 'No, sayyad. The ship is progressing well. It should be ready on time.'

'So why the visit?'

'You know we have lost the master shipbuilder, Bakr, to the pirates. Well I wondered if there was anything you could do to help us find him?'

'But he could be anywhere. Once the pirates have you there is no knowing where you might end up.'

'I know, sayyad, but one of my sons has heard a rumour that a pirate named al-Awar is planning to build a fleet of ships that he says will outstrip those of the khalifa. In other words, ships that will be better than those we are currently building.'

'Is that so?'

'It may only be a rumour, sayyad, but I have to ask myself *who* is building these ships? We know that Bakr's reputation is widely known throughout the Middle Sea and nobody has heard of anyone who could rival him. So who else could it be but Bakr himself?'

The admiral stroked his beard in silence and then said, 'Where do we find this al-Awar?'

'That is the problem, sayyad. Nobody knows where he goes in the winter to make repairs, but the fishermen are pretty confident that it is not near the Maghreb. They think possibly more to the north.'

'Well, Makoud. I owe you a debt of gratitude for the work you have done in the absence of the master shipbuilder, so I will tell you what I know. Without your assistance we would not have that fine ship, and even another one under construction. I have told you that the khalifa is very happy with the quality of his new ship, so much so that he has ordered me to find out where they have taken Bakr. He does not want him building ships for the pirates, if that is what he is currently being made to do.'

'So you're going to look for him?' asked Makoud, his heart racing.

'It's not quite that straightforward. We think he may be in the Balearic Islands,' said the admiral, pulling at his beard again. 'On the island of Dragonera.'

'If you know where he is then you can go and rescue him?'

'As I said, it's not that simple. The Balearic Islands are in a different taifa; we need permission to enter their waters.'

'But you're going to try?'

'The khalifa has ordered me to recover the shipbuilder. He has sent one of his generals to speak to the ruler of Dénia about it. That's all I can tell you. I will do as I'm commanded, if it is possible,' said the admiral.

Makoud thought he looked doubtful about his chances of success.

'And of course,' the admiral continued. 'It is possible that Bakr is not the one responsible for building the ships for the pirate captain.'

'Al-Awar,' Makoud said, to remind him.

'Yes, al-Awar. So I'm sorry Makoud, that I cannot give you a clear answer to your questions but rest assured that the khalifa and I are taking the disappearance of these men seriously.' He put down his glass on the table in a way that told Makoud that his meeting with him was over. 'Do not worry. We will do all we can to find your son-in-law.'

Makoud got up. 'Ma'a salama, sayyad. Thank you for speaking to me.'

'Alla ysalmak, Apothecary. I will send word immediately we have news.'

As Makoud made his way out of the alcazaba and down the hill to his apothecary shop, he didn't exactly feel elated, but at least they were making some progress. This evening, he would go and tell the others what he had discovered. If the admiral wasn't allowed to rescue Bakr, then they'd have to do something themselves. If they didn't, Aisha would never forgive him.

CHAPTER 10

General Rashad was extremely annoyed that the khalifa had decided to send him to negotiate with Mujahid al-Amiri. He just didn't have the time to be running around looking for some shipbuilder; he should be concentrating on the campaign. Idris thought it was going to be easy to overthrow Abbad I because this time he had the support of not just Garnata, but also Álmeria and Badajoz, but he should never underestimate that wily old campaigner. It was never going be easy to defeat Isbiliya; they had become a very powerful taifa and still Abbad wasn't satisfied. He was a ruthless and ambitious opponent, with years of experience in dealing with newcomers like Idris. But the general couldn't say all that to his sovereign; Idris was normally a reasonable man but, like most men in his position, he didn't like criticism and would certainly view it as treason if the general spoke to him in that way. Rashad was too fond of his head to risk upsetting their new khalifa.

'Quaid, take a message to the admiral for me. Tell him I have decided to travel to Dénia on horseback. I will not need one of his ships to take me. I don't see the point in wasting yet more time sailing leisurely along the coast, when a team of good horses could get me there in a couple of days.'

'Very well, sayyad.'

'Then arrange for a dozen good men to accompany me. We will need a change of horses. I do not intend to stop until we arrive at the palace of Mujahid al-Amiri. Is that clear?'

'Yes, sayyad. Will a dozen men be enough? It is poor protection if you were to be attacked,' the quaid said.

The general thought for a moment and then said, 'Make it fifty. But fifty of your best men, mind.'

'Of course, my General.'

'We leave within the hour. Is that understood?'

'Yes, sayyad. They will be ready.'

'Oh and tell Admiral al-Maraghi that I will leave word for him in Dénia. By the time he arrives I will no doubt be back in Malaqah.'

'Very well, sayyad. I will make sure he understands that speed is of the essence for you.'

The quaid was an older man who had been with the general many years. Due to his injuries in the many battles he had fought over the years, he was no longer any use in the field, but he had turned out to be an excellent personal aide-de-camp for the general. Rashad often wondered how he had ever managed without him.

*

The journey was uneventful. General Rashad made sure to by-pass the main towns of Álmeria, Qartayannat al-Halfa and Alicante, and head straight to his destination; he wanted no delays other than those forced upon them by the need to rest the horses. As soon as they arrived in the fortified port of Dénia, he and two of his men made their way to the alcázar where he asked for an audience with Sultan Mujahid al-Amiri.

Almost as if he were expecting him, the sentry took him and his men straight to the sultan, who was seated in the gardens overlooking the harbour, reading. A young boy sat by his side, playing a lute.

'Wait here,' the general told his men and bowing his head made his way towards the sultan. He had met him on many occasions because Mujahid al-Amiri had been the sultan of Dénia for almost thirty years. He was an astute and careful man, unlikely to make any precipitous decisions.

When Mujahid saw the general approach, he motioned for the boy to stop playing.

'As-salama alaykum, General Rashad. I take it you have been sent to persuade me to let you search for this man whom your khalifa is so keen to find?'

'Wa alaykum e-salam, Your Excellency. That is correct. I have come to talk to you about the men kidnapped by pirates whom we believe to be hiding on one of your islands.' He bowed respectfully.

'Sit down beside me,' the sultan said, patting the cushions where he sat. 'And enjoy this lovely music. This sweet child has the touch of angels. Don't you agree?' He waved his hand at the boy, who resumed his playing.

The young slave could certainly play very sweetly, but music was not something that Rashad knew much about. The music he liked best was the call to battle. That's what got his blood stirring.

'I'm sure it is very good, Your Excellency.'

'Well, General, I do not think that I can tell you anything more than I have already told your grand vizier. You will have had a wasted journey, I fear. I do not know where these men are. I believe there are three of them?'

'Yes, Your Excellency. The owner of the shipyard, himself a master shipbuilder, his foreman and a young apprentice.'

'Indeed. I fail to see why these three men are of so much importance to your khalifa. Are there no more shipbuilders in your city?'

'Indeed there are, Your Excellency. Many in fact. Our navy is not as great as your own.' He looked towards the harbour where more than two hundred naval ships lay at anchor, and continued, 'but shipbuilding is very important to our economy and the shipbuilder who has been kidnapped is one of the best there is in all of al-Andalus. Besides which, Khalifa Idris I believes it is important to show these pirates that they cannot do as they please. He wants to send them a message that he intends to hunt them all down and sink their ships. He will give no quarter to men who steal from him.'

Idris had no intention of doing any such thing, but Mujahid didn't know that.

'Well, I must say I'm surprised that Idris is devoting so much time to this rather trivial matter. Personally, I do not feel I can risk our own peace and stability by allowing a foreign power to land on the islands. I hope your khalifa understands this. He knows that the peace here is fragile. There are those who would like to break up my kingdom and set up independence for the islands. I cannot allow that.'

'The khalifa understands that things are difficult for you. The last thing he would want to do, is make them worse. Which is why he sent me to speak to you, to see if there is any way we could confirm that our citizens are not being held by the pirates.'

'And if they are?'

'Well then he would like to rescue them, naturally. Is it possible that I could speak directly to the governor?'

'No that is impossible. Governor Abd Allah ibn Aglab would leap on that as a provocation and incite the people of the islands to rebellion. He is just waiting for an excuse to cause me trouble. The governor has very few ships of his own; he relies on the support of the pirates. And in return he leaves them alone.'

'Surely there is some solution we can agree on?' asked the general, in his most persuasive voice. 'The khalifa would be very grateful for your help in this matter.'

'But are you even sure that these men are on the islands? And if so, which one? There are dozens of small islands. It is a wonderful area to disappear; hundreds of small coves and inlets where a ship can enter and not be seen from the mainland. That is why it is so favoured by the pirates.'

'We have two accounts that suggest that the men might be being held on Dragonera. Do you know the place?'

'Dragon Island as the locals call it? It's a lump of rock off the coast of Mayurqa. That's possible. There's nothing there. But there are many more similar places. It could be any one of them. Or none of them. It will be like looking for a needle in a sack of corn.'

'But if you put your hand in the sack and the needle pricks your finger?'

The sultan smiled. 'True.'

'Your Excellency, may I ask you something?'

Mujahid nodded.

'Are you happy to have so many pirates sheltering off your shores? What if one day they join forces with the governor and attack Dénia? Would it not be better if Idris were to wipe them all out and destroy their ships? Would you sleep better at night?'

The sultan looked at the general in silence for what seemed a very long time. Rashad began to wonder if he had overstepped the mark.

'General. Let me speak plainly. I would not like there to be any ill feeling between Idris and myself over this. I have the highest regard for your khalifa and count him as one of my few friends. He is a cultured man and we have enjoyed many pleasant exchanges in the past, discussing books and music. Like me, the khalifas of Malaqah have always welcomed the intellectuals and scholars who were banished from Qurtuba, into our cities. Like me, Idris I is a patron of the arts, a lover of good music. I would hate for anything to disrupt our friendship,' said Mujahid al-Amiri, laying his open book on the ground beside him.

The General nodded. Was Mujahid being sincere, or was this a threat? He couldn't be sure. All he could do was wait and see if he had said enough to convince the sultan to help them.

'Leave me now and I will think about what we can do to help you. Go and rest. Eat. I will send for you as soon as I have had time to ponder the best solution for both of us.'

He waved his hand and the general was dismissed.

A servant led him to a small room where food had already been laid out for him. As he looked at the colourful array of fruit, bread, nuts and the steaming dish of rice and seafood, he realised that he hadn't eaten since the day before and neither had his men. Well, they might as well enjoy this meal because there was nothing else they could do now, not until the sultan sent for him.

'Come on lads, you can help me eat this food,' he said to his men.

*

Two hours later, rested and with a full stomach, he was on his way back to the Dar al-Jund where the rest of his men were waiting. In his bag was a letter from the sultan giving Admiral al-Maraghi permission to sail in their waters, but it said nothing about allowing him to land. However, neither did it say that he couldn't land. It was worded in a beautifully ambiguous way. He smiled to himself. This would be enough for the admiral; the sultan had agreed to them sailing around the islands to look for the men. It said nothing about what they should do if they found them, so it seemed as if the sultan was going to turn a blind eye to that eventuality.

His men were in the Dar al-Jund, chatting to the local soldiers; some were grooming their horses and one or two were taking advantage of the free time to stretch out and catch up on their sleep.

'All ready, Quaid?' he asked.

'Yes, General. The men are ready to leave as soon as you give the word,' he said, aiming a heavy kick at one soldier who was sitting hunched against the wall and snoring his head off.

'Select two good men and send them to the harbour to wait for the arrival of Admiral al-Maraghi. They are to give him this document. Under no circumstances are they to give it to anyone else. Is that clear? Once they have done that they must return to Malaqah with all possible haste. We will be leaving for Écija at the end of the month.' The general handed him the scroll that carried the signature of the sultan.

He waited while the quaid gave his orders and once the soldiers had formed an orderly column, he gave the order to move out. As they trotted out of the alcazaba and headed for Malaqah, General Rashad silently congratulated himself on a mission successfully accomplished, and without promising Mujahid anything in return. The khalifa would be pleased. Especially if it led to the location of the three men who seemed to be so important to him.

CHAPTER 11

There were worse places to be than Dragonera, thought Bakr as he watched the dolphins playing offshore. The sea was a brilliant turquoise and as still as a mill pond; in the distance he could see the outlines of other islands and the hazy peaks of the mountains on the mainland. It was a truly beautiful spot; in other circumstances he would have been happy sitting there on the white sand, but here he could never forget that he was a prisoner, separated from his wife and his family. With a deep sigh, he got up and walked back to their makeshift boat yard. They had been on the island for about four months; he couldn't be sure of the exact length of time, but he had counted four new moons so he knew it was about right. Four new moons without his beloved. What was she doing right now? Did she think he was dead? Had they said prayers for him as though he was? And how were they managing? Who was running the shipyard? He knew there was enough money to keep his family fed for at least a year, but what then? He feared the captain would never let them go home. What would Aisha do then? Would she take another husband? It was like a knife to his heart when he thought of her in another man's arms.

'Sayyad, we have covered the hull in pitch. Do you want us to work on the sails while we wait for it to dry?' asked Asim.

His foreman didn't look well. He hadn't eaten for days and his skin was a grey colour, despite the fact that they were working in the sunshine every day. Young Kamil, on the other hand, was a brown as a nut and bursting with health and testosterone.

'Yes, that's a good idea. Rig up some shade over there by the palm trees and work there.'

Together they spread out the canvas sheets so that Asim and Kamil could stitch them into triangular sails. Later they would be oiled and hung over wooden trestles to dry.

'Are you feeling well, Asim?' he asked.

'I'm fine, sayyad. Just missing my own bed, that's all.'

'Aren't we all,' said Bakr with a sigh.

'Well, I'm not sure about all of us,' said Asim with a grin. He pointed across at Kamil, who was chatting to the daughter of one of the older pirates. 'I think that one might have found a new bed to share.'

Bakr laughed. His young apprentice was a high-spirited youth, always optimistic; his exuberance had helped them all cope with their new circumstances. 'I just hope her father doesn't find out,' he said. 'Kamil, come here and help Asim sew these sails.'

It had been a surprise to see women on this island; at first glance it hadn't seemed habitable. There certainly wasn't much chance of growing their own food on this barren rock, so how did they live?

'Yes, sayyad,' the boy replied, hurrying over to them, but not before giving the girl a big smile and whispering something in her ear.

'What's that?' asked Asim. 'A secret assignation?'

'Nothing's very secret here,' said Kamil with a wide grin.

'Yes, and don't you forget it. If you go messing about with the young women on this island you'll find yourself in a lot of trouble. Just because they are pirates it doesn't mean that they don't take their women's honour as seriously as we do,' said Bakr, wondering how many times Kamil was going to chance his luck. The captain had already locked him in the hold of the ship for constantly questioning his actions; he was in danger of a more severe punishment if he didn't learn to show the captain some respect. 'And no more wandering off. I expect to see that sail finished by the time I come back.'

Kamil opened his mouth to say something but then thought better of it.

During the months they had been on the island, some of the pirates had disappeared from time to time on raiding parties, from which they came back laden with whatever they had managed to steal. Sometimes they were successful, at other times, less so. One day they returned with bales of cloth, silks and satins of various colours, and swords and daggers made of fine Toledo steel. Another time they had a pair of goats and a donkey, but usually it was barrels of wine and sacks of flour that they dragged up the beach. If they kidnapped anyone, then they got rid of them before they returned, except once. One day, the captain came back from one of his forays with a young girl in tow. She didn't look much older than Maryam, and she had the same big brown eyes. He felt his stomach lurch as he thought how some poor mother must be breaking her heart over this girl's disappearance. It was unlikely she'd ever see her again.

Bakr headed for the pirates' ship; the captain wanted it careened and had ordered him to oversee the work. At the last high tide it had been dragged up onto the beach and now lay tilted on the sand, exposing its underside. A group of pirates were busy scraping barnacles off the hull. It was Bakr's job to make sure the careening went well and that any rotten parts were replaced, if not then the ship lost speed and in extreme circumstances sprang a leak and even sank.

'What's that?' he said, poking at a decaying plank perforated with holes. 'It looks like a case of Teredo worm. You'll have to cut it all out.' He marked out the area he wanted removed and then went along the length of the hull, carefully checking that the perfidious worm hadn't attacked any more of the ship.

'How bad is it?' asked the captain, peering at the hull with his only good eye.

'Not bad at all. Just a couple of patches. We can fix that easily enough,' said Bakr.

'And the new ship? How much longer do I have to wait for that? We can't live on fresh air, you know. We have to get back to work.'

'It's not possible to build a ship of the quality you require in a hurry. It takes time. It will be ready when it's ready,' said Bakr. Surely the captain knew that they wanted it finished as quickly as he did, but Bakr wasn't going to cut corners, even for a pirate.

The captain turned away from him, angry at his tone and shouted at his men to work faster. At the moment he was careful not to upset the shipwright, but once the ship was finished his attitude would change; Bakr was sure of that.

The pirates had been coming to Dragonera for so long now that a community of chandlers had set themselves up on the island to provide the pirates with rope, sailcloth, water barrels and other utensils that they couldn't always steal. Two of these men now sat under the shade of a banana plant, plaiting ropes. He squatted down beside them.

'Good day to you, shipwright,' said the older one.

'As-salama alaykum,' replied Bakr, accepting the jug of water that the rope maker passed him. He drank thirstily.

'So you're still here?' said the other.

'Yes, there's a lot to be done to complete the ship. The hull's finished but we've only just started on the sails, and there are still the galleys to construct, and the masts. Plenty to do,' said Bakr. The men on the island were very friendly towards them; they liked to have someone new to listen to their stories and to bring them news of the world outside Dragonera. Sometimes he wondered if they too were prisoners.

'Then there will be the others to do,' said the rope maker. His hands were as hard and knotted as a tree trunk from years of doing the same work.

'What others? You think the captain will want more ships?' asked Bakr, his worst fears now spoken aloud.

'He's planning to have a fleet of them. One for each of his sons and one for himself.'

'What? How many sons does he have?' He felt his stomach lurch at the thought of how long they would have to remain there.

'Oh only four,' the rope maker said with a laugh. He was amused to see Bakr's consternation. 'But don't worry, one of them is only seven. He won't need his ship for a few years yet.'

'Just make sure you do exactly what he wants,' said the older one, who had a cast in his left eye, which made it seem that he was looking at something over your shoulder.

'Well I'm trying to, but it's not always easy to combine speed and extra cargo space. I think the captain is looking for a miracle,' said Bakr.

'That was the problem before,' said the rope maker. 'The captain wouldn't take poor old Sulayman's advice.'

'What happened?' asked Bakr, feeling uneasy.

'First raid they made was a disaster. The ship was top heavy and almost sank; the captain was lucky to escape with his life.'

'As it was he lost the ship and most of his crew.'

'Not to mention the hoard of silver and bales of silk that they'd stolen. Not a good day.'

'So what happened?' asked Bakr.

'What do you think? By the time the captain had made his way back here, he was in a filthy mood. He sent for Sulayman and told him what had happened to his precious ship. Then he marched him up to the top of that cliff over there and threw him onto the rocks.'

'What?' Bakr looked to where he was pointing; angry waves lashed against the rocks at the foot of the cliff, sending up plumes of white foam. No-one could survive a fall like that.

'In front of everyone. Poor bastard lay there in agony for hours, until the tide came in and washed his body away. He'd thought he was going home once the ship was finished—he was a local man, from Mayurqa, you know. Nice chap. Instead he went off to Paradise.' The man with the cast in his eye, laughed, humourlessly. 'Doesn't do to upset the captain. He has a nasty temper.'

'I'll keep that in mind,' said Bakr.

'You'd do well to do that. And keep that lad of yours under control. He's always sniffing round the young women.'

'I know; I've spoken to him and warned him to keep away from them.'

'Problem is that the captain can be very jealous,' said the rope maker, coiling the completed rope on the ground. 'Especially when it comes to his wives.'

'The captain has wives on the island?' asked Bakr, amazed at the news.

'Two. It's the younger one that we've seen your chap sniffing around. The one with the huge brown eyes that the captain brought back here just recently.'

'Can't say I blame him; she's a real beauty,' said the other chandler.

'In the name of Allah, don't tell me she's one of the captain's wives? I thought she was a child.'

The two men smiled at him, evidently amused at his consternation.

'She is. The captain likes them young.'

'That's why you need to keep that young fellow in check. The captain doesn't like anyone messing about with his women.'

'Don't worry, I will.'

Bakr was furious. What he had taken for exuberance on the part of Kamil, now looked more like foolhardiness. He would have to speak to him at once, before things got out of control. Escape now looked more urgent than ever. There was no time to lose; they had to find a way off this lump of rock as soon as possible.

'Tell me, how is it that the pirates can live here, in sight of the mainland, and nobody bothers them? Doesn't it worry the governor of the islands that there are pirates here?' Bakr asked. He needed to understand exactly what sort of situation existed between Captain al-Awar and the people on the main island.

'No. not at all,' said the younger man, whom his companion had addressed as Ali. 'Quite the opposite. They have an arrangement.'

'What sort of arrangement?'

'The pirates don't bother the people living on the other islands and they don't bother the pirates. It works well. That's how we come to be here.'

'Yes, we would be in fear of our lives, otherwise. But they need us as much as they need a safe haven,' said Ali.

'But what's in it for you?'

The two men looked at each other. 'It's a living,' said the older one, twisting together three strands of jute while Ali held them taut.

'Our families live on the main island,' Ali said. 'They're tired of being governed by Dénia; they want to be independent. The pirates have sworn to support the governor get that independence.'

'What about the women we saw earlier? The wives? Don't they live here?' asked Bakr.

'Those whores? No, they're only here while the pirates are on the island, then they go back to Medina Mayurqa and take their offspring with them.'

'It's quiet now. You wait until the colder weather comes in, and the storms. Then you'll see a lot more activity on Dragonera and the other islands. All the pirates hole up in the winter. There'll be at least another couple of ships here, the usual ones that come every year. You never know, one of their captains might have some work for you as well,' said Ali.

Bakr's mind was racing, not with the news of their wish for independence—he had heard talk of such movements all over al-Andalus—what was much more interesting was the fact that these two men had families on the main island. Did that mean that they came and went as they wished? And the women too returned to Mayurqa. But how did they get there? The pirates couldn't take them; they would be arrested. So did the men have a boat? He had to find out more if they were going to get off the island before the other pirates arrived.

*

Bakr left the men making their rope and wandered down to the beach again; this time he set off away from the pirate ship and headed for a small cove surrounded by cliffs. For the first time the possibility of escape occurred to him as something more than a dream.

He headed inland, following the stream that came tumbling down from a mountainous ridge that ran the entire length of the island. The climb was steep but not long and he soon was walking along a stony path with the land dropping away on either side of him. Waves lapped the shore and from this high vantage point the sea was a deep turquoise, so clear he felt he could see to the bottom. He stumbled. One of the numerous small lizards that inhabited the island, scuttled out of his way, narrowly avoiding being stepped on. Bakr stopped and looked around him. Dragonera, their prison, was nothing more than a spit of rock, a mountain top rising out of the sea. He calculated that it was approximately three Arab miles long and no more than half a mile wide. As long as they were on the island, the pirates would know every move they made. Escape appeared to be impossible.

The pirates had chosen wisely. Their safe harbour was at the southern end of Dragonera, on its west coast, so they could not be seen from Mayurqa which lay only some thirty Arab miles to the east, while the coast of al-Andalus was a mere shadow on the horizon to the west. He could see the pirate ship, lying on its side as the men careened its hull, and Kamil and Asim sitting under the palm trees, the new sails spread out before them. He couldn't let them spend the rest of their lives here. He couldn't spend the rest of *his* life here; he had to find a way to get them all back to Malaqah, and soon, before Kamil ended up with his throat slit and the island turned into a haven for a pirates' reunion.

He thought about his predecessor. It sounded as though Sulayman had tried to reason with Captain al-Awar, but he'd ignored his advice. In which case, why should he expect the captain to take any notice of him? He could only hope he'd learned his lesson, otherwise there was a danger that Bakr, too, would end up as food for the fish.

He stared at the larger island; it was so close you could see the houses. He felt he could reach out and touch them; you could almost swim there. He felt the longing to be free overwhelm him. This was their only means of escape; if they could reach Mayurqa then they could disappear into the interior and the pirates would never find them.

He turned and looked back at the ship. It was like a beached whale lying there in the sand. There were at least another four weeks of careening to do before it would be sea worthy again. Now was their opportunity. If they could get to Mayurqa while the pirates had no ship they wouldn't be able to pursue them. But how could they achieve that? And could they do it before the weather changed?

CHAPTER 12

Aisha walked along the beach, her eyes scouring the horizon for signs of a ship, as she did every morning at daybreak since Bakr had gone. There was no sense to her actions; no ship was going to bring him back to her. Five months had passed; they were now in the full heat of summer and there had been no word of him. He was dead or had been taken so far away it was impossible for him to return; her head told her this but her heart refused to believe it. So every morning she retraced her footsteps through the sand and watched the waves lap along the shore; every morning she saw the gulls following the fishing boats as they came back with the night's catch; every morning she watched the red sun rise in a cloudless blue sky and every morning she knelt in the sand and prayed to Allah to bring her husband back to his family.

Aisha adjusted the weight of the baby, whom she always carried in a cotton sling across her shoulder; he was growing fat and more beautiful than ever. Already he was toddling unsteadily on his chubby legs. If only Bakr could see how happy and healthy he was.

She stopped for a moment as the nausea caught her in the throat. She still hadn't told her mother-in-law that she was pregnant again; but she would soon have no option. Even her loosest djubbahs were becoming tight. She couldn't keep the news to herself for much longer but this time the news would be bitter-sweet. Her delight at having another child was marred by the fact that Bakr would probably never know that he was to be a father again. At that thought she couldn't stop the tears from running down her cheeks.

She wiped her eyes and turned towards her home. Tears wouldn't help anyone. It was being pregnant that was making her so weak. But she couldn't give in to self-pity; she had to be strong. The last thing she wanted was for the children to see her giving up hope. Every day they asked about their father and every day she said that he would be home soon. Her daughter, Maryam stared at her when she said it; she didn't believe her anymore. Why should she? Everyone thought he was dead except her; so why couldn't she accept it too? But it was too soon to give up. She knew Bakr; he would do everything in his power to get back to them. He loved them.

Her mother-in-law and Rayya, Bakr's youngest sister, were on the patio washing clothes when she arrived home.

'Maryam and Sandi say we should have a funeral for their father,' Rayya said. 'They say the children at school are saying that it's wrong not to have a funeral for him. They are very upset. They think their father won't go to Paradise if we don't give him a proper burial.'

'What does Naila say? Does she think her father is dead?' snapped Aisha. She still felt sick and longed to sit down and put her feet up for a short while; she also wanted to get away from her mother-in-law's nagging.

'She doesn't say anything. She just cries whenever anyone mentions her Baba,' said Bakr's mother, looking at Aisha as if she were the cause of all their misfortunes. 'And who can blame her?'

'Well, I'm sorry but as far as I'm aware funerals are for dead people. We have no proof that your son is dead. Why are you in such a hurry to bury him?' Aisha knew she was being cruel, but she couldn't stop herself. She was doing all she could to help these women continue to lead the comfortable life they were used to and all they did was complain.

The sickness welled up again into her throat. This time she knew she would vomit. She clamped her hand over her mouth and rushed out into the garden. There was no way she could hide her pregnancy now.

'Aisha, are you all right?' her mother-in-law asked, her voice a little kinder now. 'What's the matter, daughter?'

'I'm pregnant,' Aisha whispered. 'The baby will be born in three months time, insha'Allah.'

'That's wonderful news, child. Why didn't you tell me sooner? You should be resting more. After all you still have the little one to look after; it's time we got him weaned, so you will grow strong enough for the next one. Rayya, bring some warm milk with ginger and honey for your sister-in-law. Here child, come and sit down.' Now she was all smiles. 'Another grandchild. How lovely.'

'Another mouth to feed. Don't forget that when you complain about me meddling in men's affairs,' said Aisha spitefully. But the thought of another child filling the house with laughter and noise made her feel happier than she had for months.

'Don't you worry about that. We will manage. You said yourself the shipyard is going well. I have to admit I am very surprised at how well you and your father are running my son's business. Bakr made a good choice when he asked you to be his wife.'

Aisha looked at her in amazement. Bakr's mother had never given her such a compliment before. In fact, she didn't remember her paying her any complements at all. She felt her eyes fill with tears again. Oh this damn pregnancy.

'Now just relax; the hot milk will soon settle your stomach,' her mother-in-law said, smiling at her.

*

The children were in school, so Aisha took the opportunity to go to see her mother. She wanted to tell her the news about the new baby before she heard it in the market; news travelled very fast in their neighbourhood. She was sure her mother-in-law would have already told all her friends and, as she had been to the market this morning, all the shopkeepers were likely to know as well.

Ibrahim was sorting through some glass vials when she arrived.

'As-salama alaykum, sister. What brings you here so early?' he asked, giving her a hug. 'Have you got any news about Bakr?'

She shook her head, sadly. 'No. Is Mama about?'

'Upstairs,' he said and returned to his task.

Aisha climbed the stairs slowly; she still felt queasy despite all the herbs and infusions that her mother-in-law made her drink.

'Aisha, what a nice surprise. Your father will be sorry he missed you; he was planning to go round to your house later.' Her mother gave her a big hug, then pulled back and looked at her with a quizzical expression. 'So, you have something to tell me, daughter?'

'How do you know?' Aisha asked, laughing at her mother's face. 'Are you a witch?'

'I know my daughter and I can see from all the signs that she is with child once more. Am I right?'

'As always, Mama.'

Her mother almost threw herself at her in her eagerness to embrace her again. 'This is good news, child. Very good news.' She placed her hands on Aisha's belly and asked, 'When is the baby due?'

'In a few months. Before the end of the year.'

'And you're happy? Of course you are. Whatever sadness there is in the world, a new child can always banish it, at least for a while. Come, sit down and take the weight off your feet. Here let me have the little one.' She lifted the baby out of his sling and began to cover him in kisses. 'What a big boy you are getting,' she cooed at him, delighted to be holding her grandson.

'Does Baba have news for me?' Aisha asked.

'I think so. He hasn't told me much, but I do know he wants to have another meeting at Avi's house this evening. He wants you to go.'

'Have they found him? 'Have they found Bakr?' She couldn't keep the emotion out of her voice.

'No, I don't think it's that. He would have gone straight round to tell you if that were the case.'

Abal lowered the baby to the floor and held his hands as he staggered across the floor towards his mother.

'But he does have something positive to tell you. He'll explain when he sees you.'

At these words Aisha felt her heart leap with excitement; her father had discovered something that would help them to find Bakr. She tried not to be too optimistic, but she couldn't help it. What had he learnt? Did they know where her husband was at last?

'Is that all you can tell me, Mama?'

'Patience, child. Go home and rest for now. Baba will explain it all to you this evening.'

*

Makoud was both pleased and surprised to learn that his daughter was pregnant again, although he wondered how she was going to cope with a new baby and a toddler, and still manage to run the business. He looked at her; her face was drawn with anxiety but otherwise she was as lovely as ever. He felt a rush of pride; she was such a determined woman. Her grief had given her an inner strength he would never have imagined her to have. He smiled to himself. It was true what they said, the she-wolf was much more dangerous than the male; she would do anything to protect her family.

Dirar had insisted he join them, so the three of them waited outside the door of Avi's house, in the cool of the evening.

'I can't see why you won't tell us what you've found out, Baba?' asked Aisha, her irritation obvious in her voice.

'Patience, child. I've told you, it's not much information on its own, but maybe with what Avi has found out it will make more sense.'

The heavy door swung open and Avi's manservant greeted them as usual and led them into an internal patio, where Avi was waiting. A foreigner was seated beside him, a man of about fifty, wearing baggy silk trousers and tunic, a yellow turban and a matching sash around his waist. His swarthy face was partially covered by a full moustache and beard, both of which were iron grey, and his eyes were as black as a hawk, and just as wild.

'Come in, my dear friends. Come in. Sit down and let me introduce an old acquaintance of mine, Captain Mustafa Bey. He's just arrived from Constantinople, bringing me some wonderful new silks. Vibrant colours. They will make beautiful robes. Beautiful. Mustafa and I have been doing business together for more years than I care to remember,' Avi added.

'As-salama alaykum,' said Makoud. 'I am pleased to meet any colleague of Avi's. May I introduce my youngest son, Dirar and my daughter, Aisha.'

'As-salama alaykum, sayyad,' said Dirar, bowing slightly to show respect to this older man.

'Wa alaykum e-salam,' the man said. His Arabic was comprehensible but his accent was a mixture, like that of people from the eastern edges of the Middle Sea. Makoud guessed that he was a Turkish Jew.

Out of courtesy to Avi's guest, Makoud didn't immediately blurt out what he'd learnt from the admiral, instead he let Avi and Mustafa continue with their general conversation about the state of their respective businesses and their families.

Once the servant had brought more glasses of Rebekah's famous lemonade, Avi turned the conversation to the reason they were there.

'Captain Mustafa has kindly joined us this evening because he has agreed to help us in our quest for your son-in-law,' he said, addressing himself to Makoud. 'But first I will tell you what I have learned. As I promised, I contacted as many of the merchants as I could and although most of them said they had neither seen nor heard anything about a new ship or any kidnapped shipbuilders, one man has sent me a message. This particular merchant trades between

Dénia and Malaqah, bringing rice—the rice from that region is of a particularly high quality—textiles and wool. I have known him a long time and have great confidence in him. He hasn't seen your shipbuilder, but he says everyone in Dénia is talking about one of the pirates, an ambitious man whose greed and ruthlessness strikes fear into all their hearts. This pirate is said to be building an enormous fleet of ships which he plans to use to outrun any naval ship that currently exists. That's what the rumours say. And the question everyone is asking, is where is he getting the ships from?'

'I too have some information which will back that up,' said Makoud. 'I went to see the admiral this morning and he has told me that they too have heard of this pirate. They think he makes his base on a small island called Dragonera, in the Balearic Islands, in the taifa of Dénia.'

'Yes, I spoke to as many fishermen as I could and they had all heard of this ambitious pirate,' said Dirar. 'They say his name is Captain al-Awar. He and his men have ravaged the villages along the north African coast for many years but that isn't where he goes to do his annual repairs. They think he sails to somewhere more northerly, for that.'

'So what makes the admiral think Bakr's on Dragonera? And if that's true why doesn't he sail there and rescue him?' asked Aisha.

'It's not that simple, daughter. The khalifa has instructed the admiral to do what he can but he doesn't want to create any problems with the sultan of Dénia.'

'Surely he can just sail there and send a landing party to search the island and if he's not there then they can leave,' said Dirar. 'What's complicated about that? You said the khalifa wanted Bakr found.'

'It's politics. The sultan of Dénia is having problems with the governor of the Balearic Islands, who wants independence from Dénia. Things are quiet at the moment and he doesn't want to stir up any trouble.'

'You mean the pirates are supporting the governor?' said Avi.

'Yes, I'd heard that, too,' said Captain Mustafa. 'He allows them to hide on the many small islands that make up the archipelago. It's not just this al-Awar; there are dozens of pirate ships which use the islands as their winter hideaway.'

'Have you all forgotten something?' asked Aisha. 'It's not winter. Summer is still with us. So where are the pirates now? Isn't that what we want to know?'

'No, sister, you don't understand. If we're right and Captain al-Awar took Bakr and the others to build them ships, then they will still be there, even if most of the other pirates have left,' said Dirar. 'They're not going to take them with them all summer while they're raiding and pillaging all across the Middle Sea. So that's to our advantage; it's a good time to go there while the islands are deserted.'

'So, we have until the weather turns, to find them?' asked Aisha.

'Yes, three months at the most. Maybe less if we have storms; that always deters the pirates. They're fair-weather sailors, all of them. Not like the fishermen who go out in all conditions.'

'After that it will be impossible to get close to the captives without being seen; the islands will be crawling with pirates,' said Captain Mustafa. 'We will have to wait until the Spring.'

Makoud saw the distress on his daughter's face; she was pinning her hopes on them finding Bakr despite the impossibility of the task. Poor woman, her husband would probably never know he had another child.

'I wonder why the khalifa is so interested in finding your son-in-law,' mused Avi. 'I would have thought he'd have more important things on his mind, the campaign to Écija, for example.'

Makoud shook his head. 'I don't know. Maybe he doesn't want the pirates to have faster ships than he does. But whatever the reason, I doubt if he would consider going to war with Dénia just to save a shipbuilder, no matter how good he is.'

'I'll sail to the Balearic Islands and see what I can find out,' said Captain Mustafa. 'I have a cargo of sweet wine and pottery that I can take; the Sultan of Dénia is very fond of the wine from Malaqah. It won't be a wasted journey.'

'I'll go with you,' said Dirar. 'There is no point worrying about how we're going to rescue them, if we don't even know if they're there. When we get to Dragonera, I can swim to the island and find out if we're in the right place.'

'You're very welcome to come along,' said the captain. 'There's always the danger of being attacked by pirates on the Middle Sea, so an extra man on board would be an advantage. Mind you, it'll be a slow journey. My old tub isn't as fast as I'd like her to be.'

'I think that's a wonderful idea,' said Aisha, brightening up. 'At last we have a plan.'

Her eyes were shining with excitement. How disappointed she was going to be if this all came to nothing.

CHAPTER 13

Bakr hurried across the sand to where Asim was busy waterproofing the sails.

'Where's Kamil?' he asked. That lad would be the death of them; he was never where he was supposed to be.

'I said he could go. We can't do any more to the sails today and the hull isn't dry yet,' said Asim, rubbing his oily hands on a dirty rag.

Bakr picked up the edge of one of the sails and examined it. The stitching was good; it would hold well in the wind. 'You've oiled them?' he said.

'Just the first coat.'

'So, where is he?'

'Kamil? He's probably with those kids. He's teaching them to read and write.'

'What? Does the captain know about this?' asked Bakr, once again astonished at the audacity of his young apprentice.

Asim shrugged. 'Their mothers know. They're very happy about it. They repay him by washing his clothes and sometimes he comes back with a few sweet pastries.'

Bakr couldn't help himself; he threw back his head and laughed. 'That young man is either going to make a name for himself or end up swinging from the gallows,' he said. 'When he comes back I want to talk to you both.'

'Very well, sayyad. I'll tell him.'

Bakr headed back towards the pirate's ship, to see how the careening was going. He was thinking about Kamil; he'd ingratiated himself with the islanders right from the start and now he was teaching the pirates' children. The lad was in an ideal position to find out when and how they travelled back and forth to the main island.

'Here's the man who will know,' said one of the pirates as he approached. 'This worm.'

'Teredo worm?'

'Yes, that's the one. He reckons you can eat them,' he said, pointing to one of the pirates busily scraping the hull. 'Is that right?'

'Well I've never eaten one,' said Bakr, twisting his face into a grimace. The thought of eating one of those disgusting creatures nauseated him. 'Where did you hear that?'

'I've travelled in the East,' the man scraping the hull replied. 'In some lands they consider these worms to be a delicacy. They soak them in lime juice and serve them with onions and peppers. Sometimes even a bit of chilli. You know the Teredo worm can grow up to an arm's span in length; it can make a fine meal. They taste much like any other mollusc from the sea. You should try one.'

'But why would you want to eat something that feeds on wood?' asked the first pirate.

'I suppose you'll eat anything, if you're hungry enough,' said Bakr. 'Now, more to the point, the ship. Have you actually seen any live ones in there? We need to make sure that we don't leave any of them buried in the hull. Remember they aren't all big enough to eat; some are very small. Look carefully.'

'Not a sign,' said the pirate. 'But how can we be sure?'

'We can't, but when you've finished repairing it, I want you to coat the hull with tar. That will stop them, for a while at least.'

'Aye, aye, boss,' said the man who'd travelled to the East.

'And if you do find any live ones, you can prepare them for the captain's supper,' said Bakr, with a laugh.

'What's that?' asked Captain al-Awar, striding across towards them.

'Nothing, Captain,' said the pirate, hurriedly moving away from Bakr.

'I hope you're not slowing down the men,' the captain said to Bakr.

'Of course not. I'm just checking that the work is being done properly.'

The pirates' captain spat in the sand and walked away.

Bakr watched until he had rounded the cliff and then headed back to where he knew the chandlers would be plaiting their ropes.

As usual they were sitting under the palm trees, with coils of newly plaited rope at their feet. They looked up as Bakr approached and beckoned to him.

'As-salama alaykum,' the oldest one of the men said. 'Come and join us for a while.'

'Wa alaykum e-salam, my friends.' He sat down beside them and leaned back against the trunk of a palm tree. 'I can't stay long or I'll have the captain after me.'

'Oh, he won't be bothering you for a while,' said one of the chandlers. 'He usually takes a siesta about now, in Isa's hut.' He nodded towards a group of huts at the far side of the beach and winked lewdly at Bakr.

'A man of habit is our captain,' said another man.

Bakr knew who Isa was; they all did. She was a striking woman of very loose morals and, despite the fact that he had two wives on the island, the captain was one of her most frequent visitors.

'I was looking for my young apprentice,' he said. 'Have you seen him?'

'The young lad who's always chatting to the women and kids?'

'Yes, that's him.'

'He's in that hut, over there. I saw him go in a short while ago.'

'I need to have a word with him,' he said, frowning.

'In trouble again, is he? Come back after you've boxed his ears,' one of them said, with a grin.

Bakr could hear the sound of children laughing as he approached the hut; it wrenched at his heart as he thought of his own young family having to manage without him. He pulled back the curtain and bending down, went inside, blinking as his eyes accustomed themselves to the gloomy interior. Kamil was squatting on the floor surrounded by half a dozen small children. The women were sitting at the back of the hut watching him. Nobody paid any attention to Bakr; they were too engrossed with what Kamil was doing. He had a large piece of flat wood, which he must have prepared himself because the surface was clean and smooth. On it he had drawn the letters of the alphabet. As he pointed to each letter, the children called out what it was and then drew it in the sand at their feet with pointed sticks. It was a rudimentary lesson but it seemed to be working. Even the mothers were reciting the letters.

'Kamil.'

The boy spun round, a look of surprise and embarrassment on his young face. 'Sayyad. I didn't know you were there.' He started to get up.

'No, stay where you are and finish the lesson. I'll wait for you outside. We need to speak,' said Bakr, stepping outside into the fresh air. The smell of all those dirty bodies huddled together in one tent was too much for him.

He sat down and leaned against a tent pole. The sing-song voices of the children floated out to him. What an extraordinary young man his apprentice was. What about his family, were they looking for him? Or had they abandoned all hope? It had been five months since the three of them had been kidnapped; surely everyone had given up all thought of ever finding them. And his lovely Aisha, was she still waiting and praying for his return? He had to escape and get back to her; he couldn't leave his family to fend for themselves. They needed him.

The flap of the tent opened and Kamil's tousled head appeared. 'I'm sorry about that, sayyad. I usually only give them lessons in the evening, but Asim said it was all right to go.'

'Don't worry, lad. I'm not angry with you about that. In fact you have given me an idea of how we can get off this barren lump of rock.'

He looked around to make sure that nobody could overhear them, then said, 'I want you to find out all you can about how and when they get provisions from the main island. The children are bound to know; kids never miss anything. What we need to find out is whether they have a boat moored here on the island or if they just rely on someone coming across with the provisions and then leaving immediately after they have delivered them. This could be our best chance of escape, so it's important to understand how it works.' He went on to explain that the pirates' ship was out of action and so even if they saw them escaping, they wouldn't be able to follow them. As he spoke, Kamil's eyes grew rounder and rounder.

'Yes, sayyad, I can do that. The children like to talk to me; I'll soon find out.'

'All right, but don't be too obvious. I don't want the pirates to know what we're planning. Remember Captain al-Awar doesn't miss much. You'd do well to remember that.'

Kamil nodded his head vigorously. 'I'll suggest that they ask for some charcoal so we can write on those flat stones they collect from the stream.' His face became serious as he added, 'It's a shame. They are just beginning to understand what reading is all about. And I'm teaching them to count; I'll be sorry to leave them.'

'Well you can stay here, if you prefer. Just get me the information so Asim and I can go home.'

'I didn't mean that, sayyad. Of course I want to escape. My father will be very worried about me,' Kamil said, hurriedly.

'Good. Now there's something else I need to tell you. And I want you to mark my words well.'

'Yes, sayyad.'

'This girl that you've been talking to, the pretty one with the big eyes.'

'She's one of my pupils, sayyad. She said she'd like to learn to read and write so I told her to join us. She was there, just now. Didn't you see her?'

'No I didn't. And don't interrupt me again or you will regret it.'

'Yes, sayyad. I mean, no, sayyad.' Kamil's face had flushed dark red with embarrassment.

'This girl, your pupil, just happens to be one of the captain's wives. I don't really think I have to spell out to you what will happen if he discovers you are teaching his wife to read, do I?' Never had Bakr seen anyone's face drain of colour quite as quickly as Kamil's at those words. Poor lad. He'd had no idea. 'You realise you're playing with fire, don't you?'

Kamil just stared at him.

'Well, I never thought I'd see the day when you were lost for words, Kamil. Perhaps now you'll keep your mouth closed when the captain is about.'

'But what do I do about her lessons?' he croaked.

'What? Are you completely mad? There are to be no more lessons for that young girl unless her husband tells you in person. And that is never going to happen, because Captain al-Awar does not want you or anyone else educating the children on this island. And especially not his wife.' Bakr groaned. 'I'm beginning to despair of you, Kamil. Do you have any idea of how much danger you are in? The captain doesn't need a reason to get rid of us; he would happily slit our throats and throw us all in the sea. So why are you trying so hard to give him one?'

'I'm sorry, sayyad.'

'Just let me know as soon as you have anything from the children.'

He stood up, stretching his back as he did so; he could feel it creaking. He was getting old; this outdoor life was not for him. Bakr wandered back to the men careening the ship; he was going to have to listen more carefully to what the pirates said if he wanted to find out how things worked here. If the chandlers were to be believed, then they would be getting quite a bit of company once the good weather was over. Insha'Allah they would have escaped by then.

*

That night, as they sat around the fire eating their evening meal of fish stew, Bakr heard one of the pirates berating the cook for the lack of wine.

'You shouldn't drink so damn much of it,' the cook said. 'Or go out and steal some. Don't come moaning to me because there's none left. I don't even drink the bloody stuff.'

'Shut up, you two. There'll be barrels of it in a few days, more than you can drink Faisal, even with your greedy thirst,' said the captain, taking a deep draught from his own beaker.

So the delivery was due any day. Bakr pretended he wasn't listening to them, and continued poking at the fire with his stick.

'Sayyad, can I have a word?' whispered Kamil.

'Meet me by our tent once the singing starts,' he muttered beneath his breath.

He saw Kamil nod, then walk away towards the water's edge.

'I hope that lad of yours isn't going to bother any of the women,' said the captain, turning suddenly and glaring at Bakr.

'I'm sure he isn't,' he said. 'He's not that stupid.'

'I don't know about that. I think he does most of his thinking with his cock. You'd better tell him that if he wants to keep his manhood, he'd better stay away from them.'

Bakr didn't reply; he knew better than to argue with the captain when he'd been drinking.

'Anyway, how's my ship coming along? It seems to be taking a mighty long time,' the captain continued.

'The hull is almost complete and now we can start on the interior. A few more months and she'll be ready to launch,' Bakr replied.

'A few more months? In the name of Allah, what's taking so long?'

'You wanted a ship as good as the khalifa's. You don't think I would rush his ship, do you? Yours will be of the same high standard and quality.'

'Will it be as fast? That's what I want to know. Will I be able to outrun the buggers?'

'It will be faster because you won't be carrying so much weight. It will outrun any ship on the Middle Sea.'

The captain glared but didn't comment. Instead he turned to the men with the organistrum and shouted, 'Right boys, how about a tune. Something to liven up this sober bunch. Even if there's no more wine, we can still have music.' He threw his empty wine beaker into the fire where it smashed against a log.

Bakr waited until they were all singing and the captain had moved away from him, then he slipped away quietly and headed for the beach.

Kamil was sitting on the shore throwing pebbles into the water. As each pebble landed it sent out silver ripples in the otherwise calm sea.

'What have you learnt?' asked Bakr, dropping down onto the sand beside his apprentice.

'The boat arrives in two days' time. It always comes on the night of the full moon.'

Bakr looked at the sky; the moon was already well rounded and as plump as a ripe peach. It hung like a yellow globe, low in the sky and surrounded by a myriad of sparkling stars. In a couple of days it would complete its cycle and then begin to wane once more.

'I told the children we needed some charcoal and one of them said he would ask his mother to tell the men to bring us some,' he said, then added, sadly. 'I feel really bad about tricking them like that. I won't even be here to see them use it.'

'Just hope that nobody tells the pirates or you'll be eating the charcoal, not writing with it.'

'No, they won't say anything. They know that the captain doesn't want them to learn to read and write, especially the girls.'

'What about the captain's young wife?'

'I told her it wasn't safe for her to come to the classes anymore. She was upset, but she understood. I just feel so bad about it.'

'You'll feel worse if he beats her. Now, did you find out anything about the chandlers?'

'Yes. They go across to the main island every three months. The boat that brings the provisions collects them and then they return the following month. Of course they don't all go at once. The captain won't allow it. They have a rota.'

'So they don't have their own boat?'

'Doesn't sound like it.'

'Are any of the chandlers due to go home this time?'

'No. But according to the children, some are coming back.'

'What sort of turn around does the boat have? The one that brings the provisions.'

Kamil looked at him blankly.

'How long is it here? Do the men just unload the boat and then go straight back?' Bakr said, impatiently. 'Or do they stay until the morning?' This was going to be trickier than he thought.

'I think they just unload and then head back. One of the boys said the captain doesn't want them snooping about. Sounds as though he doesn't trust them.'

'So we'd have to be waiting for them?'

'If you want to steal their boat, yes. But they come at night, which is why we've never seen them. And they land on the other side of the island.'

'That's interesting. Do you know where?'

'Yes, but I'd have to show you.'

'Right. We'll go tomorrow while the captain is having his siesta.'

'Siesta?'

'Don't worry about it. I'll tell you when. In the meantime, keep away from the pirates' daughters?'

'I didn't know; they never said anything.' Even in the moonlight Bakr saw Kamil's face pale with fear.

'Well keep away from them. The captain has threatened to castrate you if he catches you with any of them. Unless you want a job in the khalifa's harem, I should take his words seriously. Now get off to bed. I've got a lot of thinking to do.'

'Aye, aye sayaad.'

CHAPTER 14

Khalifa Idris I sat in the throne room going over the final plans for his campaign, the most important one of his reign. This was the best chance he would ever have to stop Abbad I, ruler of the taifa of Isbiliya for the last twenty years, from expanding his growing influence even further. It was vital not to make any mistakes. He looked at the men seated around him: his own generals, all experienced and battle-hardened men, the grand vizier Ibn Baqanna, and representatives from each of his allies.

'General Rashad, please will you outline the current situation for all of us,' he said. 'How many men will we have for the campaign?'

'Yes, Your Majesty. As you know our friends in Álmeria, Garnata and Badajoz have all agreed to support us in the attack on Isbiliya. Like us, they are angered by the unrelenting expansion of Isbiliya's territories.'

'Yes, yes, we know all that. Just bring us up to date,' he said, anxious to get everything moving as quickly as possible.

'Very well, Your Majesty. I have agreed with Sultan Abdallah's generals that they will bring ten thousand men to attack Écija from the north-west.'

Idris looked across at the general from Badajoz, who was wearing a distinctive red turban with the gold insignia of his regiment pinned to it.

The officer nodded his head in confirmation and said, 'Indeed, Your Majesty. The sultan is happy to give you his full support.'

'Not quite his full support, if he is only sending ten thousand soldiers,' Idris said. He had hoped for more men from Abdallah, whose lands stretched from the Atlantic to its border with Isbiliya.

'And Badis will bring some twenty thousand troops to attack from the south-east,' said General Rashad, hurrying to break the awkward silence that had followed Idris's words.

Once again the khalifa looked across at the others for confirmation.

'General Rashad is quite right, Your Majesty. Garnata is happy to support our old friends in Malaqah in an attempt to defeat the tiresome Abbad I,' ibn Nagrilla said, with a warm smile. He was the Jewish grand vizier of the neighbouring taifa, who also held the post of Supreme Commander of their army and had full powers to act on the behalf of Badis ben Habus, the sultan of Garnata. Idris found it strange that any ruler would devolve so much power to someone else, but he had heard that the sultan was a man who was not overly interested in matters of state. It made no difference; General Rashad had always had a high regard for ibn Nagrilla, and that was enough for him.

'And Álmeria?' asked Idris. He looked at the two generals that Sultan Zuhair had sent to his court.

'Your Majesty, our esteemed sultan sends you his cordial greetings and has promised fifteen thousand trained soldiers to join the attack on Isbiliya. They will approach Écija from the east,' the older of the generals replied.

'So all that remains is Qarmuña?' said Idris, looking at General Rashad. 'What do we know of their intentions?'

'That is more complicated, Your Majesty.'

'How so? Qarmuña is an independent taifa, is it not?'

'Yes, Your Majesty, but it has been under the influence, and some say even the control, of Isbiliya for years. But I have heard rumours that Muhammad ibn Abd Allah would like to make a clean break with them.'

'Really. And you think that instead of defending Écija and fighting alongside Isbiliya, they may use it as an opportunity to assert themselves?'

'It's possible. Écija is part of their taifa, but as we know, Isbiliya has plans to expand its territory to the east, and that could mean swallowing up Qarmuña, including Écija. Joining forces with us, could be the opportunity they have been looking for to retain their independence.'

'Have you spoken to any of their generals?' asked Idris. This was intriguing. Personally, he had no interest in expanding the borders of Malaqah, certainly not in that direction. All he wanted to achieve from this campaign was to stop Abbad I from becoming even more powerful than he already was. If they promised Qarmuña that they would return the town of Écija to them after the battle and guarantee their independence, then maybe they would agree to fight alongside them.

'No. Well not officially, but I think you may be right, Your Majesty,' said General Rashad. 'This could be an opportunity for them to get from under Isbiliya's yoke.

'Yes. They must know that Isbiliya will fall this time. Surely they want to be on the winning side,' said Idris. 'Anyway when they see Abdallah and the army from

Badajoz their doubts will disappear. No, I don't think Qarmuña will oppose us.'

'And if they do?'

'Then we attack them as well,' said Idris, more confidently than he felt. They had underestimated Qarmuña once before, when his brother was the khalifa; he didn't intend to make the same mistake.

If he and his allies joined forces against Isbiliya then their ruler, Abbad I, stood no chance; even with the support of Qarmuña his armies would be greatly outnumbered. The previously undefeated Isbiliya would at last learn what it was like to be the vanquished party.

This wasn't the first time armies had fought over Écija. The town, which according to the historians, predated even the Romans, had long been the source of disputes because of its strategic position. It lay in a wide, fertile plain, halfway between the cities of Qurtubah and Isbiliya, on an ancient Roman road, the Via Augusta which stretched from Qadis in the south across the entire Iberian peninsula, linking all the Muslim taifas, from Arcos on the Dark Sea to Tortosa on the frontier with Christian Spain. Currently Écija was within the boundaries of Qarmuña, but everyone around the table today knew that this campaign was nothing to do with occupying Écija; it was about defeating Abbad I and stopping his expansionist plans. Even Qarmuña must realise that.

'General Rashad, I want you to send someone to Qarmuña, to the court of Muhammad ibn Abd Allah to find out what he is planning to do. There is no way he can remain neutral in this fight. He has to decide if he is with us or against us. Tell him we can come to an agreement about Écija, if that is what's worrying him. I have no plans to station troops there to defend a town that is of little use to me. Why would I? And I can't see it being of any interest to our allies in Badajoz or Álmeria; they are both too far away.'

He looked across at them and saw that he was correct in his assumption. But what about Garnata. That was much closer. 'Ibn Nagrillas? What are your feelings on Écija?'

'Your Majesty, Garnata has no plans to expand her territory. If you wish to use Écija as a bargaining point with the sultan of Qarmuña, I am sure that I can speak for our ruler, Badis ben Habus, when I say that we are in complete agreement with you. Our objective, as is everyone's here, is to curtail the ambitions of Abbad I. Something we have to do whichever way we can, before he has all of al-Andalus under his control.'

'Well said. Very well, gentlemen, I will leave you to discuss the finer details of the campaign with my generals,' said Idris, standing up, ready to leave them.

Immediately they all stood and bowed whilst the khalifa made his way back to his private quarters. The meeting had gone well; the preparations for the campaign were under way and all that remained was the final outcome. He felt confident that this time he would be victorious, but despite all their careful plans and strategies, he knew in his heart that in the end it would depend on Allah. He prayed that He would hear their prayers and bring them victory.

He could hear the general laughing; he too was pleased with the support of their allies. He was a good man and it was at times like this that his long experience was invaluable. Idris felt particularly pleased with him because of the diplomatic way he had dealt with the sultan of Dénia, persuading him to allow their ships to patrol his waters; he had achieved the ruler's co-operation without compromising Idris's position. He'd promised the sultan nothing in return. Now Idris could relax and concentrate on the campaign. He would send for Yusuf and explain that he had done all that he could for his son. Now it was up to Allah if the shipwright and his men were found or not.

*

Idris and the librarian walked through the gardens of the alcázar together. It was almost dark and yet he was grateful for the cool breeze that floated in from the sea. Tomorrow was going to be hot, despite the fact they were now into autumn. But he couldn't delay the campaign any longer. It would be the same for all the soldiers; nobody liked fighting in the heat, not with all the protective clothing that they wore. Well, they would just have to put up with it; he couldn't control the weather.

So far Yusuf had not mentioned his son. Perhaps he preferred to remain in ignorance of the lad's fate; that way he could continue to pray for his return.

'I do not have any news of your son, nor of the others who were kidnapped,' Idris said when Yusuf closed the book from which he'd been reading him some poetry. 'But the admiral of my fleet is on his way to the Balearic Islands, where it is possible they are being held. I don't want to raise your hopes, my friend, because, as you must realise, the chances of finding any of them alive are very slim. But if Admiral al-Maraghi finds out anything he will get in touch with you. Anything at all. You have my word. Whether it be good news or bad.'

'Thank you, Your Majesty. You are very kind.'

The librarian pulled another scroll out of his bag. 'I found this the other day,' he said. 'It's an old Roman prayer that used to be said before going into battle. I thought, in view of the imminent campaign, you might like to read it. It has been translated into Arabic. Maybe it will bring you good luck.'

Idris took the scroll from him. This was so typical of Yusuf and one reason why he was fond of him. The librarian always treated the khalifa with respect but underneath that Idris knew there was a genuine affection for him. They shared the same passions and when they spoke of poetry, Yusuf seemed to forget that Idris was the khalifa and held the power of life and death over him; they were equals in their love of the written word. There was no-one else who behaved like that with him. Even his wives never treated him like an ordinary man.

'When I return you must read it to me in the original,' he said, as he read the prayer written to a Christian god, but one that he knew Allah would also listen to. 'I would like to continue walking in the garden with you, my friend, but tomorrow we leave at first light and I still have things to do before then. Have you brought the documents?'

'Of course, Your Majesty.' He opened his pouch and took out two scrolls and offered them to Idris. 'I copied them myself.'

'Thank you, my friend. I will only take one copy; the other I want you to keep safe for me.'

'Very well, Your Majesty.'

'And remember, this is between us. Do not mention to anyone that you have a copy of this document; it could put your life in danger. If I die in battle, I would like you to take this copy to my son, Muhammad ibn Idris ibn Ali in al-Jazira. Is that understood?'

'It is, Your Majesty. Ma'a salama and may Allah watch over you and keep you from harm.'

'Alla ysalmak, Yusuf.'

When the librarian had left, Idris signalled for his servant to approach.

'Bring ibn Baqanna to me, at once,' he said.

'Yes, Your Majesty.'

Idris had just one more loose end to see to before he left. Reading the Roman prayer had reminded him of how perilous this mission could be; he needed to be sure that justice would be done if anything happened to him.

He sat by the fountain, watching the carp swimming lazily around in the pond. Within a few minutes he saw his grand vizier hurrying towards him. There was a worried look on his lined face. Idris smiled to himself; maybe he thought he was about to be told to accompany Idris into battle. He certainly wouldn't like that. His grand vizier was wily and manipulative, ambitious to a fault, but he was not brave.

'Your Majesty,' ibn Baqanna wheezed, as he arrived, puffing from his exertions. 'You wanted to see me.'

'Yes, ibn Baqanna. I want to make it very clear to you that if anything happens to me during the campaign, if I am killed, then you must send for my nephew Hasan straight away. It is only right and proper that he should take over the throne in the event of my death. He is, as we both know, the rightful heir. If we do not make that quite clear then all sorts of cockroaches will come crawling out of their dark holes and claim the title of khalifa as their own. That would be devastating for the country.'

'But, Your Majesty. What of your own sons?'

'My eldest son has al-Jazira. The others will have to wait. They are too young anyway and have no experience at ruling. No, I wish to honour my brother's wishes and put his eldest son on the throne. I also intend to offer my daughter's hand in marriage to him. I think Jumila will be an excellent match for Hasan and, besides which, it will bind our families even closer. Insha'Allah they will be blessed with many sons and the country will see my grandson on the throne one day.'

'You are being very pessimistic, Your Majesty. Nothing will happen to you. You are still a young man and have many years left.'

'Please Allah that is so, but I want to be sure that you understand what must happen if I am killed. Is that clear?'

'Very clear, Your Majesty. Will there be anything else?'

'Yes, this document is a signed statement of my wishes. Take good care of it, and in the event of my death, I want no confusion over what is to be done. Do you understand?'

'Yes, Your Majesty, but I am sure that this is all quite unnecessary.'

He took the document and, after a cursory glance, rolled it up and slipped it into the pocket of his djubbah. Idris watched the grand vizier waddle back into the alcázar. Could he trust him? Maybe ibn Baqanna was right. Maybe he was just being pessimistic but it was as well to be prepared. He couldn't explain it, but he felt a strange foreboding about this battle and he didn't want to meet his Maker and have to explain why he had stolen the throne from his brother's heirs.

CHAPTER 15

Umar stroked Basil's muzzle and whispered words of encouragement to her. Like all the horses in the stables she could sense the excitement in the air; the army was gathering. The khalifa had sent out officers to draft in extra men from the outlying villages and they were camped on the hillside outside the Jbel Faro. He passed their camp each morning when he took Basil out for her daily exercise but despite the training that these new recruits had been receiving for the last few weeks, they still seemed an undisciplined mob. Part of that impression came from the fact that having been given no uniforms, they were still all dressed in the same clothes they wore for ploughing the fields and tending to their sheep. Some had made themselves a type of armour from leather skins which they wore over their djubbahs, but hardly any of them had protective headgear. Their only real protection was from the shields they'd been allocated—long oval shields made from leather and strengthened with iron studs. The khalifa had given the order that these raw foot soldiers were also to be well supplied with swords, maces, axes and lances, which they were learning to use with great enthusiasm, even if their prowess was more a question of verve than actual skill.

Most of the recruits would be used as infantrymen and sent out as a buffer between the regular soldiers and the enemy. The usual battle formation was that the infantry was at the front, with the archers behind them and the cavalry in the rear, and he hadn't had any instructions to the contrary. They would wait for the enemy to approach, the foot soldiers sheltering behind their shields, and once the enemy was within range the commander would give the signal and the archers would stand up and fire a barrage of arrows, while, at the same time, a rain of steel flew from their infantry's javelins. Then both the archers and the infantry would move aside to allow the jinetes, men like himself, to charge through and attack with sword and spear. After that it was usually a free-for-all, every man fighting for himself.

But not all these conscripted men were there to fight. Some were expected to drive the herds of animals that were required to feed the army, mostly sheep and oxen. Some were butchers. Others were cooks. Many of the villages were completely depleted of their menfolk because a military campaign required much the same support as a village did, so they took all the able-bodied men that could be of use to them. Only the women, children and old men remained until, if they were fortunate, their sons and husbands returned home.

Umar was impatient to leave. It was always the same feeling of exasperation. The preparations for the campaign took months, sometimes almost a year, and it seemed as though the order to leave would never come. That morning the khalifa had called together all his commanders and told them to be ready to leave the next day at dawn, and now the alcazaba was buzzing with excitement; everyone was on the move. Preparing for a military campaign was a task of epic proportions. The blacksmiths had loaded up their wagons; the heavy siege machines had already begun to trundle their way out of the Jbel Faro and onto the mountain road, and the armourers, doctors, grooms, carpenters and an assortment of men from the sculleries were preparing to leave. For many this wasn't the first campaign they had been on, and all were silently praying that it wouldn't be their last.

'Talib, I'm going to go home to see my family before we leave; I need to find out how my sister is coping. Don't worry. I'll be back in good time,' Umar said.

He led Basil into the stable and shut the door. 'Stay here, my friend. You need to rest. We have a long journey in front of us.' The mare looked at him with her large brown eyes and whinnied softly.

*

As usual, his father was in the dispensary at the back of the shop. What was he concocting this time? Whatever it was, it smelled foul.

'Baba. How are you?' he called, pulling aside the curtain.

'Umar. What a surprise. As-salama alaykum, my son,' Makoud said, putting down the mixing bowl and covering it with a muslin cloth.

'We leave tomorrow,' said Umar. 'I thought I'd call by to see how Aisha was before I left.'

'Much as expected,' Makoud said with a sigh. 'She refuses to give up hope that her husband will return. I think it's being pregnant that makes her so stubborn.'

'Pregnant? Is she expecting another child?' Umar asked in astonishment. His sister was an incredible woman; he was still amazed at how she had managed to keep Bakr's business running, despite all the odds. But then she'd never been a woman to let adversity get the better of her.

'Yes, it's due in a couple of months, or maybe less. It was a surprise for all of us. I'm not sure how she will manage, what with the business and the other children as well.'

'She'll be fine, Baba. After all there's a houseful of women, most of whom, from what I can see, do nothing at all anyway. She'll manage.' He dropped his voice and added, 'I don't suppose there's any news about Bakr?'

'Nothing. It's not for want of trying. Your brother Dirar has gone to the Balearic Islands to see if he's there. It's a wild goose chase if you ask me. We are all going to have to accept the inevitable one day; Bakr is gone. He's either dead or too far away now for anyone to find him. The Middle Sea is a big place and if the pirates don't want him found then he won't be found. And that goes for his men too.'

'I heard that the khalifa sent the admiral of the fleet to look for him. Is that true?' asked Umar.

'Yes, but we've heard nothing. It's been too long now. But you can't say that to Aisha. She refuses to accept it. Maybe when she's had the baby she will be able to see things more rationally,' said his father, turning back to his task. 'Your mother is upstairs. You'd better go and say your goodbyes, even though she won't like it.'

'She's still upset with me then?'

'Of course. But more than that, it's me she blames for bringing us all here in the first place. "Malaqah the city of dreams" she says, "More like a city of nightmares." And now that Dirar has gone to search for Bakr, she's even more angry with me.'

'Don't worry, Baba. I'll put in a good word for you,' said Umar with a grin. His father liked to adopt this martyred tone when he spoke about Basma, but it was all an act really. There was only one head of their household and that was his father.

'You take care, son. I will pray that Allah watches over you and protects you, and brings you safely back to us. I don't think any of us could bear it if something happened to you, least of all your sister.'

'I'm a soldier, Baba. It's inevitable that there will be danger, but don't worry, Allah will be with me and if it's my time to go to Paradise, then so be it,' Umar said, a little more confidently than he felt.

It didn't do to dwell on what might or might not happen. Luckily once the battle started there was no time to be frightened. That was the moment when all the hours of training came into their own; there was no time to stop and reflect, no time to consider options. You fought to win and to stay alive. It was attack and counter-attack until the battle was over. You relied on your commander, your comrades and your own reflexes to get you through it, and in his own case, on his faithful Basil. But this time was different for him. This time he had the responsibility of looking after his men. Only sixteen of them, it was true, but he'd trained them and come to know them well over the last six months. He felt his duties keenly; he couldn't let them down.

His father didn't reply. Perhaps he was already saying a silent prayer for him.

*

By the time Umar returned, the Dar al Jund was quiet. Most of the men were taking advantage of spending their last night with their families, or if they didn't have any family to go to, then they were in a comfortable bed somewhere and probably not alone.

He decided to go to the stables and check on Basil; he liked to spend some time with his mare on the night before they set off. It calmed both of them and, in Umar's case, it helped him to focus on what he had to do. Leading a squad of men into battle was a new responsibility for him and he wanted to perform his duty to the best he could; mistakes could cost lives. He was lucky; they were a good group of men, all regular soldiers and men who had fought alongside him before.

Apart from a torch, lighting up the entrance, the stables were in darkness, but Basil knew straight away that it was him and whinnied softly in greeting. He slipped into her stall and began to stroke her muzzle, rubbing gently around her eyes; something she enjoyed. He leant his head against hers and whispered in her ear, telling her and only her, his secret fears. She nuzzled him, pushing her head against his shoulder, a signal that she wanted him to groom her, so he picked up the curry comb and began to brush her back, in wide, circular strokes.

Suddenly Basil's ears pricked up. She had heard something. Umar stopped brushing her and listened. At first all he could hear was the usual nighttime sounds of the stables, the noise of a stallion kicking against its stall door, the occasional whinny from a sleepless mare, and the snoring of Talib's horse who could fall into a deep sleep anywhere. Then he heard a voice, whispering. Perhaps someone had had the same idea as himself and come to see his horse. But whoever it was, wasn't talking to a horse, because a second voice, a rather imperious one, answered him. Umar crept to the door of the stable and looked out. At the far end of the passage he could see two figures, deep in conversation. They weren't his men; he could tell from their dress. One of them looked like a member of the khalifa's personal guard; he could make out the green and white chequered pattern on his tunic. What was he doing down here? And who was the other one?

He opened the stable door as quietly as he could and, keeping in the shadows, crept towards them. The light from the torch shone on the guard's face so he could see him quite clearly. It was not a face he recognised, but it was one he wouldn't forget. The man had a livid scar across his mouth, giving him a grotesque grin. Poor sod. Without doubt a battle scar, and from its curved shape, one caused by a scimitar. But why was he meeting someone here, in the stables, in the middle of the night? And who was the other man? Their negotiations seemed to be over. The man with his back to him handed a purse to the guard, who thrust it into the pocket of his djubbah and turned to leave. At that moment the stallion decided to give its stall door another hefty kick; the noise reverberated through the stables like a slingshot.

Instantly the men both turned in Umar's direction. He held his breath, not daring to move.

'It's just a horse,' said the guard. 'No need to worry; there's no-one here at this hour.'

'There had better not be. We'd both have some explaining to do,' said the other man. He was old, with a long beard and white robes. A large ruby on his right hand glowed in the light of the torch.

Who was he? There was something familiar about him; Umar was sure he'd seen him before. He wasn't a soldier; that was clear. More like a scholar or one of the khalifa's ministers. Whoever he was, he was rich; that ring was worth a ransom. And why was he talking to one of the khalifa's personal guards in the middle of the night? In the stables?

CHAPTER 16

The children had told Kamil that the boat was due that night. They were very excited at the prospect of getting their charcoal and had scoured the island collecting anything they could write on: smooth stones from the river bed, banana leaves, the huge flat leaves of the elephant ear plant, fig leaves and scraps of bark. Kamil wished he'd asked for parchment as well as charcoal, but he knew that would be too costly and would come to the captain's attention. Maybe next time. He stopped himself; if their plan went well then there wouldn't be a next time. Much as he wanted to go home to his family and friends, he didn't want to leave this tiny island paradise and the children, his eager little pupils. He had become very fond of them, particularly one lad who was exceptionally quick at learning; Kamil never had to repeat anything to him. His memory was astonishing. What that child could achieve with a proper education. He wished his father was here to see the boy's potential; he'd know what to advise him. And then there was the captain's young wife. He felt he was abandoning her to a life of ignorance; she had been so keen to learn. But what else could he do? The captain could read and write—he'd seen him working on the plans for the new ship with Bakr—but that didn't mean he wanted others to learn as well. He knew the power of education and he had no intention of handing it over to anyone on this island. Already Kamil could see the children's confidence growing as they learned to master the strange symbols that were letters and numbers. One day they would begin to ask questions. The captain wouldn't like that. Bullies didn't like to be challenged and that's just what Captain al-Awar was, a bully.

The week before, knowing that he was leaving, Kamil had started teaching them to count with the shells they had collected from the beach and he'd prepared a board with the numerals 0 to 9 written on it in the same tar they used to caulk the hull of the new ship. He wanted to leave them with something they could refer to and, he hoped, a thirst for more knowledge.

As Kamil wandered over to Asim and Bakr, who were sawing planks to fit into the new boat as galley seats for the rowers, he noticed a ship come over the horizon. It was heading straight for the island.

'Look,' he called. 'There, coming towards us. A ship. We're going to be rescued.'

Bakr and Asim put down their tools and ran down to the beach. Already some of the pirates were gathering at the water's edge; they didn't seem concerned at the sight of the approaching galley. In fact they appeared to be delighted.

'I don't think that ship has come to rescue us,' said Bakr. 'It's a pirate ship.'

More pirates so soon. What would that mean for them and their planned escape? Kamil knew they were relying on the fact that the pirates' ship was out of action; the arrival of this ship could change everything. He looked across at Bakr, but his expression gave no clue to what was running through his mind. Would he risk it and steal the provision boat anyway? The captain would treat them harshly if they were caught. He might not punish Bakr and Asim, but he would certainly take it out on him; he'd been threatening Kamil with all manner of unpleasant things ever since he'd arrived there. He had already spent a night locked in the punishment cage; and this was said to be a warning. What would he do to him if he caught him trying to escape?

'What are we going to do, sayaad?' he whispered. It was obvious that this was a ship that regularly called at the island because nobody seemed surprised to see it. Maybe it was their resting place as well. But why come now? According to Bakr, more pirates would come to the islands for the winter, but that was still a long way off, even though the nights had begun to lengthen.

'That's scuppered our plans, then,' said Asim, starting to cough.

The foreman had developed a persistent cough that racked his body until he could hardly breathe. Whatever sickness had got hold of him, it was taking a long time to shift.

'Here, drink this,' said Bakr, handing him a flagon of water.

The foreman held the flagon above his head and tilted it so that a stream of clear water ran straight into his mouth and not a drop was spilled. Whenever Kamil tried to do that he managed to get his tunic wet.

'Take a rest, Asim, Kamil can help me with this part,' said Bakr, handing the plane to his apprentice.

'What are we going to do about him?' asked Kamil once Asim had gone to sit in the shade of a palm tree. 'He needs some medicine. Shall we ask the captain if we can send for a doctor?'

Bakr stared at him as though he'd lost his mind. 'Can you hear yourself? You're talking about the man who has threatened to castrate you for just looking at their women, the man who would slit another's throat as soon as look at him. You would do well to remember that we are only alive because we are of use to him. If Asim can't work, if we suggest that he is sick, never mind actually ask for a doctor, then the captain will get rid of him. No, we must help Asim as much as we can and keep his illness hidden from the pirates. Do you understand?'

Kamil felt like a child who'd just been scolded by his father.

'Yes, sayyad. But what about tonight? Are we still leaving?' he whispered.

'At the moment, I don't know. Let's see what this ship is doing here, first. In the meantime, I want to get this wood prepared; the captain is bound to come over and if he sees little progress he won't be happy.'

'Aye, aye boss.'

*

Bakr knew the captain would never let them go home; it wasn't in his interest to do so. The new ship was a lot nearer to completion than he had admitted, but what did that matter? The captain had already made it plain that he wanted more than one ship from them. When Bakr had broached the matter of allowing them to leave, he'd just laughed and said, 'Maybe after the next one.' Now a new pirate ship had come into the harbour. How would that affect them? Did the other captain have plans for increasing his fleet too? Without meaning to, Bakr let out a loud groan; this was beginning to feel like the labours of Hercules. How many years was he going to be slaving away for these blood-thirsty cut-throats? He knew it was risky to attempt to escape tonight but he had to weigh the risks against what could happen to Asim when the captain found he wasn't pulling his weight. And then there was Kamil, who was pushing the captain's patience to the limit. No, the sooner they got off this island the safer they would be. And if they didn't go tonight, they had another month to wait for the next boat. Could they keep Asim's condition hidden until then? And what if more pirate ships arrived on the island? The chances of escape would be even less.

'Everything all right, shipwright?' asked the captain, staring at him with his one eye as though he could read his thoughts. 'Where's the rest of your team?'

'Cutting planks for the interior,' he said, 'I think we can start to fit some of them tomorrow.'

The captain nodded.

He seemed to be in an amiable mood so Bakr pointed towards the galley that had just weighed anchor in the harbour and asked, 'Friends of yours?'

'Not exactly.'

'Have they come in to do repairs to their ship as well?'

'Now why would you say that? Worried that they'll steal you away from us? Well no need; they have their own carpenters.'

'Captain, what I don't understand is why you need me? You, too, have plenty of carpenters who could build you a new ship,' said Bakr.

'I do indeed. But you underestimate two things: your own renowned skill and my ambition.' He looked across at the recently arrived pirate ship. The captain was being rowed ashore by two of the crew, while the rest waded through the waves to the beach. 'That scoundrel, on the other hand, has no ambition at all. He is content to live from day to day, raiding the villages along the coast and attacking merchant vessels. He is weak and cowardly, but I wouldn't turn my back on him for a single moment because he's the most treacherous man I know. He doesn't want to win fame and glory; all he wants is to take what he can with the least effort.'

'Is that what you want, Captain, fame and glory? Is that why you want a fleet of ships? Is it power that inspires you?'

The captain turned on him and for a moment Bakr thought he was going to threaten him with his sword. Instead he adjusted the patch he wore over his right eye, and said, 'What's wrong with that? Don't all men want power? Don't you? I intend to have the fastest ships on the Middle Sea. No-one will be able to catch me. My name will be known from Constantinople in the east to the coast of Iberia. The name of Captain One-Eyed will strike terror into the hearts of all men; they will throw down their weapons, and their women and children will run and hide when they hear it.'

Bakr could see that al-Awar was a man obsessed with his dream. There was no way he was ever going to let them leave this island even when he had his fleet of ships.

'Well I must get on with my work or you'll never get your wish,' he said, smiling as pleasantly as he could at the captain.

'You know the choice,' snarled the captain, his mood changing as quickly as the sun going behind a cloud. He slapped his hand against the hilt of his sword to emphasise the point.

Yes, as far as Captain al-Awar was concerned they had no choice but to do as they were told, however he hadn't counted on Bakr's determination, which had been doubly renewed after their conversation. He must get Kamil to talk to the children again to make sure that they hadn't missed anything. Tonight they would make their escape or die in the attempt.

*

Kamil and Asim were working under the shade of an old piece of sailcloth which Kamil had strung up between two coconut palms. A stack of already planed planks lay to one side and while Kamil sawed at a roughly hewn log, Asim was smoothing another plank with the plane.

'How are you feeling, Asim?' Bakr asked.

'Right as rain, sayyad.'

'Good.' He looked around him to make sure no-one was within earshot, then said, 'We're leaving tonight. It could be our only opportunity and we have to take it.'

He waited for their response, but the two men continued with their work in silence.

'Kamil, I want you to go and see the children again. Make sure that you have all the information that we need. How long do the men stay? How many men are there? Do they always land at the same place? What do they do with the provisions? Do the pirates collect them, or the chandlers?' His apprentice looked up and was about to speak. 'I know you have already asked them, but I want you to be sure that there isn't anything we've forgotten.'

'If they land on the other side of the island it will take them a good while to carry the goods across to here,' said Asim. 'That should give us plenty of time.'

'But that's the problem,' said Kamil. 'They don't do that. They are not allowed to; the captain forbids them to land. He sends some of his men to collect the supplies. All they are allowed to do is unload everything onto the beach then they head for home; according to the children, they have never been over to this side of the island. The captain doesn't like too many inquisitive eyes.'

'So that's that. We'll never make our escape,' said Asim, with a choke in his voice.

'Not so. We just have to wait for the right moment. How many men are usually in the boat?' Bakr asked Kamil.

'Only two.'

'How can you be so sure?' asked Asim.

'I made it a counting game. I asked the children a variety of questions, such as "How many brothers do you have?" "How many coconuts are on that tree?" And then I slipped in, "How many men are in the boat that brings the supplies?" They all answered "two." And I believe them,' said Kamil.

'Two men. We can manage that,' said Bakr.

'We're not going to kill them, are we?' asked Kamil, looking shocked.

'Not unless we have to, lad. We'll just pull them into the water and steal their boat.'

'But sayyad, how on earth will we do that?' asked Asim.

'Ah, well. I will have to think about it. I need to have another look at the place where they will be landing. You two keep working here and if the captain wants to know where I am, you don't know. All right?'

'Yes, sayyad.'

Neither of them looked very confident about the plan, and if he were honest with himself, he wasn't that sure that it would work either, but they had to try. The arrival of the second pirate ship had certainly complicated things, but despite that his gut was telling him that it had to be now or never.

*

Once Kamil had finished the work that Bakr had left him, he headed for the hut where he knew the children would be playing. He was sure that no-one would see him; they were all busy getting drunk with their visitors.

'Kamil, is that you?' one of the girls asked, looking up. 'What are you doing here? Have you come to do some more counting games?'

'Yes. I just thought I'd see what you have remembered.'

The children gathered round him, evidently pleased to have some diversion, so Kamil squatted down to talk to them. But before he could say anything, he felt someone grab his arms and haul him to his feet. A voice he recognised said, 'So this is where you sneak off to, is it? Does your boss know what you get up to? I hope he doesn't or he will feel the sharp end of my sword as well.'

Kamil felt his stomach turn to water. It was Captain al-Awar and he wasn't alone. Two of his crew held Kamil firmly in their grasp, while another had the captain's young wife fast by her hair. The girl was weeping and trying to wriggle free but the pirate just yanked her to her knees. She looked at Kamil, beseechingly, but there was nothing he could do to help her.

'I've warned you many times about hanging around the women, my lad, but you wouldn't listen. I've been a very patient man. Too patient. And this is how I'm repaid. Well enough is enough, as I always say. You have had your fun and now you must pay for it.'

The captain turned to Kamil. 'You're a law-abiding Muslim, I believe. What would you do to a wife who betrayed her husband with another man? What is the punishment for adultery? Come on, speak up, boy. You know what it says in the Quran.'

'But she hasn't done anything. I was only teaching her to read,' Kamil stammered. He was terrified that al-Awar was going to kill them both. 'There was no adultery.'

'Well, the Muslim would say that wouldn't he? What about you my dear? What do you have to say for yourself?' The captain's tongue slithered over the words like a snake.

The girl cried even more; by now she was visibly shaking.

'I beseech you, captain, let her go. She's only a child and she hasn't done anything wrong.'

'Answer my question. What does the Hadith say about adultery?'

'I'm not sure?' Kamil whispered. 'It depends.'

'Depends? Not much of a law then. Come on lad, spit it out,' the captain shouted at him, now.

'Stoning,' he whispered, the word drying in his mouth. Surely the captain wouldn't stone them to death.

'Ah, rather barbaric, I'd say. What do you think? Is it a fitting punishment for someone who breaks the law?'

There was no way Kamil was going to answer that, no matter what the captain did to him. He was so unpredictable, who knew what he'd do.

'But you're lucky. I don't like things like that. I am not a man who likes to see people suffer, not even that faithless whore. A quick death is always preferable. Don't you agree?'

Even if Kamil had wanted to reply to the captain's question he couldn't; his mouth was too dry to utter a sound.'

'Enough of this. He looked at the men holding Kamil. 'Take him out and string him up,' he said.

'What about her, captain? What shall we do with her?'

'Take her to my tent. I'll deal with her, myself.'

Kamil tried to struggle free, but his arms were pinned to his sides. One of the pirates was their big, burly bodyguard, and he seemed to be enjoying this opportunity to inflict some pain on Kamil.

'Don't hurt her. She hasn't done anything. In the name of Allah, don't hurt her. Please.'

'Don't bother your head about that little whore. Think about your own salvation. Time to pray to your Maker to save your skin, I should think.'

The captain motioned for the pirates to drag him away. What were they going to do with him? Hang him? Allah save him. He didn't want to die and certainly not at the end of a rope.

'What's your boss going to say when he realises he will have to work twice as hard now, because he'll be one man short?' said the captain, pulling a whip out of his belt and cracking it in the air.

CHAPTER 17

Dirar was so excited at the prospect of going with Captain Mustafa that he was quite unconcerned about losing his job as a fisherman, but to his surprise, the captain of the fishing boat simply clapped him on the back and said, 'Good luck, young lad. If you can do anything to help those unfortunate men, it will be worth losing a few fish.'

'Yes, give them one in the eye from me, too,' said an old man, who sat most of the day with the fishermen while they were mending their nets. His right hand was twisted and bent like a claw from where he'd been stung by the spine of a weaver fish many years earlier and now he hardly ever went out fishing. 'Don't you worry. I'll take over for you.' He gave Dirar a toothless grin.

'We probably won't even miss your tiddly catch,' said Yusuf, whom he considered a friend.

'Yes, what difference will a handful of boquerones make?' said the fourth man in their boat.

For a moment he felt disappointed that his contribution to the boat's nightly haul could be dismissed so lightly, but then he saw the smiles and realised they were joking.

'Take no notice of them. Just make sure the pirates don't kidnap you as well,' said the skipper.

News travelled fast round the harbour. Already everyone was talking about the plans to rescue his brother-in-law.

'Yes, don't rely on the khalifa sending a war ship to rescue you,' said Yusuf.

'He won't need to,' said Dirar, with a bit of a swagger. He had to admit he was enjoying the attention.

He hurried back home. It had been easier telling his boss than it was going to be to tell his mother. She was already in a state because Umar was going off to Écija any time now, and spent half her day berating his father for allowing her eldest son to enlist in the first place and the rest of the time weeping and wailing. If that was how all women carried on whenever their husbands or their sons had to face any danger, then he wasn't going to get married. Ever. He'd be like great-uncle Rafiq and remain a bachelor.

It was still light, although the night was already far advanced, and he knew he was going to get little sleep because he'd arranged to meet Captain Mustafa the next morning at dawn. It was going to be a long journey, some four hundred and fifty nautical miles so the captain wanted no delays in setting off.

'Dirar, is that you?' his mother called, as he climbed the stairs to their home.

'Of course, Mama. Is there anything to eat?'

'At this time of night?'

'Sorry I missed dinner. I had to speak to the skipper before I leave tomorrow.'

'So now you're going to tell me about this foolhardy trip, are you? I thought maybe you were just going to leave it to the gossips in the market to tell me that my youngest son was going to fight pirates?'

'Mama, don't exaggerate. I'm going to look for Bakr. Not to fight anybody.'

'I don't understand why all my sons are turning into warriors. They have a death wish. Why is that? Are they unhappy at home? Have I not been a good mother to them?

Have I not looked after them and cared for them since they were tiny babies? And now they want to throw themselves under the hooves of the first horse that passes by, so eager are they to enter Paradise.'

'We don't have any horses on the ship, Mama,' he said, grabbing a piece of bread and heading for his bedroom. 'Tisbah ala-kheir, Mama. I have to be up early tomorrow.'

He left her sitting on the patio, chuntering to herself, angrily. There was no sign of his father or Ibrahim; they knew from long experience to keep out of her way when she was in this mood.

*

Dirar's excitement only increased when he boarded the merchant ship. It was massive and built to withstand bad weather. Because it was designed to carry as much freight as possible there wasn't a lot of space for the oarsmen; the captain had been right when he said that she wasn't very fast. With only two men to each oar they would have to rely on the sails and a following wind to get up any speed.

'Welcome aboard, young man. I would like to treat you as my guest but I'm afraid that isn't possible on this ship. Space is limited and every man has to pull his weight,' the captain said. He looked at him as if he were sizing up a bale of cloth, then added, 'You'll be no good at the oars. Not enough muscle. Sorry but it will have to be slops or galley for you. You choose.'

Dirar stared at him. He hadn't expected to be working as a galley slave. In fact he hadn't given a single thought to what he'd be doing during the voyage. 'Galley,' he said. He didn't fancy "slops," whatever it was.

'I hope you can cook better than the one we have at the moment. It's a long way to the Balearic Islands.'

'How long will it take us?'

'Ten days if we make no stops.'

'Good, we'll be there before the new moon,' Dirar said.

'I said if we make no stops,' said Captain Mustafa. 'I have cargo to deliver.'

Dirar's heart sank. This was not what he was hoping for, a slow cruise along the coast of the Middle Sea, cooking—something which he had never done in his life before—for the crew of a merchant ship. He sighed. Well how hard could it be? He'd watched his mother sometimes when she was making churros for their breakfast. He'd manage.

*

Life in the galley was hot, cramped and chaotic. There was barely enough room for one man, never mind two and the cook was a bad-tempered individual who didn't take kindly to a young fisherman entering his domain.

'Chop these,' he said, slamming a sack of aubergines and onions in front of Dirar. In the corner was a huge pot, already half full of an assortment of vegetables. 'Put them in there when they're done,' he added, pointing at the simmering pot.

The cook was a short, rotund man who smelled as though he hadn't washed in weeks, and took up more than his share of the space in the cramped galley. His hair was long and greasy and tied back in a pigtail. Just looking at him made Dirar lose his appetite.

Dirar took the knife offered him and began to peel the onions.

'Not like that. You'll be here all day. Just chop them up as they are.'

He grabbed the knife off Dirar and quickly chopped the onion into quarters and tossed them into the pot, skin and all.

Exactly what he was cooking was a mystery to Dirar. It contained many vegetables, including copious quantities of garlic and ginger, but there was also a fishy smell to it. Fish stew maybe? So far he hadn't seen anything other than vegetables in the galley.

When he had finished chopping the onions, he asked, 'Would you like me to prepare some fish?' That was something he did know how to do.

'Fish? There ain't no fish. Whatever gave you that idea?'

'Meat?'

'Meat neither. Where do you think you are? We only eat meat when we stop off in port. And fish when we catch it.' He glared at Dirar as if he were mad. 'Here. No point you standing around. Take this mop and swab down the galley. I'm going up on top.'

While he was gone, Dirar took the opportunity to taste the broth. It was just as unsavoury as it looked. He poked about the tiny space, looking for anything that would improve the flavour. What did his mother add to her food? Rosemary and thyme. He couldn't see anything like that anywhere. In fact he couldn't find any herbs and spices at all. No wonder the captain didn't like the food. It was tasteless. When they stopped at the next port he would look for something to improve the flavour. He'd starve to death if he had to rely on that unappetising mess for his daily meal.

*

Three days later they pulled into the busy port of Qartayannat al-Halfa. He doubted that the pirates would bother to attack here because the harbour was well protected on both banks, with watch towers on either side of the narrow entrance. He saw the soldiers looking down at them from the ramparts as they rowed past. One waved at the captain as if he were an old friend.

'Do you want to go ashore?' Captain Mustafa asked Dirar as the ship approached the quay. 'It wouldn't hurt to make some enquiries about the men you're looking for. I very much doubt they're here, but, you never know, someone may have heard of them. I've work to do but you're free to do as you please. Make sure you're back on board tonight because I plan on leaving early in the morning.'

'Yes, Captain.'

Dirar felt a surge of excitement. He had only ever been in two places in his life, the sleepy town of Ardales where he'd been born, and Malaqah. This was quite different. There were no mountains encircling Qartayannat al-Halfa, no forests of trees as there were in Malaqah. Instead the hinterland was flat and dry, an arid plain that stretched inland. Even the air smelled different, hotter and drier. The harbour was crowded with naval vessels—all carrying the flag of the taifa of Mursiya—and other merchant ships like their own, some moored alongside the bustling quay, others about to leave the harbour.

He grabbed his bag, slung it over his shoulder, then clambered over the side and waded ashore. The crew of the merchant ship were busy sorting through the cargo, selecting the items that were to be unloaded in Qartayannat al-Halfa and re-stacking those that were destined for Dénia. The rowers had shipped their oars and were now stretching their backs and arms. He couldn't help thinking that they certainly looked strong enough to defend themselves, even though the captain had said they weren't fighting men; all had bulging biceps gleaming with sweat, and thighs the size of a bull's. They wouldn't have any problem fighting off the pirates.

The port was swarming with people eager to see the newcomers; the arrival of Captain Mustafa's ship had caused great interest, and traders and merchants were gathering on the quay to find out which wares he'd brought with him this time. It was obvious that Mustafa was well known here; he was greeting people like long-lost friends. Dirar waited a while as the crew unloaded casks of wine and boxes filled with pottery from Malaqah. The wine in particular seemed to be in high demand. Others were lining up to persuade the captain to buy their own goods, some of which were meant for the crew: vegetables, fruit, and many loaves of bread. No sign of any meat. Other merchandise was obviously destined to go on to other ports: young palm trees in pots of soil, bales of wool and crates of oranges, for all of which the captain paid in silver dirhams. One man wanted the captain to buy his rice. Mustafa opened one of the sacks and ran his hands through it and then shook his head; he didn't want it. The man was plainly angry at this and shouted something at the captain, but by then Dirar was too far away to hear what he said. It obviously made no difference to Captain Mustafa as he just turned away and spoke to the next trader.

By now Dirar's stomach was complaining; he could hear it rumbling. He'd eaten none of the tasteless stew that the cook made him serve the men at midday and now he was starving. Luckily his father had given him some money before he left and so he made straight into the town to find a tavern where he could get a decent meal.

Before long he came across a rather scruffy looking inn, but the delicious smell coming through the open door was good enough to entice him inside. The tavern was dark and dingy, but crowded with men, all eating from a long, low, wooden table.

'That smells good,' he said to a burly man who was busy ladling some aromatic stew into bowls and passing them down the table to the men.

'It is,' he said. 'I take it you want some?'

Dirar nodded his head.

'Sit down then lad and I'll get you a bowl.'

The men moved up and left enough room for him to squeeze in beside them. By the look of their clothing and their strong arms they were all seamen, probably rowers. He soon learned that they had arrived in the port that morning from Alicante, and were on their way to the Mahgrib.

The innkeeper placed a bowl of kid stew in front of him, and cut him a hunk of bread. It smelled so good that he sat for a moment just enjoying the spicy aroma of meat and rice.

'What's wrong? Don't you want it?' asked the sailor on his right. 'Pass it along to me, if you don't like it.'

Dirar picked up his spoon and said, 'Not likely. This looks delicious.' It was as good as it smelled and in no time he had eaten it all, and wiped the bowl clean with the bread.

'Beer?' asked the inn-keeper. 'Or wine? We cater for all sorts here.'

'Just water, thank you,' said Dirar. He'd never drunk wine or beer before and this probably wasn't the time to try it.

He turned to the seaman next to him and said, 'So you're on your way to the Maghrib?'

'That's right. Do you know it?'

'We fish along the coast there. I'm from Malaqah.'

'You're a fisherman? What the hell are you doing up here then?' asked the man opposite. He had a long scarf wound around his head, in the manner of a Berber turban. 'Don't think you'll find any tuna in these waters.'

'I'm looking for my brother-in-law; he was kidnapped,' he said. Instantly the table went quiet; all eyes were on him. He smiled to himself; there was nothing mariners liked more than a good tale and they could see the makings of one here. 'We think the pirates brought him north. I hoped someone might have heard something or knew where the pirates could have taken him.'

The man with the turban laughed. 'Well good luck with that. You'll never find him if pirates have got him.'

'When was he kidnapped?' asked the man on his left.

'Three or four months ago.'

A burst of laughter came from the sailors. 'Forget it, lad. Go home to your fishing. Your brother-in-law could be anywhere by now,' said the man opposite.

'If he's still alive,' said another.

'I know. But we think there could be a reason that the pirates would keep him alive,' said Dirar and went on to tell them the theory about the shipbuilding.

The sailors listened attentively and when Dirar had finished explaining what he believed had happened, one of them said, 'What was that name again?'

'Al-Awar. Why? Have you heard of him?'

'A couple of years back, the ship I was on was attacked by pirates. They stole the ship, all our cargo and murdered the crew. I only escaped by jumping overboard and swimming for my life,' he said. 'I'm pretty sure the captain's name was al-Awar. Big guy, with a patch over one eye.'

'So what happened to you?' asked another of the sailors.

'I was swimming for most of the day when I got picked up by a patrol that was on the look out for pirates.'

'Sounds as though they were a bit late.'

'Yes, but not for me. I was grateful to see them. I'd drunk so much salt water by then that I felt like an anchovy.'

'I've heard of him,' said one of the sailors at the end of the table. 'He's a ruthless devil. But nobody knows where he comes from.'

'Have you seen him?' asked Dirar.

The man shook his head.

'I used to be a fisherman,' said a slightly built man with an enormous beard. 'Pirates raided our village and took my younger brother and sister. I never saw them again. They killed my father and my grandmother. My mother only escaped because she was washing the clothes in a nearby stream and when she heard their screams she hid in the woods until it was quiet.'

'Was that al-Awar?' asked the man next to him.

'Don't know. There was nobody left to say who they were, only my mother and she hadn't seen anything.'

They all wanted to help Dirar, and everyone had a story about pirates but no-one knew Captain al-Awar or where his hideout was, and nobody had heard of any pirate captain wanting to build more ships.

'They usually just steal them,' said the mariner who'd had to jump overboard. 'That's what they did with our ship.'

The innkeeper brought out jugs of wine for the sailors, and a pot of mint tea for Dirar. And so he passed the evening, talking to the seamen, whose tales became more outlandish the more wine they drank.

'Closing up now, boys. Time you made your way back to your lovely wives,' said the innkeeper, clearing the table.

Dirar suddenly realised how late it was and bidding his new friends good night, he rushed out of the door and began to run back to the quay. He hoped the merchant ship was still moored where it had been when he came ashore; he certainly didn't fancy swimming out to it in the dark.

*

The captain was furious. 'Where the bloody hell have you been? The next time you keep me waiting, I'll sail without you,' he shouted as Dirar clambered aboard.

'Sorry, Captain. I got talking to some sailors.'

'Well, did they have anything useful to tell you?'

'Not really. Some of them had heard of al-Awar but nobody knew where he was,' Dirar said, realising that he had gained nothing from his interlude in the tavern, except a decent meal, but he decided not to mention that. 'I thought you weren't leaving until the morning?'

'We're not, but I'm not spending the night moored alongside the quay, so that any thief and cutthroat can climb aboard and help himself to our cargo,' said the captain, signalling for his first mate to cast off.

Someone began to play a drum and the rowers, who'd been patiently waiting for Dirar's return, picked up their oars and began to row in time to the beat. They rowed to the middle of the harbour and then shipped their oars. By then the night was well on and the sky was filled with bright stars. Now everyone was eager to get some rest; they had a long journey ahead of them the next day and each man had to find his own spot to sleep. As usual the cook had taken over all the available space in the galley, so Dirar curled up in a corner of the hold, between some barrels of wine and a large sack of silver ore that Mustafa had bought from the silver mines in Qartayannat al-Halfa. It was hard and uncomfortable, but the fumes from the barrels began to make him feel drowsy and he was soon asleep.

A sharp pain in his side woke him up. The captain stood over him, a malicious grin on his face.

'Time to get up, young man. The cook is shouting for you,' he said.

Dirar rubbed his ribs and sat up. 'But it's still dark,' he muttered. It seemed as if he'd only just fallen asleep and now he was being told to get to work again.

'Get on with you. And try to persuade that poisoner in the galley to give us something edible for breakfast.'

Dirar looked around him. Most of the men were still asleep. He staggered over to the water barrel and splashed some cold water over his face and hands and then went back to his corner to say his morning prayers.

He had just finished when he heard the cook shouting for him. He rummaged in his bag and pulled out a small bag of spices that he'd persuaded the innkeeper to sell him. At least they'd have some flavour in their food today.

Captain Mustafa decided that they would sail directly to Dénia and make no further stops; they had only enough cargo for one more port and he said they'd get a better price for the wine and olive oil in Dénia than anywhere else. Whatever his reasoning, Dirar was heartened to learn that the journey was going to be less meandering. Within a few days they should be in the Balearic Islands and Dragonera. He prayed that somebody there would have news of Bakr and the men, and that they were not too late.

CHAPTER 18

Bakr waited until he was sure there was no-one about—all the pirates, including their bodyguard, had gathered on the beach eager to talk to the newcomers—and then made his way to the grove of pine trees that stretched from the beach all the way to the top of the ridge. Once hidden by the trees he began to scramble his way up the stony path and then walked along the narrow hilltop until he stood opposite the landing site. A small stream ran down into a sheltered cove with a sandy beach, ideal for landing a light boat. The entrance to the cove was narrow and guarded by outcrops of rock, against which the waves were now breaking in cascades of white foam. It didn't look the easiest of channels to navigate, especially at night, so the men would have their full concentration on manoeuvring the boat. If the moon wasn't too bright, it would be easy for them to hide in the rocks and attack the boat as it was leaving. He looked up at the sky; there was not a cloud in sight. With a full moon tonight, it would be almost as bright as day; that was going to complicate matters. They needed to find a secure hiding place where they could wait without being seen by either the men in the boat or those collecting the supplies. He clambered down the path to the cove and then set off along the rocks looking for a suitable spot. At last he had it. A jagged rocky outcrop stretched out into the sea like a three-fingered hand. As he slithered and slid his way across the rocks he realised that he was now completely out of sight of the beach. As long as they were in position before the boat arrived no-one would know they were there.

*

The pirates were all in good form that night. Their lives were so isolated from the world that the chance to swap stories with a new group of men was a rare treat and they were determined to make the most of it. Besides which the newly arrived pirates had a goodly store of rum with them, which they claimed to have stolen from a merchant ship on its way back from India. So already they were sitting on the beach together, singing and getting steadily drunk.

Bakr walked over to where Asim was still working and said, 'Time to pack up now. Make sure you lock up the tools.' He looked across at their bodyguard, who was sitting watching their every move. He looked very pleased with himself for some reason. We've finished for today,' Bakr shouted over to him.

Without saying a word, the pirate got to his feet and held out a sack into which they deposited their remaining tools, then he tied it up, slung it over his back and walked away. He too looked eager to get to the party.

'Where's Kamil?' whispered Bakr.

'He's not back from the children, yet. I thought maybe he'd gone to look for you.'

'No. I've not seen him. Where, in the name of Allah, has he got to? We need to leave soon. Did anything happen while I was away?'

'Not really. We finished planing the planks and then Kamil said you wanted him to talk to the children again. I stayed here, finishing off one or two little things, and waiting for you to come back.'

'And nothing else? What about our friendly bodyguard?'

'He disappeared. I thought he'd gone to join the party with the others but then he came back again, smirking all over his face.' He stood up and stared at Bakr. 'You don't think something's happened to Kamil?'

'I don't know. It's possible. I should never have made him go back to the children; there was always a risk that Captain al-Awar would find out what he was up to.'

'So what do we do? We can't go without him.'

'No. But first we need to find out where he is. You know Kamil; he's probably chatting to some girl and forgotten the time.'

'What if he isn't? What if he's in trouble? What do we do?'

'Leave it to me, Asim. You go and pick up the weapons and head for the trees. The plan is still the same, for the moment at least. I'll join you as soon as I can,' Bakr whispered. 'Just keep hidden and wait for me.'

Kamil had previously wrapped two axes, a plane, three long knives and a large bag of iron nails in a piece of sailcloth and buried them in the sand near the edge of the pine forest. They didn't plan to take anything else with them; in fact they had little else to take and if they took any more of their tools the pirates would know they were up to something. They also had three cudgels which they fashioned out of stout oak branches and kept hidden in their tent for some weeks now. Bakr decided to pick up one of them on his way, in case he needed it.

The two men walked as casually as they could away from their makeshift workshop. The pirates were having a great time, singing and drinking around the fire, but it was hard to make out who was who; there were so many of them. Was Captain al-Awar with them? He hoped he was because he didn't want to walk into him now; the captain had taken to suddenly appearing when he was least expected and engaging Bakr in long discussions about the ship. That was the last thing he wanted right now; he had to find Kamil and get into position before the boat arrived with the provisions. The weak point in his plan was that he didn't know exactly what time the boat would arrive.

He watched as Asim disappeared into the trees; the man could hardly walk. How on earth was he going to escape from the island? He hardly had the strength to make it across the beach so how was he going to climb up to the ridge? And now Kamil had disappeared to Allah knows where. It was hopeless. Why was he deluding himself? They would never make it back to Malaqah. Why couldn't he just accept the fact that he would never see his beautiful Aisha again?

Whether they made it or not, he still had to find Kamil, so he cautiously approached the hut where the children lived and pulled back the curtain. A dozen curious faces turned towards him.

'As-salama alaykum, children,' he said but they stared at him blankly. 'I'm looking for Kamil. Have you seen him?' He smiled at them, encouragingly. 'Do you know where he is?'

'The captain is angry with him,' said one little boy, at last.

'And with Mina,' added another child. 'He took her away and she was crying.'

'They were pulling her hair,' said another small child.

'Did the captain hurt Kamil?' Bakr asked. He prayed that nothing bad had happened to him.

They all nodded.

'Did he take him away too?'

'The pirates took him. But he wasn't crying.'

'He was angry,' said another boy. 'He didn't like the man pulling Mina's hair. He shouted for them to let her go.'

Oh dear. Kamil never knew when to keep quiet. Bakr guessed that Mina must be the captain's child-bride.

'Do you know where they took him?' asked Bakr.

They shook their heads in unison and then one boy, older than the rest, spoke, 'I know where he is. I followed them.'

'Good lad. Can you show me? Can you lead me there?'

'The captain might see me,' he whispered nervously.

'If he sees us, I'll tell him I forced you to take me to Kamil. But I don't think we'll see any more of the captain tonight; he's enjoying himself with the other pirates.' He hoped for all their sakes that this was true.

'Kamil's at the far end of the beach.'

Together they crept out of the hut. It was already dusk and the ghost of the full moon could just be seen creeping over the horizon. They had to hurry. The sound of the organistrum floated towards them; by now the party was getting rowdy and he hoped that nobody would be sparing any thoughts for the shipwright and his men. But you never really knew what was going on in Captain al-Awar's mind. He just prayed that the arrival of some rum had gone to all their heads and they would soon be slumped unconscious where they sat.

The boy led him to a clump of palm trees near the foot of the cliff where, according to the chandler, the previous carpenter had met his death. Bakr couldn't stop himself shivering at the thought.

'There he is. Over there,' said the boy. 'They said they're going to throw him off the cliff at sunrise. I don't want Kamil to die. You'll save him, won't you?'

'I'll try.'

'I'm going back now.'

'Thank you. Don't tell anyone about this, will you?' whispered Bakr.

'Do you think I'm mad? Do you know what the captain will do to me if he catches me? I'm only doing this for Kamil; he was very kind to us.'

'Go carefully,' said Bakr, praying that the child would get back without being seen.

'I hope you get away,' whispered the boy, and then he was gone.

Bakr looked towards the palm grove. Everything was silent. He strained to see any sign of movement, but it was too dark under the canopy of trees. Had the boy made a mistake? He crept forward, hoping it wasn't a trap.

'Kamil,' he called softly, pushing aside the fronds that hung down from the palms. 'Kamil.'

There was no reply, but as he edged closer he became aware of a large shape hanging from one of the trees. Suddenly it moved. Bakr froze, hardly daring to breathe.

'Kamil?' he whispered, at last. 'Can you hear me? It's Bakr.'

'Sayyad. Praise be to Allah you've found me. Get me down from here before I die of cramp,' whispered a voice.

Bakr reached out his hand and touched the dark shape; it was a net. The pirates had hung his young apprentice from a palm tree, inside a piece of fishing net. Kamil swung from the tree, doubled over, his head pressed against his knees and his arms tied behind his back.

'What the hell have you got yourself into this time?' he asked, relief softening his tone, despite his anger.

Bakr's rage was directed as much at himself as Kamil. Sending him back to double-check had nearly cost the lad his life; the boy had said that al-Awar intended to throw Kamil off the cliff as soon as it was light. If they were caught they'd all end up on the rocks. He pulled out his knife and cut through the twine from which the net was suspended and caught Kamil as he fell to the ground.

'Lie still, while I get you out of there,' he said, pulling the net apart so that Kamil could crawl out of it.

'My hands, sayyad,' Kamil said. 'I can't feel them; I think the circulation's dead.'

Bakr sliced through the ropes that bound him and pulled him to his feet. 'Come on, we must leave before anyone comes back. You can tell me what happened later. If we don't hurry, we'll miss the boat.'

He dragged the uncomplaining apprentice, tripping and stumbling into the woods, and began to head for the spot where Asim was waiting. Earlier Bakr had explained his plan to them in detail and, although apprehensive, they had agreed to go along with it. As Asim put it, 'Better that than spend the rest of our miserable lives on this forsaken lump of rock.' One way or another, they all agreed that they had to get off this island and luckily, what they lacked in strength they made up for in desperation. Now he hoped that Kamil's actions hadn't scuppered those plans. This was their one opportunity and they mustn't miss it. If they couldn't do that, it didn't bear thinking about. In the original plan, if anything went wrong there was always the possibility of sneaking back to the camp without the pirates knowing. Not now. There was no way that Kamil could return to the pirate camp; it would be certain death for them all.

Luckily nobody noticed them slip into the trees and make their way stealthily through the forest and up onto the ridgeway. As he'd hoped, nobody missed them; everyone was having too much fun to notice. They walked in silence, Kamil, limping as he led the way and Bakr bringing up the rear.

'A moment,' gasped Asim, wheezing and coughing like a man twice his age. He sat down on a rock and put his head between his hands.

Bakr and Kamil looked at one another; the foreman wouldn't be much use if it came to a fight. And if they had to swim for it, well, with his lungs like that, there was no way he'd be able to make it. They had to steal the boat and their only chance of that lay in the element of surprise. For that they had to get in position before the men arrived.

*

The sound of voices floated across the water towards them; a small rowing boat was approaching. Instinctively the three of them crouched even lower behind the rocks that separated them from the sea and, they hoped, kept them hidden from view.

'It's like I said; there are only two of them,' whispered Kamil. His voice seemed to reverberate in the cave-like formation where they had taken refuge.

Bakr put his finger to his lips and frowned at his apprentice. The boat was very flimsy; it would take them across to the main island but no further. Still, one step at a time. He peered through a gap in the rocks and watched as the rowing boat, heavily laden with sacks of provisions, passed within touching distance, then rounded the bend and vanished from sight. He heaved a sigh of relief; the first stage had passed without mishap. The entrance to the cove was so narrow that the rowers would have to take the same route when they left. The only problem would be if there were still some pirates on the beach when they made their assault; sound carried easily over water.

'Kamil, climb up there and see if you can see the beach where they're unloading the goods. Are the pirates there yet?'

He waited anxiously while his apprentice clambered over the rocks and disappeared from sight.

'He's taking a long time,' whispered Asim.

'Maybe he's waiting until they leave again,' Bakr said.

'It will take them a while to unload all that stuff,' said Asim.

'Not if the pirates are helping. The boat could come back any minute.'

As he said that, Kamil slithered down the rocks and hissed at them in what he thought passed as a whisper, 'There are about six pirates; I couldn't see all that well but I could hear them moaning about missing the party. Anyway, they've unloaded the provisions and now they're heading back to their camp.'

'What about the boat?'

'I think the men were counting their money, but then I heard them shout goodbye to the pirates, so I think they're on their way. I couldn't hang about in case they saw me.'

'Well done, Kamil. I think if you can get onto that rock there, you should be able to jump straight onto the boat. Asim and I will go down to the water's edge and when you are on board I'll swim out to you. Here take this.' He handed him the cudgel. 'You've got a knife?'

'Yes, sayyad.'

'What about me? What do you want me to do, sayyad?' asked Asim, stifling a cough.

'You can wait on the rocks until we have secured the boat, then I'll come for you. I don't think you're in a fit state to take an active part in the attack, do you?'

'I'm fine, sayyad. I...' he started to say, but a fit of coughing threatened to choke him. He clamped his hand over his mouth and did his best to stifle the sound.

They waited, listening for any shouts but the night remained quiet, and all they could hear was the splash of the oars as the boat grew closer.

'Remember, make as little noise as possible. Our only chance is to take them by surprise. Here, Asim, take the axe and this cudgel. I hope you don't have to use them but look as though you fully intend to.'

The men moved into their positions just in time because the boat was suddenly upon them, gliding past like a phantom. The rowers were oblivious to the waiting men, and rowed, heads down, their pockets full of money, intent on getting home. Suddenly the silence of the night was broken by an enormous crash as Kamil leapt from the overhanging rock, directly into the boat. For one awful moment Bakr thought the boat would sink. It rocked wildly from side to side as the two men at the oars fought to steady it. He lowered himself into the water and swam across to them, his knife held in his teeth.

'What in the name of Allah,' shouted one of the men. 'Who in damnation are you?'

'Sit down and be quiet,' said Kamil.

'It's just a skinny kid. Toss him over the side and let's get going,' said the other. 'Go home to your mother, boy.'

'Not so fast,' said Bakr, hauling himself into the boat and brandishing his knife at the two bewildered rowers. He pulled his cudgel out of his belt and pointed it at the men. 'This is where you get out and we take over.'

'What do you want?' asked one of the men. 'Money? You can have money, but don't take our boat.'

'No, you can't leave us here,' said the other, fear making his voice tremble. 'They'll kill us.'

'Out,' barked Bakr. 'Before I make you.'

The men remained seated at the rowlocks, staring at him in disbelief.

'Who are you?' asked the first man, whose face was partially covered by a white scarf. 'Where do you want to go? Maybe we can take you?'

'I know who they are. That's the shipbuilder we've been hearing about. He's had enough of building pirate ships and he wants to go home,' said the other man, who was younger and wore an untidy black beard. He laughed bitterly. 'You won't make it, you know. Nobody ever gets off this island. Even if you get to the main island, they'll find you and then I wouldn't want to be in your shoes.'

'So we'd better not let them find us then, and the best way to do that is to get rid of you two,' said Bakr.

'There's no need for that attitude,' said the man with the scarf. 'We're peaceful people. We don't want any trouble. We can take you to the main island; there's plenty of room in the boat for two more.'

'Make that three,' said Asim, pulling himself up into the boat. He lay there panting for a few minutes and then sat up and pulled his axe out of his belt.

The sight of the cold steel glinting in the moonlight looked far more menacing than it actually was—Bakr knew that Asim barely had the strength to lift it, never mind bury it anyone's head— but it had the desired effect on the two men.

'Now, now. There's no need for that. We can take three. That's no problem,' said the bearded one.

The men were obviously terrified of the pirates and preferred to risk their chances with Bakr rather than remain on the island, where, no doubt, the captain would have them flayed alive for allowing Bakr and his men to escape.

'Very well. But if you try anything you'll be sorry. The pirates aren't the only desperate men around,' said Bakr, lying down at the bottom of the boat. 'And remember I'm right here,' he said, pressing the blade of his knife against the man's leg. 'Row us to a deserted beach and then you can go home to your families.'

The men rowed in silence for a while. From the position of the moon's reflection on the sea, Bakr knew they were heading straight for the main island.

'Can we sit up now?' asked Kamil. 'My back's killing me.'

'Not a good idea; we're still in sight of Dragonera. Wait a bit longer. We'll row along the coast; I know the perfect place to drop you off.' As the man said it, Bakr felt the boat turn towards the south-east.

'What is this perfect place?" asked Bakr. 'I hope you're not planning on betraying us?'

'No. Why would we?'

'You really don't understand, do you? It's not only us the pirates will punish for helping you, it's our wives, our children, our parents and grandparents. It wouldn't bother them to wipe out our whole family,' added the man with the white scarf. 'And our neighbours.'

'They like to leave a message,' added the other.

'What sort of message?' asked Kamil.

'That nobody can double-cross a pirate and get away with it. Especially that pirate.'

'You mean Captain al-Awar?'

'Yes, Captain One-Eyed. He's a wicked bastard.'

The rowers shipped their oars and let the current take them for a bit.

'This looks like it. Stay down until I tell you, then we'll drop you off on the beach. After that it's up to you. Don't worry; you don't have anything to fear from us. It's certainly not in our interest to tell anyone we've seen you. Quite the opposite; we'll deny any knowledge of you.'

'If you know what's good for you, you'll forget you've ever seen us,' said Bakr.

The men steered towards the shore and once they were in the shallows, Bakr, Kamil and Asim clambered out of the boat and waded through the clear water to the beach.

They had done it. They'd escaped. Even though it was only the first step, they could all feel the euphoria of being free. Asim and Kamil threw themselves down on the sand to stretch their aching limbs, while Bakr watched the little rowing boat head back along the coast. Had he been right to trust them? Would they tell the pirates where they had taken them? His head ached; he was not sure whom he could trust anymore. And now what were they going to do? He'd been so focused on getting off Dragonera that he hadn't considered what they would do when they reached the island of Mayurqa. Not only was it over two hundred Arab miles to the mainland but they would have to pass Dragonera on the way. They had little money—just a handful of coins that Bakr had in his djellaba when he was kidnapped—no food and no proper weapons. What in the name of Allah had he got them into?

CHAPTER 19

Captain al-Awar woke late; the sun was already over the horizon and the cockerel had ceased to crow. One of his wives was chasing the children out into the yard, shouting at them to fill the buckets with water from the stream, while the other was clattering about the room, preparing the breakfast. It was mayhem inside the hut and it stank; he'd be glad when the ships were ready and he could get back to sea. Life on the land did not agree with him.

He splashed some water on his face, ran his fingers through his rather matted hair and pulled on his boots; his head was pounding. Their visitors had brought some pretty awful rum with them yesterday, rough as a porcupine's backside. It was a good job the men from the mainland had arrived with the new provisions last night. He groaned. Had anyone bothered to lock them away? He couldn't remember. There were a lot of things that were hazy about the previous night. Well, they would have to be checked this morning; he'd send the first mate to see to it. From the throbbing in his head, he had the feeling that between them they'd drunk quite a lot of the new Malaqah wine.

'Captain, sayyad. The prisoner's vanished,' said his first mate, pulling aside the curtain and stepping into the hut.

'What? What's that you say?' He pulled on his beard and stared at his first mate through bleary eyes. 'The boy, you mean?'

'Yes, Captain. Someone cut him down. He's gone. We went along at first light to throw him off the cliff, as you instructed, but he'd gone.'

Al-Awar let out a roar of rage. 'Gone? Where to? How can he have gone? We're on an island, damn it. He can't have gone anywhere.'

'Shall I get the men to look for him, Captain?'

'Yes. Wake them all up. I want every one of them out there looking for him. And bring the shipwright to me, and that sickly chap he calls a foreman. Bring them both here. Now.'

Who had been foolhardy enough to do this? One of the children? They were stupid enough and they had developed a liking for the lad; he had heard them talking about him. It wasn't one of his own men; they knew only too well what their punishment would be if they tried to cross the captain. Would the shipwright be stupid enough to do it? He was bold but was he that bold? Whoever it was, he would get to the bottom of it and then they would rue the day they'd been born.

'Well?' he shouted when he saw the first mate approach. 'Where are they?'

'They're not in their tent, Captain. They've gone too. Not a sign of them anywhere. No-one's seen them since yesterday.'

'What both of them?'

The unlucky first mate nodded his head. 'Yes, we can't find any of them.'

Al-Awar picked up his cutlass and thrust it into his belt.

'Are all the men searching the island?'

'Yes, Captain. Don't worry; they can't have got far. We'll find them.'

'You had better find them or it won't be me that's worried. What about our visitors? Get them to join in the search. And ask their captain if I can have a word with him.'

The first mate stared at him. 'He's gone, Captain. He and his crew. They sailed off this morning before it was light. I thought you knew.'

'What? No, I didn't know. Are you sure? Maybe he's just moved his ship round the headland?'

'No, Captain. He sailed north.'

'The snake. The bloody thief. Have you checked our supplies?'

'No, Captain. I haven't had time to think about it; we've been looking for the prisoners.'

'Haven't had time. You'll have enough bloody time to think when you're dangling on a rope from that tree. Hurry up man. See if those thieving pirates have taken our provisions.'

Why else would they sneak away before anyone was awake? He'd never liked that Captain Yazid. Not a man to be trusted. He'd seen the supplies arrive and decided to take them for himself. Damn and blast his eyes.

Captain al-Awar brushed some straw off his pantaloons and pulled a rather grubby, red silk-lined cloak, once the property of a rich merchant, around his shoulders; it had rained in the night and the air was cold. He took down a whip from a hook on the wall and cracked it in front of him. It had a leather handle and was made up of nine separate ropes, each one knotted at various stages along its length. It was the ideal punishment tool when he wanted to inflict a lot of pain but didn't want to kill the offender. Bakr would have taste of this. As for the others, they weren't worth bothering about; when he found them he'd slit their throats and throw them to the fish.

Still cracking the whip in front of him, he stepped out into the damp air. The first mate approached and stopped, just out of range of the whip.

'You're right, Captain. They've taken all the new supplies. Everything. All the Malaqah wine.'

'The bastard. What a way to repay our hospitality,' the captain said.

He was angry that Captain Yazid had stolen their food and wine, but not really surprised; it was exactly what he would have done in his place. What made him so furious was the fact that he had been so drunk last night that he'd let that moron take advantage of him.

Then it dawned on him. Yazid was not the only one to take advantage of the comings and goings of last night. Bakr. There was only one way he could have left the island and that was on the boat that brought the provisions.

'Any sign of the shipbuilder yet?' he asked.

'No, nothing. We've searched every cove and inlet, and there are men walking the ridgeway. So far, they've found nothing.'

It was as he feared; his prisoners had escaped. They had managed to get off the island; something he had thought impossible. He smiled to himself. Well they would not get far; he guaranteed that.

Al-Awar marched down the beach towards his ship, which still lay like a stranded whale on the sand.

'How long to get this finished?' he bellowed at the two men scraping the hull.

'The shipbuilder said about another three weeks, Captain,' replied one of them, staring fearfully at the whip which al-Awar still flourished in his right hand.

'Is it sea worthy? Can we put to sea right away?'

'We just have to put some tar over those new patches, otherwise, yes. There are still parts to clean but it will be watertight.'

'Get the tar on those patches, and as soon as it's dry I want my ship back in the water. Is that understood? Tomorrow morning we sail.'

'Aye, aye, Captain.'

Al-Awar wandered along the beach, deep in thought. He didn't like to be humiliated and that's what had happened today. First Yazid and then Bakr. Both were men whom he thought respected him. He didn't expect friendship; pirates didn't live long enough to make friends. He wanted men to fear him and to respect him. Yazid feared him because he knew the depths of al-Awar's cruelty but he had failed to show him any respect. He would regret that.

As for Bakr, he was an intelligent man and yet he neither feared him nor respected him. He had taken advantage of the fact that al-Awar didn't have a sea-worthy ship. He had used the distraction caused by the arrival of the other pirates to slip away unnoticed and to free that kid. And he had escaped on the very boat that brought them their monthly provisions. Was it desperation that led him to challenge al-Awar in this way? Or did he merely underestimate what the captain would do if he was thwarted? Well he would soon learn what sort of man Captain al-Awar really was and then he would rue the day that he chose to humiliate him.

First he would track down the men who had taken his prisoners to the main island in their boat and he would display their dead bodies so that all could see what happened when you crossed Captain al-Awar. Then he would set out for Malaqah and find the ship builder. He knew where he lived and he would have his revenge, even if it took him a lifetime.

CHAPTER 20

Bakr lay in the sand looking at the tree covered mountains which ran along the west coast of the island. They needed to get into the forest and head north. But what then? Al-Andalus lay directly to their west but without a ship there was no way they could get there. A ship? In the name of Allah what was he thinking? He was a shipbuilder after all. He'd make one. It didn't have to be anything very special, just sea-worthy enough to get them across to the mainland. And in the summer they were much less likely to have any storms; they would have a calm crossing. It would take a while but what alternative did they have? Just as long as they could finish it before the winter.

Already the sky was brightening; a silver glow lay along the horizon. Very soon the sun would rise from behind the mountains and a new day would have begun. They couldn't stay there any longer; they were far too exposed on the beach. He sat up and looked back at Dragonera. He thought he could see something moving along its shore. They had to get under cover. Right away.

'Wake up. We need to move,' he said, shaking his companions.

'What? What's happening?' asked a groggy Asim. He had slept the sleep of the dead all night and still he looked as though he needed more.

'I can see movement across on the island. It's probably nothing but I don't intend to sit here and wait to find out.'

'Where are we going, sayyad?' asked Kamil.

'Up there, into the trees.'

'But that's the wrong way,' said Asim. 'Al-Andalus is over there.' He pointed back the way they had come the night before.

'What do you suggest, Asim? We swim back to Dragonera and ask them to take us to the mainland? Come on, man, you're not thinking straight. We're free. Our main objective is to remain that way. Once we know the pirates can't find us then we can discuss how to get back home.'

There was no point telling them that they would probably have to build a ship in order to do so, not yet anyway.

'Very well, sayyad. But I hope you have a plan,' said Asim. 'I'm starving.'

Bakr didn't reply. He had a lot to think about; they needed food, water and a safe place to hide and he had no idea how he was going to find any of it. The only firm idea he had in his head was that they weren't going to be taken by the pirates again. He'd had enough of pirate life. More than anything he wanted to get home to his family and especially to Aisha, before she gave him up for dead and married someone else. Nothing and nobody was going to stop him.

*

It was slow going through the forest. Asim was getting weaker and weaker. His cough was tearing him apart and Bakr was beginning to doubt that he would make it much further.

'I'm sorry, sayyad. I must stop for a moment,' his foreman said, spitting an enormous gob of blood-streaked phlegm onto the woodland path. His face was ashen.

'That's all right, Asim. We'll take a break here. I'll go ahead and see if I can find somewhere for us to spend the night. Kamil, you take care of things,' he said, looking pointedly at Asim.

'Yes, sayyad.'

Bakr made his way through the pine trees, his feet crushing the pine needles and releasing their pungent perfume. It was cool in the forest; the stone pines formed a wide canopy through which the sunlight struggled to find its way. Bakr stopped and filled his bag with pine cones; the pine nuts from them would provide some sustenance but wouldn't fill their bellies. A squirrel watched his progress with a quizzical eye.

After a while the ground began to slope downhill. Bakr pushed through the scrub that covered the hillside until he had a clear view of what lay ahead of him. The land was as dry as a tinder box; one spark and the whole mountain would be alight. The stone pines had thinned out allowing some stunted palm trees and clumps of coarse grass to take hold. A snake, disturbed by his heavy footfalls, slithered across the path and disappeared into the brush. Then he saw it. A narrow stream of fresh water cascaded down the rocks in front of him. Bakr threw down his bag and put his head under the miniature waterfall. It was the sweetest water he'd ever tasted and despite the noonday sun, it was icy cold. When he'd drunk his fill, he held his flask under the cascade until it was full, tucked it into his bag, then he doused his head one final time in the stream and set off downhill, keeping to the path.

After a short distance the stream disappeared underground, but he could still see its path by the line of oleander bushes that wound their way down to the shore.

Wherever there was oleander, there was water. He hurried on, anxious that he might lose trace of the stream, but once again it rose to the surface and this time he could see that it led to a small cove bordered by a shoreline of white sand. The beach lay like a tiny gem on the edge of the turquoise sea. He stared at it, his eyes dazzled by the sparkling surface of the water and for a moment he forgot everything as he basked in its beauty. If only he could capture that image and take it home with him to give to Aisha, his own precious jewel.

The screech of seagulls brought him instantly back to his present and pressing predicament. They needed somewhere to hide while they made their plans and where Asim could rest. This looked as good a place as any; here they could build themselves a ship and Asim would have a chance to recover his strength. There was no view of Dragonera from the beach and it looked as though they would have a clear crossing to the mainland. It was perfect.

He slung his bag across his back and began the climb back up the hill to the forest and his waiting companions.

*

Asim seemed to be sleeping and Kamil was leaning against a pine tree whittling a piece of wood with his knife when Bakr arrived back.

'Everything all right, sayyad?'

'Yes, I've found somewhere for us to spend the night. Here have some of these,' he said, throwing the bag of pine nuts on the ground.

'What are these? I'm not a squirrel you know.'

'Pine nuts, you idiot. Haven't you eaten pine nuts before?'

'Of course I have but they didn't look like this,' Kamil said, holding up one of the pine cones and looking bewildered.

'In the name of Allah, what did your mother teach you?'

'She didn't teach me to steal food from the squirrels,' he said with a laugh. 'What am I supposed to do with it?'

'Here, I'll show you,' said Asim, who had woken up at the mention of food. He took one of the pine cones and tapped it against a large stone until the seeds fell out. Then he peeled off the husk of one of the seeds and handed it to Kamil. 'There you are, my son. Food for the gods.'

Kamil popped it in his mouth. 'As good as my mother buys in the market,' he said.

'How are you feeling Asim? Do you think you can walk a bit further? I've found a place with fresh water and a secluded beach. It's not far and most of it is downhill.'

He wasn't keen on having to carry Asim. Even though he was thinner than he'd been before, he would still be a heavy weight and the path was uneven and stony.

'I'll manage, sayyad. Just let me go at my own pace.'

'Here, have some of the squirrel food; it'll give you energy,' said Kamil, passing a handful of nuts to the foreman.

'As long as I don't have to climb any trees to get them,' said Asim, attempting a smile.

*

The next morning, after a good night's sleep on the beach, a wash in fresh water and a meal of fruit and nuts, Kamil felt like a new person. He had said his prayers, and now he wanted to be active. Yesterday when they reached the beach, he'd gathered branches from the forest, chopping them off with the axe and trimming them into shape to build a shelter. It had been sufficient to keep the wind off them but still needed some improvements.

'Good morning, sayyad. What do you want us to do today?' he asked. 'Shall I gather some more branches so we can finish the shelter?'

'Have you spoken to Asim?' his master asked.

'Not yet. Why?'

'He doesn't look at all well. I'm worried about him. We need to get him some medicine.'

'But how can we do that?'

'I want you to go into the town and buy him some.'

'Me?'

'Yes, you. Use this money. And if you have anything over, buy some bread. You will be quicker than me. And with your charm I'm sure that you will convince someone to help you.'

Kamil felt a rush of excitement. 'Very well, sayyad. I can do that. But what about the shelter?'

'Don't worry about that. I can manage on my own. Now, if I remember correctly, we passed a town on our right as we headed for the cove where they dropped us off. So head along the ridgeway until you can see it and then drop down and go into the town. You're sure to find an apothecary somewhere. Don't take any chances. Only speak to someone if it is really necessary; this is a small place and they won't get many strangers. A handsome lad like you will stand out. Pull your scarf around your face and if you think anyone is staring at you, just leave. I don't want anything to happen to you. We need you back here. Is that understood?'

'Yes, sayyad.'

'And keep away from the girls.'

'Of course, sayyad,' he said and gave Bakr his most winning smile.

He picked up his cloak and turned to leave.

'What are you going to do while I'm away, sayyad?' he asked.

'I'm going to strengthen the shelter and then I'm going to do what I always do,' said Bakr. 'Build a boat. How else are we going to get out of here?'

'Ma'a salama, sayyad. I will be as swift as the wind,' Kamil said and bounded away up the path towards the forest, his heart racing with the excitement of being free.

*

It didn't take Kamil long to arrive at the cove where they had landed two nights previously; it was deserted. From his hiding place in the trees he could see across to Dragonera. It looked deserted. They said it was an uninhabited island and from this viewpoint that was exactly what it looked like. There was no sign of pirates, no sign of the children Kamil had been teaching, no sign of anybody at all.

What were the pirates doing now? Were they searching the island for them? Dragonera was only about three Arab miles long; it wouldn't take them long to realise that they were no longer there. But would the captain bother looking for them? Maybe he'd think it wasn't worth the trouble and he'd get his own men to finish the ship. No, he was fooling himself if he thought that. Captain al-Awar was a ruthless man and a violent one. He imagined the captain storming about the island looking for Bakr and getting angrier and angrier. He had trusted them. But he'd also underestimated them. He thought they couldn't escape so although he locked up their tools each night, he let them wander freely around Dragonera. They had made him look a fool in front of his men; he wouldn't stand for that. It was nothing to do with building the ship now; he would want his revenge. He would hunt them down and kill them one by one. He'd probably kill Kamil first; he'd been itching to do it since day one. The sayyad had been right when he said to be careful. For the first time the enormity of the risk he was taking came home to him. A slight movement along the ridge of hills that ran along Dragonera's spine made him move further back into the trees. A glint of sunlight on a sword was all he needed to know they were still searching for them. Soon they would have to face the unbelievable, that Bakr and his men had managed to get off the island. Then they would turn their attention to the provisions' boat. There was no time to be lost. He must get the medicine and return to Bakr as soon as possible.

CHAPTER 21

Kamil wound his scarf around his face as Bakr had instructed him and walked nonchalantly into the town. Compared to Malaqah, Andrach was no more than a small village. He walked with his head down, convinced that everyone in this place knew everyone else and they would know instantly that he was a stranger the minute they saw him. At any moment he expected someone to run over to him and grasp his arm and march him to the Muhtasib, or worse still, to Captain al-Awar, but no-one even glanced his way.

As he walked through the quiet streets he realised that there was no way in which he could tell if there was an apothecary in the town or not. Unlike in Malaqah, the shopkeepers in Andrach mostly kept their wares inside their houses and as everyone knew everyone else there was no need to advertise them. Behind one of those curtained doorways was an apothecary, of that he was sure, but which one? He stopped by the town fountain and had a drink. This was impossible. He would either have to ask someone or knock on all the doors until he found one.

At that moment a young girl sat down by the fountain and began to bathe her arm. It was covered in dark bruises and blood from a long cut on her forearm was dripping into the water. Her right eye was bruised and swollen, giving her a lop-sided look. She'd been crying.

'Are you all right?' he asked before he could stop himself. Bakr had specifically said not to talk to anyone, but if he didn't say anything then how was he going to get the medicine for Asim. 'How did you get those bruises?'

The girl looked at him and then began to sob again.

'Maybe you should go to the doctor,' he said. 'He would put some salve on them.'

'I can't,' she said eventually. 'It's because of the doctor that my father gave me this.' She pointed to her partially closed eye.

Apart from her bruises she was a pretty girl with a light complexion and dark hair twisted into a long plait. Her djubbah matched the colour of her eyes, a blue as clear as the sky.

'What's your name?' Kamil asked.

'Mayy.'

Her accent was thick and not easy to understand.

'So what was the problem with the doctor? Is he your betrothed?'

She looked at him in horror. 'No, but he wants to be. He is older than my father and he wants me for a wife.'

'But what's so wrong with that? You would have a comfortable life as the wife of a doctor.'

'You sound like my step-mother. My family is furious that I have refused to marry him. My father says I *will* marry him, willingly or unwillingly; he doesn't mind which. But I don't want to be wife number four. I will be no better than a slave. I would sooner be dead.'

'You should get something for that eye,' Kamil said. Matrimonial problems were outside his experience. As far as he was aware, every girl wanted to get married to a rich husband. He couldn't see what was so terrible.

'I will. My uncle is an apothecary. He will give me something.'

'Do you mind if I come with you? I have need of some medicine.'

'Really? You look fine to me,' she said, with a flirtatious smile.

He blushed and said, 'It's for a friend. He's very sick.'

Gingerly the girl took her arm out of the water and wiped it on her djubbah.

'You're not from Andrach,' she said. 'Where are you from?'

'Do you know everyone in the town?' he asked, as he followed her down a shady side street. He had no intention of answering her question.

'Everyone worth knowing.' She laughed. 'It's hard not to; there are not many of us. Although things are better since the governor made a pact with the pirates. We used to get raided almost every month before that. It was bad enough that they took our food and livestock, but then they started kidnapping people: men to become pirates and women and children to sell as slaves. That's when the governor came up with a plan.'

'He let them make their base on Dragonera,' Kamil said before he could stop himself.

'Yes, how did you know?'

'I heard some men talking. So do the pirates ever come here?'

She shook her head. 'No, that's part of the agreement. They can live on Dragonera and in return they will keep away from the main island, Mayurqa.'

Kamil heaved a sigh of relief.

'Why do you ask?'

'No reason.'

'Are the pirates after you?'

'Why would pirates be after me?'

'Well, it just seems strange that here you are, a foreigner, wandering about my town looking for an apothecary. Where have you come from? You didn't answer my question earlier. And what are you doing in this town?'

She was very perceptive, but she didn't seem to be worried by her deductions. She was neither frightened of him, nor likely to betray him. There couldn't be any harm in telling her who he was. Just as he was about to reply, they stopped outside a curtained doorway, identical to all the others they had passed.

'We're here,' she said. 'Do you want me to get the medicine for you? Or are you brave enough to ask for it yourself?'

'No, I can do it, thank you,' he said, tugging his scarf tighter around his face.

He pulled back the curtain and stepped inside. The room was dark and smelled strongly of incense; candles burned in candle holders which hung from the ceiling and swayed slightly with the draught from the open doorway. They produced an acrid smell of burning tallow and plenty of smoke, but little light.

'As-salama alaykum, stranger. What can I help you with?' asked an old man, sitting cross-legged on the floor.

'Wa alaykum e-salam, hajj. My brother has a cough that he cannot get rid of. Have you anything that would help him?' he asked.

'Does he have a fever?'

'I think so. He is very weak; he can hardly walk.'

'And this cough, does he bring up any phlegm when he's coughing? Is there any show of blood in it?'

'Yes, he does and there is a little blood, but not much. What can you do for him?'

'Have you been to see a doctor?'

'No. He's too weak. I thought you might be able to help.'

The old man struggled to get up from the floor and then disappeared into the gloom. A few minutes later he reappeared, carrying a small package.

'I've made up a mixture of thyme and myrrh which should reduce the fever, and here is some habba souda which will cure his cough. Give it to him with a little milk. If he is no better within three days you will need to take him to a doctor. Apart from this I don't think there is much else I can do to help your brother.'

'Thank you, hajj,' Kamil said, and counted out the money Bakr had given them. There was still a few dirhams left; enough to buy some milk and a couple of loaves of bread.

'And you, young lady? Here again, I see,' the apothecary said, taking Mayy by the hand and leading her closer to one of the candles, so he could see more clearly.

Mayy stood silently while the apothecary applied a salve to her cheek and her arm. He then took a small vial and trickled a few drops into her damaged eye.

'It's time you learned to obey your father, my dear. Or one day he will do you serious harm and then no-one will want to marry you,' the apothecary said. 'Or worse.'

'Can I come and live with you, ammu? Then he won't be able to hurt me.'

'No, child. You must fight your own battles. It is not my place to come between you and my brother. Here take this, it will help to ease the pain. And remember, you are fourteen now; your father has every right to expect you to marry.'

'I am happy to become a wife and a mother, ammu. I just don't want to be the fourth wife of an old man. I've told my father that, but he won't listen to me. He says the doctor is a good man and I am an ungrateful daughter,' Mayy said, beginning to cry again.

Kamil followed her out of the apothecary's shop. He stopped for a moment, blinded by the bright sunshine. 'I must go now,' he said. 'I must get back with the medicine.'

'To your brother?' she asked. He could detect the tone of disbelief in her voice. 'Where is he, this brother?'

'He's in the woods.'

She stared at him. 'You're running away from someone, aren't you? Are you an escaped slave?'

He laughed. 'No, of course I'm not. Do I look like a slave?'

'Not really. So who are you and what do you do?'

'I can't tell you.'

'Take me with you,' she suddenly said. 'I don't mind where you're going, but take me with you. I have to get away from this town and my father.'

'What about your mother? Surely you don't want to leave your mother and your family?'

'My mother and my sister were taken by pirates when I was only six-years-old. There are only my father, his new wife and my half-brothers at home. Nobody would miss me. Please take me with you. I can help you to care for your brother.'

'He's not my brother. He's a friend,' snapped Kamil. His head was doing somersaults. How could he take her with him? He looked at her bruises and the tears in her eyes. How could he leave her? It was probably true what her uncle had said, one day her father would end up killing her. 'It's not safe.'

'I'm not safe here. I have to get away from this town.'

'Very well, you can come but don't ask any questions,' he said, wondering what Bakr would say when he saw Mayy.

Suddenly Mayy caught hold of his arm. 'I know who you are. You're one of the men the pirates are looking for. It's the talk of the town, everyone is wondering how they escaped from Dragonera. Nobody has ever succeeded in getting off the island before. You're heroes.'

Kamil listened to her excited voice in amazement. He didn't feel like a hero. Anything but. 'So everyone knows about the men who got away from the pirates?' he asked. 'Already?'

'Yes, of course. News like that travels fast. They say that Captain al-Awar is furious. He is offering a reward of twenty gold dinars for their capture, but no-one will accept it. Nobody trusts the pirates. You're as likely to get run through with a rapier as given a bag of gold for your efforts. That's why there's no-one on the streets. Everyone is staying close to home until the men are recaptured. No-one wants to help the pirates but neither do they want to go against them. That captain is a brutal man. If he finds the men who helped them escape, he'll not only kill them but all their relatives as well.'

Kamil felt faint. They had put so many people in danger by their actions. 'He thinks someone helped them to escape?'

'Yes, it's obvious. Unless they are exceptional swimmers they had to have a boat, and nobody has reported a boat stolen. I think it was the men who take them the rum that helped them to escape.'

'What will Captain al-Awar do to them?' Kamil asked,

'If he finds them. They've disappeared and taken their families with them. No point waiting about for a visit from the pirates.'

'But I thought the pirates never came to this island?'

'Not usually, but they say that Captain al-Awar does what he wants when he wants to. Nobody is going to try to stop him.'

'What about the governor?'

'Who knows? I've never seen the governor; he doesn't visit our little town, not ever.'

'Maybe they were.'

She looked at him.

'Exceptional swimmers,' he said. 'Maybe nobody helped them to escape.'

'I doubt it. So where are we going when we collect your friend?' she asked.

'I said, no questions.'

'All right.'

'I need to get bread and some milk. Can you go into a shop and get it for me?'

'No problem. But first you must tell me your name,' she said, with a winning smile.

'Kamil. It's Kamil. Now, hurry up. The sooner we're out of this town the safer I'll feel.'

'Just wait a few minutes; I have to collect some things from home.'

*

As they trudged through the forest Kamil began to feel his stomach churning. What had he done? How would Bakr react when he saw Mayy? Now their escape would be even more difficult because there were four of them, and what if Mayy's father came looking for them? Or someone had seen him and told the pirates? Twenty gold dinars was a lot of money. Surely Bakr wasn't worth that much to the captain. Or was it because he felt humiliated? They had tricked the notorious Captain al-Awar and escaped. How would that affect his reputation. He felt his stomach contract, and not from hunger; if the captain was looking for revenge for his humiliation then he wouldn't stop until he had it.

'Is it much further?' Mayy asked, stopping and taking her shoes off. Her feet were red and sore.

'What's the matter?' asked Kamil.

'My feet hurt. And I'm tired,' she pouted. She looked even younger than her fourteen years as she sat there, with her shoes in her hand.

'Well you can stay here, then. Nobody is forcing you to follow me,' he said, too concerned about his own situation to worry about her.

'You know I can't stay here. What would I do when it got dark?'

'Go home?' He strode ahead, then called back over his shoulder, 'Are you coming or not?'

'I don't know why you're behaving like this; I haven't done anything to you. I could have told everyone that you were the one the pirates were looking for, but I didn't.

You're just worried what your boss will say when you tell him I'm going with you.'

Once again she was right; he was taking his anxiety out on her.

'Look it's not much further. Put your shoes on and give me those blankets; I'll carry them.'

When Mayy had returned to her house to get her things, she had also come back with a basket of food and four blankets. He took the roll of blankets, tucked them under his arm and once again set off along the path.

'So what do you do?' she asked, running to catch him up. 'How did the pirates capture you?'

There didn't seem a lot of point in keeping it secret now, so he began to relate how he had ended up in this predicament, marooned on the island of Mayurqa a long way from home.

'Is it far to Malaqah?' she asked.

'Far enough. Have you heard of the city before?'

'Yes, I've heard it mentioned. Sometimes our fishermen go down there looking for the tuna, but I have no idea where it is. So, how are you going to get back there?' she asked.

'I wish I knew. I just hope the sayyad has a plan.'

'What's he like, your sayyad?'

'He's...' Kamil hesitated. He'd never been asked that before. He thought of Bakr and how angry he was going to be when he saw Mayy. Then he thought about how he had supported Asim. He could have left him behind; it was obvious even before they escaped that Asim was not strong enough for the venture. But Bakr had never even considered abandoning his foreman. And Kamil, he could have left without Kamil, but he'd found him and rescued him. Yes, his boss was a man to be relied upon. 'He's a master craftsman. There's no-one better at his job,' he said.

'Yes, but what is he like? Is he kind? Will he beat you when he finds out about me?'

'No, of course not. He's not that sort of man. He commands respect because he is a fair man. Anyway he needs me. He said so.'

'He sounds nice. Do you think he wants a wife? I wouldn't mind marrying someone like that.'

Kamil stopped and spun round. 'You say such stupid things. You have no idea what he is like. How do you know if he'd be any different from the doctor whom you're so keen on running away from? Anyway he has a wife and lots of children. I don't think he's looking for another wife just yet. All he wants is to get back home to the one he has.'

'I'm not running away from the doctor. I'm running away from my father.' Again she pursed her lips into a childish pout, and once again he thought how vulnerable she was, despite all her brave words.

'Well don't tell him that or he may feel duty bound to return you to him.'

They continued in silence. Mayy was sulking and he was angry with her. Why would she ask if Bakr was looking for a wife? He thought she didn't want to be married to an old man. Wasn't that why she had run away?

At last Kamil could see the beach where he'd left his companions but there was no sign of anyone, or even that anyone had been there. No footprints in the sand, no trace of where they had slept, nothing. For a moment he wondered if he'd arrived at a different cove, but then he recognised the configuration of rocks at the water's edge. It was definitely the same place. So where were they?

'We're here,' he told Mayy. 'This is where I left them.'

'I can't see anyone,' she said, peering down the path at the beach. 'It's a pretty beach though. Maybe the pirates have found them.'

'Follow me and keep quiet,' he told her. It was possible that Bakr was keeping well hidden, but there was also the possibility that they had been discovered. He pulled a knife out of his belt and carefully made his way down the stony path.

'When we get to the sand, hide behind those rocks. And keep quiet,' he told her.

Once on the beach he headed for the place where they'd slept the night before. As he grew closer he realised that Bakr had built a shelter so well camouflaged that he was almost on top of it before he could see it. He saw Bakr sitting under the shelter grinning at him.

'Did you think we'd go without you?' he asked. 'After all the trouble we'd gone to save you from Captain al-Awar.'

'For a moment I thought he'd found you. That's a brilliant shelter. You're completely camouflaged. Nobody will see us from the sea or from the woods,' said Kamil.

'Did you get the medicine?'

'I did. How is Asim? The apothecary said we should take him to a doctor if this doesn't work.' He took the herbs out of his bag and handed them to Bakr. 'I got some milk as well. He has to take the pills with a little milk.' He couldn't stop talking. It was nerves. Any minute now Bakr would notice Mayy.

'Asim is much the same. I think a good night's sleep has helped him a little, but I'm glad you have some medicine for him.' He was not looking at Kamil as he spoke, instead he stared straight past him.

'I see you've found yourself a companion,' said Bakr, calmly looking across at Mayy. 'Do you never listen to anything I say?'

'It's not what you think, sayyad. I had no choice.'

'You always have a choice. In this case you chose to disregard my instructions. So what is she doing here?'

'She wants to come with us.'

'In the name of all that's holy, have you gone mad? Allah protect me from fools and madmen, because here I have both in my apprentice.' He got to his feet and stormed across the beach to where Mayy was crouched behind a rock, trying to look invisible. 'Get up,' he shouted.

Mayy crept out from behind the rock and smiled at Bakr. 'I've brought you some food,' she said sweetly. 'And blankets for your friend.' She held the basket of food in front of her like a peace offering. Kamil heart seemed to stop as he waited to see Bakr's reaction. The shipbuilder stared at her for a moment then took the basket from her outstretched arms and marched back into the shelter.

CHAPTER 22

Admiral al-Maraghi had replenished the ship's store of food and water in Dénia, at the same time as he collected the written permission from the sultan to enter his waters. Now they were heading for Dragonera. Allah seemed to be on their side today and the weather was fine; even the sea was relatively calm—a good thing because he'd brought one of the smaller ships in his fleet, with a low freeboard that was not good in rough seas. He'd calculated that this bireme dromon was probably the best choice as they would need to get in close to the shore if they wanted to find any trace of the kidnapped men. He noticed that the sultan's authorisation said nothing about being able to land on the island, and to be honest, he hadn't expected it to be otherwise. It was fortunate he'd decided to bring the bireme. It was fast and extremely manoeuvrable and could turn on its axis if required—in case they needed to make a hasty retreat. This was what was needed if they wanted to outwit the pirates, who also favoured a similar type of bireme. With this ship he could search the entire coast, entering in all the tiny coves and even sail into the estuaries. He knew from past experience that there were many small islands in the Balearics and if the pirates weren't on Dragonera, it was very likely they would be on one of the others.

He was standing on the bridge watching the rowers, and feeling content. It was good to have a mission; too much of his time these days seemed to be spent in Malaqah organising the fleet, overseeing the purchase of new ships and making sure the regular coastal patrols were adequate. There hadn't been a naval battle for years; the khalifa was much more concerned about his army. He sometimes wondered if he really understood the potential of having a strong navy, as all they ever seemed to do was protect their coastline from pirates.

Ahead of them was the island of Dragonera, as yet a barely distinguishable shape on the pale horizon, but none of the rowers could even see that; those below decks could see nothing anyway, shut as they were in the dark, and those above decks faced towards him, their backs to the island. All the rowers relied completely on the coxswain and the rhythmic sound of the pipes. This ship required three men to each oar and every time the piper gave the signal the rower on the inner seat stood to push the oar forward and then sat down again to pull it back. He noticed that one man near the bow was always a second or two late in standing up. He signalled for the coxswain to come up onto the bridge.

'Yes, Admiral?' he said, saluting his commanding officer.

'See that man there,' the admiral said. 'He's either not well or tired. Move someone else to the inside oar.'

'Aye aye, Admiral.'

The rowers sitting in line with the man shipped their oars while he moved into the middle. It took a matter of minutes and then they were back into their rhythm. The dromon was making good speed, at least eight knots and they could increase it to ten if they hoisted the sail, but he didn't want to do that; it would make them more conspicuous. If there were pirates on these islands, the admiral wanted to take them by surprise; without a sail they lay close to the water and wouldn't be visible until they were almost upon them. He wasn't looking for a fight with the pirates; that was not his purpose. He just wanted to rescue the shipbuilders and get them back to Malaqah with as little confrontation as possible. But if it came to a fight, he was ready for it. There were some four hundred men on board, including forty marines. If the pirates attacked he knew he could rely on the rowers above decks to go to the aid of the marines; together they were a match for any raiders.

*

As soon as they reached Dragonera, the admiral instructed the captain to take the ship in close to the shore. He chose a spot where the mountains disappeared into the sea, and the waves crashed against the rocks. No ships could land here. There was no point heading for the obvious landing places until he knew whether the place was deserted or not. At the moment they were on the side of Dragonera that faced the mainland and completely hidden from the large inhabited island of Mayurqa, which lay only a few nautical miles away.

'I want us to row around the island, all the time keeping as close as possible to the shore,' he said to the captain. 'And don't run us aground, or let the waves take us onto the rocks.'

'Aye, aye Admiral.'

'Position four good men on the forecastle as lookouts. I want to know if they see any sign of life. Anything at all. Goats, sheep, smoke, anything that suggests that someone is living here.'

'Yes, Admiral. I'll see to it straight away.'

The island definitely looked deserted but you could never tell. The pirates were wanted men. Criminals. They weren't going to advertise their presence. It was better to be cautious.

The men rowed around the coast of Dragonera until mid-afternoon. They had visited every small cove and inlet, every beach, every stream that tumbled down from the mountains that loomed over them. But there was no sign of any living soul.

'It's no good,' the admiral exclaimed in frustration. 'The place looks empty enough but we can't be sure. I don't care what this bit of parchment says or doesn't say, we're going to investigate.'

He turned to the ship's captain and said, 'Send six of your crew and ten marines to take a closer look.'

'But Admiral, we don't have permission to land,' said the captain.

'I know that, you fool. But if we stay out here, we'll never know if this is their hideout or not. We haven't come all this way for nothing. Do you want to be the one to tell the khalifa that we weren't sure if they had been here, because we were frightened to land without express permission?'

'No, Admiral, but we've been right around the island now. There's no sign of any habitation, never mind pirates.'

'It's not pirates that we're interested in, man. It's signs of recent shipbuilding. If they're not here now, I want to know if they have ever been here. On this island. Do you understand? I want to know if anyone has lived here in the last four months. If they have then they will have left something behind them. There will be animal bones, empty houses, broken pottery, cooking fires; something will be there to betray them.'

'But even if there is any of what you have just described, what good is it if they're not here now?' asked the bewildered ship's captain.

'It will mean we're on the right track. Then we'll look for evidence of ship repairs, new wood cut into planks, traces of tar, sailcloth, anything that suggests that Bakr might have been on Dragonera.'

'Very well, Admiral.'

'We will anchor here, just off the cliffs. The men can wade ashore and make their way along those rocks. First I want them to search the harbour just behind the headland. That seems to me to be the ideal place to hide out; it's sheltered and the entrance is well protected. If the men find nothing there then they will have to move on to the next inlet.'

'What about the mountains? Do you want them to search there?'

'Not yet. If we find evidence of any shipbuilding activity then yes, we may have to do that. However I think we can guarantee that they wouldn't have built a ship half way up a mountain. Not unless this Captain al-Awar is a complete idiot. We'll worry about whether they are hiding up there later. First let's see what we discover on the beaches.'

The captain relayed all that the admiral had said, and once the men had started to wade ashore, the ship moved further away from the coast and dropped anchor.

*

Daylight was fading by the time the first of the marines clambered back on board, and stars were already lighting up the night sky.

'You were right, Admiral. People have been living there but the place is deserted now. We found a number of shacks built from canes and reeds; they were on the edge of the forest, which is why we couldn't see them from the ship.' the marine told him.

'How long ago do you think they abandoned the island?'

'Not long. I'd say just a few weeks. Days maybe. Looked as though they'd left in a hurry. There were even pots with traces of uneaten food in them. Not much, mind you. I think the rats had helped themselves to most of it.'

The rest of the search party began to climb on board, pleased that they had something positive to report.

'Any sign of our kidnapped men?' asked the admiral.

The marine pulled out something from his bag. 'I found this,' he said. 'I think it's a woodworking tool, or part of one.' It was an awl without its handle.

The admiral took it and examined it. 'It could be. Was there nothing else?'

'Nothing that revealed that the shipbuilders had been there, no sayyad. Then it became too dark to see and we didn't want to light any torches in case we gave ourselves away.'

'I understand. Well done, man.' He turned to the ship's captain and asked, 'What do you think, Captain?'

'It sounds to me as though they knew we were coming. Surely that's the only reason they would leave in such a hurry.'

Perhaps their attempts to approach without being seen had failed. Or maybe the governor had heard that they were coming and alerted the pirates. Whichever it was, the admiral knew they had arrived too late.

'At first light we will sail into the harbour and search the place thoroughly. If the pirates took our men there then they must have left some trace of them behind. And if they did then we will find it.'

'But Admiral, even if pirates lived on the island, we don't know that it was al-Awar and his men. They could have been other pirates; they say that many of them winter in the Balearic Islands.'

'That's true Captain, but what else can we do? We're here now. Let's make sure that there is no trace of Bakr and his men before we abandon the search.'

'Aye, aye, Admiral.'

*

At dawn everyone was awake and ready to continue the search. The admiral stood on the forecastle alongside the captain. The coxswain instructed the piper to begin his plaintive call and the bireme began to move forward. It glided silently over the calm sea towards the headland. The sun was already staining the purple night sky a brilliant orange and against this backdrop the dark outline of Dragonera loomed, more like a sleeping dragon than ever. The admiral had already said his morning prayers but now he whispered another one, asking Allah to protect them from whatever sleeping dragons they might be about to waken. He knew that the khalifa would not protect him if he were caught making an unauthorised landing on the territory of a rival taifa. Mujahid al-Amiri, the sultan of Dénia was supposed to be a friend of the khalifa, but the admiral had been around long enough to know that such friendships did not really exist. These men were powerful because they were ruthless. Friendships and loyalty were conveniences that could be discarded when necessary. No, he could expect no protection from Idris I. But neither could he turn around and go back to Malaqah without completing his mission, even though it was looking more and more like a hopeless one.

The captain steered the ship into the quiet harbour. The admiral could see right away why the pirates would be attracted to this haven. There was a freshwater stream tumbling down from the woods that covered the mountainside and the beach was wide and sandy. It was ideal for making ship repairs, something every pirate had to consider from time to time as his ship was his livelihood, even if it was a dishonest one.

He waited until he heard the anchor drop and then he turned to the captain and said, 'Leave a few men aboard to look after the ship. The rest I want on shore. If we have to search the whole island we will need them all. And I don't want to be here a moment longer than necessary.'

'Aye, aye Admiral.'

The captain divided his men into four groups. The smallest group were to stay on the ship while the other three searched the island; one to search the mountains, one to go along the coast checking the coves and bays and the last one to stay here on the beach.

*

The marines had been right; there had definitely been people living here, and not long ago either. His heart quickened; were they going to be lucky after all? Was Allah going to help them against these godless heathens? If he went back to Malaqah with Bakr and his men, the khalifa would be delighted. And when he was delighted he was always very generous.

'Captain, Captain. Over here,' one of the rowers shouted. He was a big man and he was kneeling on the beach shovelling the sand with his bare hands.

The captain and the admiral hurried across to see what they'd found. Were the men dead? Had the rower discovered their bodies?

'What is it, man?' snapped the captain. 'What have you found?'

'I think it's a ship. Look. But it's not finished.'

Sure enough, there was the prow of a wooden ship; it was unmistakable. And the wood looked like newly cut oak that hadn't been fully waterproofed.

'Get some men over here and uncover this ship right away,' the admiral told the captain.

'Yes, Admiral.'

So the pirates had had enough time to bury their new ship. They knew someone was looking for them and they'd tried to cover their tracks. Luckily for them the pirates hadn't made a very good job of it. While the men dug at the dry sand, some with their bare hands, others with iron spades, the admiral waited impatiently. For what seemed like hours, he paced back and forth across the beach until at last he heard the captain cry, 'Admiral. Look at this.'

The hull of an enormous partly-finished trireme galley lay on the sand; the quality of the workmanship was outstanding. The admiral instantly knew this was the work of Bakr. He bent down to examine it more carefully. Yes, it had to be him. The way the joints were made, and the overlaps on the planks, all meticulously cut and joined. No-one else could have built such a magnificent ship. No wonder the khalifa was so anxious to rescue Bakr; he didn't want the pirates to own ships like this. This one alone could carry three, maybe four hundred men. Even without a sail it would be faster than most of the ships in the khalifa's navy.

'Do you think our men built it?' asked the captain.

'Very likely, Captain. I can't think of anyone else in this part of the world who could build such a vessel. The question is, where are they now? And are they and the pirates coming back?'

'What shall we do with the ship, Admiral? Do you want us to bury it again? It will take quite a while.'

The admiral stared at him. 'Are you completely mad? Burn it. All of it.'

'But the smoke? We'll be seen on Mayurqa.'

'I don't think so. The wind is blowing to the west; it will take the smoke towards the mainland. That's far enough away for it to have dissipated before it reaches land.'

'Very well, Admiral.'

The admiral could see that the captain found it disgraceful to destroy such a beautiful ship, but nevertheless he gave the orders to his men and within minutes the wood was burning brightly and a tar-filled column of smoke was rising into the sky. What a waste. But there was no way he could leave it intact. The pirates had buried it because they intended to come back and finish it. He couldn't allow that to happen.

Gradually the rest of the crew arrived back on the beach. No-one had seen any trace of Bakr or anyone else for that matter, not in the mountains, nor in the coves. The island was deserted. So did that mean the pirates had taken Bakr and his men with them? It looked like they had been alive at some point but were they still? What was he going to do now? He couldn't risk landing on Mayurqa.

'Captain, I've found something else,' called one of the marines. 'Tools.' He pulled out a heavy sack that had been buried next to the ship. 'It says Alfarería Mahood, Malaqah.' He held it up for the admiral and the captain to see. It was an old sack that had once been used to carry clay, some of which was still engrained in the hessian.

'So these are Bakr's tools?'

'It certainly looks like it. I would say that is proof that Bakr and his men were here and were working on this ship until something made them stop,' said the admiral. 'The question is, where are they now?'

The hull had burned quickly, aided by the tar coating it had received, and now was reduced to a smouldering wreck at the bottom of its pit.

'Bring the tools with you,' said the captain. 'If we do find these men, they may want them back.'

Once everyone was accounted for and back on board, the admiral told the captain, 'Move the ship out into deeper water. We'll spend the night there and in the morning we'll head for the mainland. Then we can refurnish our stores before we set off for home.'

'So we're returning to Malaqah, Admiral?' asked the captain. The tone of his voice held a hint of disapproval.

'What else do you propose? If the pirates are not here, then where are they? And do they still have our men with them?'

'Admiral. I bet we'd find out where they are if we went to Medina Mayurqa. It's so close to Dragonera, someone must have known the shipbuilders were here.'

'No doubt you are right, but would they tell us anything, even if we were able to land there? No, captain, tomorrow, I want you to set course for Malaqah.'

He had done his duty and now it was time to return home.

CHAPTER 23

Aisha had just waved goodbye to the children as they set off for school, when her father arrived. She stifled a groan, her back was giving her a lot of pain this morning; it was as though her muscles weren't strong enough to support the enormous weight of her stomach any more. She felt irritable and weepy and had hoped to lie down for a while. Nevertheless she forced herself to greet her father as warmly as she could, 'Baba, how nice to see you. But why so early?'

'Aisha, I have good news.'

Her heart gave a leap. They had found Bakr and the others. Praise be to Allah.

'He's safe?' she cried.

Makoud's face dropped. 'No, sorry, princess, it's not that.'

She felt the tears start again, and tried to shake them away. This pregnancy was turning her into an emotional wreck. 'So what good news do you have for me?' she asked, with a watery smile.

'Yesterday, I was ordered to go to the harbour to speak to the vice-admiral. He has placed an order for two more ships. He was very friendly and said that they are really pleased with the work you are doing, my dear.'

'Hardly my work, Baba. It's down to the men. Anyway, is he authorised to order more ships?' she asked. 'We don't want to start something that's then cancelled when the admiral returns.'

'The admiral himself has agreed to it.'

'Does that mean he has returned? Does he have news about Bakr?' she asked, her voice trembling with emotion. If the admiral could send messages about new ships, surely he would have let them know how the search was going.

She saw her father look down at his feet. A certain sign that he had bad news.

'There was some news, but it's not good, my dear. They found the pirates' hideout but they were too late. They had all gone.'

'But was there any sign of Bakr? Had he been there?'

'I don't know, Aisha. Apparently, they found some of his tools and evidence that someone had been building a ship, but no sign of the men. So there is a real possibility that the men were on the island but they were too late to rescue them. The trip to Dragonera has proved to be a dead end, so the admiral is on his way back to Malaqah. There is nothing more he can do. The pirates could be anywhere now. And only Allah knows what they have done with Bakr and his men.'

Aisha choked back a scream of pain. This was so much worse, to know that he was alive and they could have rescued him if only their ship had arrived sooner. Now what? Was he dead? Had the pirates decided to cut their losses and get rid of him? She had heard of pirate brutality; horrific stories abounded in all the ports along the Middle Sea. She tried to shut them from her mind, but the images crowded in: men shackled and thrown into the sea, men hung feet first from palm trees and left to die a slow death, men buried in the sand up to their necks watching the tide come in to take their lives.

'Don't upset yourself, princess. He's probably still with the pirates. If he's working for them, then they may let him go once he's finished building their ship.'

'You don't really believe that, do you Baba? What, you think the pirates will say, "Thank you Bakr, now you can go home. But make sure to tell no-one where we are?" Pirates are cruel, greedy and vicious men who don't care about anyone. No we're never going to see him again,' she said and began to sob.

'Come now, Aisha. You have to be strong, for the children, for the new baby. You are the one who has always maintained that Bakr wasn't dead. You have to hang on to that thought, no matter how bleak it seems.'

She looked at her father through her tear-filled eyes; he looked old and tired. She knew how much he loved her and it was killing him to see her so unhappy.

'I can't Baba. I can't carry on being strong for everyone, not while my heart is breaking inside. I just can't.'

In the long, lonely months since Bakr had been kidnapped, she had never felt as inconsolable as she did now. If it weren't for the children, she would give up completely. It was too much to bear. Why did Allah want her to suffer so much? He had taken Daud, her first love. Now, when she had found happiness and purpose in her life again, he had taken Bakr. The imam had tried to offer her solace by talking about Paradise, but it didn't help. She prayed that Daud had found peace and now resided in Paradise, but Bakr, with him she had found paradise here, on earth. She wanted him to come home.

'Of course you can, my dear. You have the strength of a dozen men. I know you won't let your children suffer. You and the men in the shipyard are doing a wonderful job and these orders will mean you will have enough money to last you through the coming year. Bakr would be so proud of you,' said her father.

'Makoud. I didn't hear you arrive. As-salama alaykum,' said her mother-in-law, coming through to see who was there. 'Can I bring you something to drink?'

'Wa alaykum e-salam. No, thank you but I must get back to the shop. I just came to tell my daughter that we have two more orders.'

'Excellent.' Her mother-in-law turned towards her and said, 'Aisha, you look worn out. Go and lie down for a while, child. I will see to the food. You must rest.'

What a difference being pregnant had made to her relationship with her mother-in-law; now she couldn't do enough to help her.

'Very well, hama.'

'Ma'a salama, daughter. Take care of yourself,' said Makoud.

'Alla ysalmak, Baba. Will you tell al-Najjar about the orders?'

'I'll go there now, on my way home.'

A sudden kick from her unborn baby made Aisha jump. Her mother-in-law was right; it was time she rested. She waddled over to the sofa and sat down. The baby was becoming very active; it seemed to be trying its best to kick its way out of her. She placed her hand on her distended belly and smiled as she felt the child moving inside her. It wouldn't be long now before the baby made up its mind to enter the world; soon her waters would break and the birth pangs would begin. She choked back a sob. What was supposed to be a very happy event was cloaked in sadness. Bakr was never coming back; she had to face it. He would never see this child, the fruit of their union. He wouldn't even know that he or she existed. It broke her heart to think that they would have another child together and he would never even know.

'Are you all right, Aisha?' asked her mother-in-law, bringing her a glass of herbal tea. 'You mustn't upset yourself; it's not good for the baby.'

Aisha wiped her eyes and managed to smile. 'Yes, I'm fine, hama.'

There was no point making her mother-in-law miserable as well. She thought back to when Maryam was born; that had been more than seven years ago. Aisha had been terrified and although her mother had explained the whole process to her, it had made no difference; she was certain that she would die. Mama had stayed with her all through the birth, and Daud, who was not allowed in the birthing room, sat outside listening to her screams. But now she knew exactly what to expect and was ready for it.

'Drink some tea, while it's hot,' her mother-in-law said, leaning over and putting a cushion under her feet. 'It won't be long now.'

She meant the birth. She was more excited about it than her daughter-in-law. She never mentioned her son. She never asked if there was any news of him. She had resigned herself to the fact that her son was gone and she would never see him again. Maybe it was time that Aisha did the same.

CHAPTER 24

Bakr couldn't believe that Kamil could be so stupid. Their situation was even worse now. What if the girl's father came looking for them? His apprentice had already admitted that the apothecary he bought the medicine from was the girl's uncle. It wouldn't take a genius to link her disappearance to the arrival of a stranger in their town. They would know they were still on the island. So now, not only did they have pirates out for their blood, but they had an angry family to deal with and maybe even a jilted suitor. Could it get any worse? They seemed to have been here, isolated from the world for so long.

Still he had been grateful for the blankets and the food. Asim was starting to get some colour back in his cheeks. His fever had abated and he was eating at last. By the time they had the boat ready he should be well enough to travel. That was supposing that they managed to keep their presence undiscovered until then.

They had found some suitable trees, felled them and dragged them into a clearing where they could work undisturbed. He still shuddered when he remembered that tremendous crash when the first tree hit the forest floor. He was sure they could hear it in Medina Mayurqa. They'd been frightened to move for ages until he realised that nobody had heard anything and no-one was coming. After that he and Kamil worked steadily until they had the planks cut. There was still a lot to be done but at least now they didn't have to worry about keeping an eye on Asim and preparing the food, those tasks had been left to Mayy. If she was disappointed that they were still on Mayurqa she never said anything. Her bruises had faded and she seemed to be very relaxed in their company. Bakr had taken it upon himself to be her guardian and had told Kamil in no uncertain terms, that his behaviour towards her had to be with the utmost propriety. She would want to marry one day and he needed to be sure she went to her wedding a virgin. In the absence of the rest of his family, Bakr had come to look upon her as if she were his own daughter.

'Sayyad, I'm going to check the traps,' called Mayy.

Kamil had set a number of lures for rabbits, and the fresh meat was a welcome addition to their sparse diet. It was Mayy's job to check them every morning, dispatch the animals caught and prepare them for the meal. Bakr had thought she might find the work distasteful, but she was a pragmatic young woman and did the task without complaint. Although she had shed a few tears the first time Bakr had showed her how to remove the animal without damaging it and then promptly wrung its neck.

'What about Asim?'

'He's still sleeping.'

'Very well, be careful,' he called. It was easy to become complacent in this peaceful cove, but he knew that Captain al-Awar would never give up looking for them. They had demeaned his position as captain, and he wouldn't forget it.

'I will.' She skipped up the path looking as happy as if this was a normal way to live. Her life must have been pretty dreadful if she preferred sleeping on the beach with three strangers who were hiding from the pirates and catching her own food.

Kamil had set the traps deep in the forest, well away from their hideout. It would take her most of the morning to check them all.

'Give me a hand, Kamil. We need to soak these planks in the stream and then we can bend them into shape.'

They were using pine, not the best wood for a durable ship, but much easier to work with than the harder, more compact oak that he usually used. But they weren't building a ship to last, just to get them to the mainland. It wouldn't be much use in bad weather either. They would have to pray to Allah to give them a calm sea and clear skies when they were ready to leave.

'It's going to take months to finish this,' said Kamil. 'Why don't we steal a boat instead? We should have stolen the fishermen's boat when we had the chance.'

'It wasn't strong enough to cross to the mainland.'

'But we could have strengthened it.'

'You don't know what you're talking about. It would have taken just as long to take it apart and rebuild it and we probably wouldn't have such a seaworthy vessel in the end, anyway,' said Bakr. He knew it was slow, frustrating work. They were all desperate to get off the island but this was the only way he could think of to achieve it. 'Put your back into it, lad. The quicker we work, the sooner we will be able to leave.'

They worked in silence for a while, until all the planks were soaking.

'Isn't that Mayy? What's she doing back so early?' asked Kamil.

Mayy was running down the path to the beach; she seemed upset.

'What is it child?' asked Bakr, going over to meet her.

'Someone has taken the rabbits out of the traps. I tried three of them and they were all empty,' she said, her voice shaking. 'There's someone in the forest.'

'We were probably just unlucky. It doesn't always work. I'll move them to another place, tonight,' said Kamil.

'No, it's not that. Someone had sprung the traps and taken the rabbits. It's obvious.'

'Kamil, go and check the area. Look for any footprints, broken branches, any sign that someone has been there. And don't touch the traps. Leave them exactly as they are. If someone is looking for us, I don't want them to know we're still here. Mayy, help me clear the beach of anything which might tell someone we've been here. We're going to have to move deeper into the forest.'

'What's happening?' asked Asim.

He looked stronger than he had for weeks.

'Probably nothing to worry about, but someone has found our traps. We need to remove any sign that we've been here.'

He watched as Kamil bounded up the path into the forest, a cudgel in his hand; he hoped he'd taken his knife with him as well.

'Asim, can you help me move these planks out of sight.'

'Yes, sayyad. But why don't we just cover them with some branches? Then they can continue to soak a while longer.'

'Good idea. Cut some branches and drag them over here.'

In the meantime, Mayy had removed the tools from the clearing and hidden everything in the trees. Now she was walking backwards towards their hiding place, sweeping away her footprints as she did so. By the time she had finished the beach looked as though no-one had ever been there.

'Excellent. Now I think we'll move further away from the shoreline,' said Bakr.

They collected up their belongings and headed inland until they came to an enormous rock face and could go no further. They could no longer see the shore.

'This will do for now. Asim help Mayy put up the tent. I'm going back to find Kamil,' he said, tucking an axe in his belt.

He made his way back towards the beach but skirted round the sand until he reached the path. He stopped and looked back. There was no sign that anybody had been there and no sign of the boat building. All they had to do now was find out if this was a real threat or just some local who had stumbled on their traps.

*

Kamil was squatting over one of the lures when Bakr found him. He spun round and said, 'What the devil! Oh, it's you, sayyad. I thought I was about to be attacked.'

He had his cudgel raised to strike.

'What have you found?'

'Well, I don't think it was pirates. They would have made much more mess. Someone has definitely been here, but I think it was just one person, probably a hunter. Look here are some feathers. Pigeon, I'd guess. I would think he was out hunting with his falcon when he came across our traps. Decided it was his lucky day and took our catch.'

'I hope you're right. Have you seen anyone about? Heard anything?'

'No, nothing.'

'Very well, let's get back. I just hope it's as you say.'

'Do you want me to put out any more traps?'

'No, not for now, in case he comes back. He might tell his friends and then the news would get back to the village. If that happens the pirates will get to know.' Kamil had told him about the reward for their capture.

They walked towards the path that led down to the beach. Bakr studied it carefully. Mayy had done a good job of removing any sign that they had ever been there.

'Sayyad. Look. Is that a ship?' asked Kamil, fear making his voice break.

Bakr looked towards the horizon. Yes, it was definitely a ship, but whose was it? From where he stood, it was impossible to make out any details.

'Is it the pirates?' asked Kamil. 'Have they found us? We need to tell Mayy that she must hide. The pirates mustn't find her. Who knows what they'd do to her?'

He leapt up and was about to race off to look for the girl, but Bakr caught him by the arm and said, 'They mustn't find any of us. Get down. Let's wait and see if it comes any closer.'

They hunkered down in the scrub and watched. The ship was travelling towards Dragonera. It wasn't that large but had two lateen sails and, with a following wind to help it, was moving quickly.

'That's not a pirate ship,' said Bakr. 'And it's not a merchant ship. What the hell is it?'

He peered hard at the vessel, trying to look for distinguishing marks that would help to identify it. Slowly it began to dawn on him that it was a naval ship. In fact he recognised that ship; it was part of the khalifa's navy. One he'd designed himself for close shore work. What was it doing here? Was this a general patrol or were they looking for pirates? And why so far north?

'Do you think they're looking for us?' asked Kamil.

'Looking for us? I doubt it. No naval vessel is going to sail all this way looking for three shipbuilders. They don't know where we are, anyway. They probably think we're in North Africa. No, they're just making their presence known to the pirates, a show of strength I expect. Or maybe they're making a visit to the governor.'

'But they'd help us, wouldn't they? If they knew we were here and had been captured by the pirates.'

Bakr doubted that they would bother with anyone as insignificant as them, but nevertheless he said, 'Yes, I expect they would. But how can we let them know we're here?'

'A signal. We have to send them a signal. Or I could swim out to them.'

'It's too far. They'd have gone by the time you got out there, but you're right; we need to make a signal, something to let them know we're here,' said Bakr. There was a slim possibility that they had come to look for them. After all, the boy had told him once that his father was friendly with Idris I and went to visit him regularly in the alcázar. Even if they weren't looking for them, they might come to their aid. 'We'll light a fire,' he said, at last.

'What? But we're supposed to be in hiding. A fire will tell the pirates that we're here.' Kamil looked at him as if he were mad.

Maybe he was. Maybe living with the pirates had taken away his reason but he was prepared to risk anything to get home.

'Come on. Hurry before they round the bend and are out of sight,' he called, sprinting down the path.

This time he was heedless of the pristine sand and raced across it, leaving his large footprints for all to see.

'Get the wood we cut for the oars. That should burn well. Hurry,' Bakr said. His heart was pounding. The dark cloud that had dogged him for weeks had lifted. This could be their opportunity to get back to Malaqah.

While he built a mound of dry ferns and bracken, Kamil dragged out the pine logs they had prepared as oars. Then Bakr piled twigs and pine cones on top of the mound. 'Here light it,' he said, tossing Kamil the flint. 'It should burn well. And when it's going, add the oars. I'm going to get Mayy and Asim.'

He could hear the pine cones crackling and spitting as the flames took hold. Pine might not be the best wood for building a ship but it made a very good bonfire. He looked behind him, the oars were blazing now and a column of smoke was curling towards the sky. It would be impossible to miss. They had to see it. He watched the ship continue on its way; it never deviated from its course and kept set for Dragonera. Disappointment was bitter in his mouth. The others would be devastated; he knew he was. He hurried to the spot where he'd left the foreman and the girl and stopped in astonishment. There was no sign of them and nothing to indicate that they'd even been there. He looked around him. Had he taken a wrong turn? No. He was sure that this was the place he'd left them, right under the rock face.

'Sayyad. We're over here,' Mayy called.

'What in the name of Allah are you doing over there? And where's all our stuff?'

'We found a cave, sayyad,' said Asim, coming out of a small entrance in the rock. 'It's a perfect hiding place. Come inside and see for yourself.'

Bakr bent down and crawled into the cave. It was enormous. Somehow, together, Asim and Mayy had dragged all their belongings into the cave and laid them out.

'It's completely dry and comfortable, but we'll have to cook outside. And we've collected some bracken for us to sleep on and there's only one way in and that's it,' she said, prattling like a small child.

'Well done. It looks a good place for us to stay. But now I want you to come with me. There's a naval ship close to the island. We're trying to get them to notice us. Hurry.'

He crawled back out into the forest. They had discovered an excellent hideout, one where it was impossible to see the entrance unless you knew what you were looking for. But if Allah was protecting them, then they wouldn't need it. They would soon be on their way home.

CHAPTER 25

Khalifa Idris I had taken leave of his family: kissed his wives and reminded his sons to take good care of their mother. He had said his prayers both privately and together with his army as they stood on the parade ground listening to the words of the imam. They had asked for Allah's blessing and prayed that he would give them victory over the army of Isbiliya. Now, as the sun rose over the mountains to his right, he led his troops out of the city of Malaqah and up through the winding passes towards the small but very significant fortified town of Écija. This was where the fate of Isbiliya, and his own, would be determined. It would take his commanders at least a couple of weeks to assemble all the army and its equipment in position for the attack. His allies in Badajoz had already sent word that they were on their way, and so had Zuhair from Álmeria.

'Any word from Garnata?' he asked General Rashad, as he pulled his horse alongside him.

'Not yet, but I am sure they will be there at the pre-arranged time.'

'And Qarmuña? Do you think they will keep their word?'

In the end, Qarmuña had sent a message to say that they would fight alongside Malaqah and against their old ally, Isbiliya. He wondered what Abbad had thought when he'd heard that news.

'Their army is moving into position,' replied General Rashad. 'What we don't know yet is where the armies of Isbiliya are? Our scouts have seen clouds of dust on the plain, heading for Écija, as though a great army is on the move. I can only assume that is Abbad and his troops.'

'What about inside the town? How many troops are there?'

'When Abbad got wind of what we were planning he sent three regiments of men to Écija. As far as I know they are still there, but the rest of his army is on its way. Most of Muhammad's army is still in Qarmuña.'

'So the battle will be fought outside the town, on the open plain?' said Idris. 'Then when we have defeated them we will head for the city of Isbiliya and take that as well.'

'Has that been agreed with our allies, Your Majesty? I don't think anyone wants to attack Abbad's city.'

'Why not? If that falls as well then he will know that we all mean business.'

'Our allies have only agreed to support us in the attack on Écija, Your Majesty. We must be careful not to take on something we cannot fulfil.' The general spoke carefully. Idris could see he didn't want to contradict him but he seemed worried that the khalifa's enthusiasm would lead them into trouble.

'Don't let's concern ourselves about that now, General. We will concentrate on the battle to come. When we have defeated Abbad and his armies then we can decide what to do next.'

'Very well, Your Majesty,' replied his second-in-command, but he didn't look wholly convinced.

*

The battle was hard and fierce. It had been raging since dawn and already the sun was heading for the western horizon. The soldiers were tired but still the infantry were locked in hand-to-hand fighting. Gradually they were pushing the enemy back to the banks of the Genil River. With the help of their allies they were squeezing Abbad's army into an increasingly small area. Those that still fought were going to be caught like rats in a trap. They were surrounded. Even Isbiliya's mighty force couldn't beat off this four-sided advance. Some sought to escape their attackers by jumping into the water and swimming downstream, but if their armour didn't pull them down into its murky depths to drown, then Idris's archers picked them off one by one. There seemed to be no escape for the troops of Isbiliya. The air stank of blood and sulphur, of death and putrefaction, of guts and viscera; it resounded with the cries of the battlefield: the screams of the wounded, the clash of steel on steel, the shouts of anger as men whipped themselves up into the frenzy of battle amid the death cries of wounded horses and dying men. Umar heard it all but listened to none of it. Even the stench did not distract him. His mind was focused on two things only, staying alive and making sure his men stayed alive. He thrashed wildly to the left and right, cutting his way through the enemy lines, heedless of who they were; all he needed to know was that it was either him or them. His mare, the gallant Basil, was steady and fearless. An enemy foot soldier lifted his broadsword to strike at Umar, but before he could make contact, Basil had reared up on her hind legs, her hooves pawing the air and the man fell to the ground, blood gushing from a blow to his face.

Umar pulled on Basil's reins and turned her away from the fallen soldier. Where were his men? He could see three of them in front of him and rode across to help, throwing his lance at one of their attackers and pinning him to the ground.

'Behind you, soldier,' he shouted as the youngest of his squad wheeled round just in time to parry a blow from an axe-wielding infantryman.

'Everything all right, Nazir?' asked the quaid, reining his horse in next to Umar. 'Have you seen the khalifa? There's no sign of him. What can have happened?'

The battle was almost over. Men were laying down their arms or collapsing with exhaustion. Umar could still make out isolated pockets of fighting on the banks of the Genil, but it seemed that the main battle had ended. So where was the khalifa and the royal standard?

He turned and looked back to where he had last seen their Supreme Commander on a raised hillock which gave him a panoramic view of the battleground. There was no sign of the standard bearer and the group of men who'd been protecting their khalifa were now engaged in close combat fighting. Of Idris himself there appeared to be no sign. Umar and the quaid galloped towards the group and fought their way through. The ground was slippery with blood and gore; men lay all around them, the dying and the dead. And there, in the middle of it all, trampled into the mud like an old rag, was the green and white checkered standard of Idris I. Umar leant down from his horse and grabbed it; the flag was stained with blood. He held it aloft so that the pennant fluttered in the wind.

The battle was over. Instead of the incessant cacophony of the fighting, now he could hear the individual cries of agony, of men dying, of desperate prayers to Allah, of fear. White flags were being raised and men were throwing down their arms. The enemy had surrendered. The allies had won. Écija was theirs. Isbiliya was defeated. He felt the elation course through his veins. It was all over. They had won. The words ran round and round in his head.

'The khalifa? Where's the khalifa?' he shouted to the quaid. His commanding officer had dismounted and was walking towards a group of their own soldiers who were staring silently down at the ground. As the men parted to let the quaid through, Umar saw the prostrate body of their Supreme Commander lying at their feet. He was dead. A broken and blood-stained lance lay beside him.

Umar watched as the quaid turned the body of their ruler over onto his back. The hilt of a dagger was protruding from his neck. As the quaid gently pulled it free, blood spurted out and ran into the mud beside the khalifa's body, then it stopped. Carefully the quaid lifted the dead ruler and laid him across the back of his horse.

'What happened here?' he asked the men who were supposed to have been guarding their supreme commander.

Fear was in all their eyes as they looked at the officer. Then one of them said, 'A lance caught the khalifa on the shoulder.' He pointed to the broken weapon on the ground. 'The blow knocked him from his horse and while we were defending him…' He stopped and looked down.

'What happened then, soldier? Speak or you will be in even more trouble,' said the quaid.

'We didn't know, sayyad. We thought he was one of us. There are so many new people in the army, we thought he was someone the khalifa had brought in. He seemed all right. Same as us, we thought.'

'What are you gabbling about, man? Who is this person?'

One of the guards kicked at the dead body of a soldier lying close by. 'Him. We thought he was helping the khalifa to get up, but instead he stabbed him with that dagger. In the neck, just pulled up the khalifa's hauberk and stabbed him. There was nothing we could do.'

'He murdered the khalifa?'

'Yes, sayyad. It all happened so quickly.'

'So, who is the ugly bastard? What was his motive for killing our supreme commander? Was he one of Abbad's men?' asked the quaid.

The soldiers looked at their feet but no-one spoke.

'You don't know who he is or why he has committed this crime, and yet here he lies, dead at your feet. Why is that?'

'I killed him, sayyad. Before he could do any more damage,' said a young lad, who looked as though he should still be in school.

'You killed him? Was that necessary? Could you not have arrested him and then we could have found out why this man would want to murder our khalifa?' the quaid asked, struggling to control his anger.

'I didn't think, sayyad. I believed he was the enemy. What else was I supposed to do?' The young boy looked as though he was about to burst into tears.

'Take this man's body away. Find out if anyone knows who he is, even if it means taking him back to Malaqah with you,' he bawled at the men. 'I will deal with the rest of you later. Especially you,' he added, staring at the boy.

He turned to Umar and took the royal standard from his hand and draped it over the khalifa's bloody corpse. 'He was a brave man,' he said. 'It is a great shame he didn't live to see our glorious victory. But now he is in Paradise.'

Umar barely heard the quaid's words; he was staring at the body of the dead assassin. He knew that face. It was unmistakable. Even in death the man continued to smile his grotesque smile. Umar's head was swimming as he looked around him at the dead bodies littering the battlefield, at the crows that were already feasting on men who, until a few hours ago, had been his companions, at the dead horses, once so proud and beautiful and were now nothing more than carrion. Was it really a glorious victory? And for what? So that their khalifa could say that he had put a stop to the expansionist ambitions of Isbiliya? Would one battle stop Abbad I? He doubted it. And Idris I hadn't even survived to enjoy his victory. He was dead. Murdered. Someone had planned this and now their ruler was dead. Was it really that glorious?

'Are you hurt, Nazir?' the quaid asked him.

Umar looked down at his tunic. A reddish brown stain was slowly spreading across his chest, soaking into the padded cotton vest that was supposed to protect him. He touched it lightly, wonderingly. Blood? Why was he bleeding?

'Here, you'd better get down off that horse. Hey, you. Come and see to this man. He's hurt,' called the quaid.

An orderly who was trying to bandage the arm of a wounded soldier, lifted his hand and shouted something that Umar couldn't hear. The man's words drifted away on the wind. Umar gripped at Basil's mane. He tried to dismount and felt himself falling to the ground. His legs seemed to have no strength in them. Then the quaid's strong arms were helping him lie down on the damp earth and he heard him shout again. Umar looked up at the sky; a solitary cloud, tinged red by the setting sun, looked back at him as though reflecting the blood spattered battlefield. Someone was speaking to him but he couldn't concentrate enough to understand what he was supposed to do. He would just have to wait for the quaid. He would help him. His eyes began to close and the last thing he remembered, before it all went dark, was the sight of a huge black crow watching him.

CHAPTER 26

Bakr could see the frustration written on all their faces; he felt it himself. The fire had burned down to a pile of white ash but still the ship hadn't seen it. It had continued sailing for Dragonera and hadn't even slowed down.

'We'll have to cut some more wood for the oars,' Kamil said, trying to sound positive. 'I can't imagine there will be many more ships sailing past us today.'

'No, you're right. But why was that ship sailing along the coast? If it had been going to Medina Mayurqa it would have gone straight across from the mainland, nowhere near Dragonera. There would be no need to be sailing so close to the shore, certainly not on this side of the island. They had to be looking for something,' said Bakr.

'Or someone,' said Asim.

'We'll cut some more wood but not for the oars, we'll build up the fire and keep it burning in case they come back this way.'

They looked at him in surprise.

'But isn't it dangerous?' asked Mayy. 'What if someone else sees the smoke?'

'It's a risk we have to take. This could be our only chance,' he told them, trying to sound more confident than he felt. If the pirates found them then they'd pay with their lives and Mayy would soon be regretting the day she joined them.

'Well at least there's plenty of wood,' said Kamil. 'And we could cook our rabbits on the fire, if we had any.'

'Do you want me to see if I can find anything for our supper?' asked Mayy.

'Yes, good idea, but don't stray too far from the camp. We still don't know who took our catch,' said Bakr.

He watched as she picked up a knife and slipped it into her bag, then set off up the path. What did she think she'd find? Perhaps some berries or some fruit. Not more pine nuts, please. He'd turn into a squirrel if he ate any more of them. What he wouldn't give right now for a nice slice of slow-cooked kid, in that delicious sauce that Aisha made with almonds and honey. He sighed. If he wanted that then he had to get off this damn island. He was beginning to think that they would have been better off staying with the pirates; when they had completed all the ships al-Awar wanted then he might have let them go. Or then again, he might not have. He sighed. Well, there was no point dwelling on what could have been. There was work to do.

Kamil and Asim were already hard at work in the trees, cutting down the saplings and dragging them towards the remains of the bonfire. Most of the wood was too green to burn properly, but there were a lot of broken branches and twigs which would get it started and then the fire would burn slowly, sending up lots of smoke. That's what they wanted, a column of smoke that the ship couldn't miss.

He straightened up and stretched his aching back. A flash of something bright caught his eye. There was someone at the top of the path and it wasn't Mayy.

'Get under cover,' he hissed at the others. 'I think someone's watching us. Don't hurry, just make it look as though you're going for more wood. I'll follow you.'

He waited until Kamil and Asim were hidden in the trees and then he walked towards them. He longed to turn and see if whoever was watching would follow him but he didn't want to let him know that he'd been spotted. Once Bakr was in the wood and out of sight he hunkered down and waited for the figure to reveal itself, but there was neither any movement on the path nor any sign of anyone. If, as Kamil had suggested, it was a hunter, then he would be used to waiting; he was probably trying to work out who they were before he left. That couldn't happen. If he went back to the town and told people that he'd seen three strangers on a deserted beach, it wouldn't be long before someone came to investigate. They had to stop him.

Bakr crawled across to where Kamil and Asim were crouched and whispered, 'Asim carry on gathering the wood for the fire. Kamil, I want you to try to get around behind that man, whoever it is, and stop him from leaving. I think he's at the top of the path and it's possible he may be the one who stole our dinner. I'll stay here and help Asim with the fire. Shout if you get into trouble.'

'I'll bring the rabbits back with me,' whispered Kamil.

It wasn't going to be easy for Kamil to make his way through the scrub without being seen, but he'd have to try. He waited while Kamil moved towards the cliff, keeping under cover of the trees for as long as he could, then he saw him drop down on his belly and disappear from view.

'Come on Asim. We must behave as naturally as we can.'

They began collecting branches and taking them to the bonfire, sometimes calling out as though Kamil was still in the woods cutting down trees. There was still no movement at the top of the path.

'What about Mayy?' asked Asim. 'Will she be all right?'

Bakr had forgotten all about the girl. That was even more reason to apprehend this intruder. 'I expect so. She won't be back for a while yet.'

Suddenly the screech of a falcon broke the silence. And then he heard Kamil shout. He picked up a stick and began to run up the path towards the noise. An old man lay slumped on the ground, still clutching at the jesses of a falcon who was screeching and flapping his wings in fear, as he desperately tried to get away from him.

'What happened?' he asked Kamil, who was standing over the man with a cudgel in his hand.

'He's frightened my bird,' the old man said, sitting up and trying to sooth the agitated bird. 'I've only just got her used to coming out with me and now look what he's done.'

'What are you doing here?' asked Bakr.

'What do you think I'm doing? Training my falcon, of course. Trying to get it to hunt me some nice fat partridges. More to the point, what are you doing here? And why is there a bonfire on the beach?'

'Did you steal our rabbits?' asked Kamil, still brandishing the cudgel.

'Your rabbits? Since when were they yours? I've been hunting these woods since I was a boy. Those rabbits don't belong to no-one.'

'Are you alone?' asked Bakr.

'Yes and no,' he said, his weathered face breaking into a grin that doubled the number of wrinkles on his cheeks. He continued to stroke the falcon. 'Me and young Arra here were alone, but now I reckon we have a companion.' He nodded to where Mayy was trying to hide behind a pine tree. 'That young lady has been following me for some time. I used to attract the girls in my youth, but I thought those days were over.' He smiled a toothless smile.

Mayy stepped out onto the path; she had her knife in her hand.

'I think you can put that away, Mayy. We can handle this,' said Bakr.

'I was waiting for him to catch something and then I was going to take it,' she said. 'But that bird is useless. It couldn't catch a fly. No wonder he had to steal our rabbits.'

'Get up,' said Bakr. 'You're coming with us.'

Kamil took the old man's arm and yanked him to his feet.

'Watch what you're doing. I've just got her calm. I don't want you upsetting her again,' the old man said. 'What do you want with me, anyway? And who are you? I don't think I've seen you around here before.'

'We haven't seen you either, old man. Are you working for the pirates?' asked Kamil.

Bakr glared at him. When would that lad learn to keep his mouth shut?

'Pirates? Oh, is that who you're hiding from? You must be the men they're searching for. But who's this young lady with the knife? I didn't hear they were looking for a woman as well,' said the old man.

'Enough chatter. Just get a move on,' said Bakr, giving him a shove. What on earth were they going to do with him? They couldn't let him go. He might go straight into town and get word to Captain al-Awar. There was no way he could risk that.

The old man staggered down the path, the falcon sitting calmly on his gloved hand. Now he was beginning to look worried.

'Good old blaze you've got going there,' he said, stopping by the bonfire. 'Looks to me like you want the pirates to find you.'

'Never mind about that. Tell me where you're from before I begin to lose patience,' said Bakr. 'Are you from the town?'

'Me? No, I never go into that crazy place. Haven't been in a town for twenty years.'

'So how do you know that the pirates are looking for three men?'

'News travels fast on this island; it even reaches an old hermit like me.'

'That doesn't answer my question. Let me make myself clear. Either you co-operate with us or that girl over there will slit your throat and we'll toss you to the fish. Do you understand?'

The old man continued to stroke his falcon, but said quietly, 'Yes. I understand. If you must know, I met two men yesterday who asked me if I had seen anyone in this part of the woods.'

'What did you say?'

'I said I hadn't. I didn't want them tramping all over my woods and scaring the wildlife. What do I care if some poor souls have managed to make a fool of the pirates? Good for them, I say. But I didn't say that to them.'

'Did you tell them about the traps?'

'No. I've seen your traps for a few days now. I reckoned you'd caught enough rabbits so I helped myself to some,' he said with a smile.

'I knew it was you,' said Kamil, menacing him with the cudgel.

'Put that cudgel down, Kamil. And you, what's your name?'

'Wasil. And this is Arra,' he said, looking down at the falcon.

'Well, Wasil. You're going to have to stay here with us for a while. We can't take the chance that you might tell anybody about us. So make yourself comfortable,' said Bakr. 'And don't try to escape or I will have you tied up.'

'Don't worry about me. I'm not in any hurry.'

Bakr felt like banging his own head against a rock. It had been difficult enough to feed and plan for three of them to escape. Now they were five; it was becoming very complicated.

'The ship,' cried Asim. 'I can see it. It's coming back.' He threw some more bracken on the fire and stood back as the flames flared up again.

Sure enough, the same ship was returning and sailing closer to the shore this time. Someone would surely see them now.

'Kamil, Mayy go and get the blankets. We need to attract their attention.'

The youngsters ran back to the cave and within a couple of minutes they had returned and were waving the blankets wildly at the ship and hollering like lunatics.

'They're not slowing down,' cried Kamil. 'Surely they can see us.'

He started to jump up and down, waving his arms and shouting louder than ever, but either the captain of the ship didn't see them or he wasn't interested.

In the end, exhausted and disappointed they stood on the beach by the remains of the smoking bonfire and watched the ship slowly sail out of sight.

'So that's that then,' said Asim. 'They weren't looking for us after all.'

Bakr didn't say anything. The disappointment was hard to take. He had been so sure that they would stop and help them, but it was not to be. Now the only thing they could do was return to the original plan; it was all they had left.

'What are we going to do now?' asked Kamil.

He saw his young apprentice look across at Mayy, who smiled shyly at him. Was something going on between them? Young love? He groaned. As if he didn't have enough to worry about.

'Just continue as before, but first we need to cut more wood. And put your back into it, Kamil.'

'Good job the planks were wet, or they'd have been burned as well,' said Asim.

'I know it's disappointing, but we can't give up. Let's just get back to work,' said Bakr.

'What about Wasil?' asked Kamil. 'What are we going to do about him?'

'You keep an eye on him, Mayy. If he tries to get away, just shout and one of us will come and help you,' said Bakr.

He couldn't let them know how disheartened he felt. If they were ever going to get off this island it was important to keep their spirits up.

CHAPTER 27

Prince Hasan ibn Yahya ibn Ali was seated in his garden high above the town of Sebta, playing chess with his friend Aqbal when his brother suddenly appeared.

'As-salama alaykum, brother.' said Prince Idris Ben Yahya, 'Aqbal.' He nodded at their friend and threw himself down beside them. 'So, who's winning?'

'Wa alaykum e-salam, my brother. What brings you here so early in the morning?' asked Hasan. 'The sun is barely over the horizon and yet here you are already. Is something wrong?'

'I take it you haven't heard the news then? Too wrapped up in the game of kings? Be careful; it looks as though check-mate is imminent.'

'Stop the tomfoolery and tell me why you're here. What news are you talking about?' Hasan looked across at the servant standing by the entrance, who shrugged his shoulders in puzzlement.

'About our dear uncle Idris, of course. What other news would be of interest to us?'

'Well?'

'He's dead. Rumour has it he was killed in the battle of Écija.'

'Rumours? You should know better than to listen to rumours,' Hasan said and turned back to the chess board.

'No brother, listen to me. It's more than that. He really is dead. Killed in battle, so they say. What's more, he's made his son, Yahya ibn Idris, his heir. Can you believe it? He will be the next khalifa of Malaqah. Now are you interested?'

Hasan motioned for his servant to approach and asked, 'What do you know of this, Razi? Is it true?'

'I have heard nothing about your uncle, sayyad. No news at all, except that they were victorious at Écija.'

Hasan could feel the rage building inside him, but he was determined not to show it, especially not in front of Ben Yahya, who would enjoy his brother's humiliation. He picked up his king and laid it down carefully on the chessboard. 'You win, Aqbal. I cannot concentrate on this game while there is a real kingdom at stake. I must set sail for Malaqah as soon as possible. I need to see for myself what's happening. I can't rely on rumours.'

'Why bother? There's nothing there for you and even less for me,' said Ben Yahya, smirking at him.

'What are you saying? I should do nothing? Are you suggesting that I accept this without a fight? No. He can't do that to me, to us. He can't cut us out of the line of succession just like that. That isn't what Baba wanted.' Hasan knew that his father would never have passed over his two sons for his uncle and even less for his nephew. He had told Hasan, just before he died, that he was his heir. But Baba had died too soon. According to Mama it was only the interference of that meddling ibn Baqanna that had stopped Hasan inheriting the throne immediately on his father's sudden death. The grand vizier said he was too young to rule and so the council of ministers agreed to make his father's brother, Idris ibn Ali al-Mutaayyad, the ruler until Hasan came of age. But everyone had agreed, including Idris, that Hasan should have the throne when he was old enough, in accordance with his father's wishes. In a few days time he would be fifteen and able to rule his kingdom. Now it seemed he'd been betrayed again. 'Well he's not going to get away with it,' he muttered, more to himself than his disinterested brother.

He started to get up but Aqbal put his hand on his arm. 'Wait. These may just be rumours. Maybe you should find out if there is any truth in them before you go rushing over to Malaqah,' he cautioned his friend. 'After all if this news hasn't reached Razi's ears, then maybe there really is nothing in it. You know how the servants are always the first to know what's happening. Come. Play another game of chess. It's a wonderful way to calm the emotions and focus the mind.'

'Mmm. You're probably right, as usual. Very well, let's wait to see what transpires.'

'Anyway, you don't have enough soldiers to fight anyone,' said Ben Yahya. 'You've never listened to me. We should have built up our army years ago. How can we defend our rights if we have no army? You're too weak to be khalifa, brother; our uncle knew that. What good is all that education if you haven't the balls to fight for what's yours? Idris did it to us once before, and now he's doing it again.'

'We have the army of the Barghawata. They're supposed to be governing this place on behalf of Idris. We could ask them to send an army to Malaqah,' Hasan replied, determined not to rise to Ban Yahya's taunts.

After his meeting with Abu Mansur he wasn't sure whom he could trust. Although the Barghawata ruler had suggested that Hasan go to Malaqah to reclaim the throne, he doubted that the old man would give him any military support. All he really wanted was for Hasan and his brother to leave Sebta for good.

'And how would you pay them, anyway? Those Berbers won't do anything unless you reward them handsomely. Do you have a pot of gold that you're not telling me about, brother?' asked Ben Yahya.

'Of course not. You know our uncle has always kept us poor,' replied Hasan. His brother was being tiresome as usual. Ben Yahya had always put on this air of disinterest whenever the question of their inheritance came up, but underneath the pretence it was obvious that he wanted the wealth and power that had been denied them as much as Hasan did. 'Do you think I'm happy about that? Here we are, exiled to North Africa with only a handful of soldiers for our protection. How can we look after our inheritance if we have no army? And how can we build an army with no money? But I expect that's what our uncle intended all along.'

'I'm sure you're right but that doesn't mean we have to accept it. In the meantime, I think you should listen to your friend. You need to find out more about what's happening in Malaqah and whether Idris is really dead before you go rushing over there.'

For once Ben Yahya was making sense. 'You're right, brother. We need to know exactly who our adversary is, our uncle or his grand vizier.'

'Better the cunning of the wolf than the recklessness of the bull,' said Ben Yahya. 'Why don't we send someone we can trust to the city. Tell them to find out all they can, but under no circumstances let it be known that we sent them.'

'For once you have good advice, little brother. I will speak to Naja al-Siqlabi and ask him to commission the fastest ship he can find.'

That was the difference between them. Ben Yahya was the cunning wolf and he was the bull, but not a reckless one; quite the opposite. He was going to consider his next steps very carefully. Very carefully indeed.

While his brother hurried back into the alcázar, Hasan looked out across the Narrow Straits towards al-Jazira and the rock named Jabal Tariq. The ancients believed that beyond the Pillars of Hercules lay the unknown. Well it was no longer uncharted territory but there were still many unknowns. Who knew what could happen to the taifa of al-Jazira if Idris really was dead? And Malaqah? Even Sebta? Would the Barghawata seize this opportunity and take Sebta for themselves? Or would they support him in his bid to claim his throne? Uncertain times indeed.

He sat down opposite his friend and said, 'Very well, Aqbal. One more game but don't think it will be easy for you just because I have other things on my mind.'

'Nothing in this life is easy, my friend,' Aqbal replied, setting out the chess pieces on the red and black board. 'Think of it as practice in case you do have to go to war.'

*

Fatima sighed. She was sitting in the zenana, embroidering the hem of a new djubbah her maid had made for her, something she hadn't had to do since before she was married. When she was a young girl her mother wanted her to be accomplished in all the womanly arts. Personally she didn't consider embroidery to one of them, but her mother, who was a strong-minded woman when it came to her daughters, thought differently. How was she to know that one day her eldest daughter, who had been married to the khalifa of Malaqah and borne him two sons, would be spending her days in an insignificant little place like Sebta embroidering her own clothes.

In Malaqah Fatima had ten personal maids and many other servants. She ruled over a harem of hundreds. Her clothes were of the finest silks and cottons, her shoes made of hand-stitched leather from the youngest lambs. Her jewellery was beyond price: emeralds from India and rubies from Persia. She had necklaces made from beaten gold encrusted with diamonds and wore sapphire rings on her toes. Musicians played for her day and night and she was never without delightful company. Now what did she have? A solitary maid, whom Fatima had only just enough time to bring with her, and a few clothes. Luckily the maid had enough sense to grab the bag where she stored her mistress's most precious jewels, otherwise Fatima would have nothing with her to denote her rank and the fact that she was the mother of not one, but two male heirs to the throne of Malaqah. By rights she should now be addressed as al-Sayyida al-Malika, the mother of the khalifa. She threw down the djubbah in disgust. Her anger against her brother-in-law was growing daily, fuelled by the fact that Hasan was now ready to take his rightful place as khalifa of Malaqah and Idris was blocking it, aided, she was sure, by that weasel ibn Baqanna. But that wasn't the only reason for her hatred towards her brother-in-law; it went back many years.

Fatima's father Qasim, had been the younger brother of Khalifa Ali ibn Hammud al-Nasir, the founder of the Hammudite dynasty. When the khalifa suggested that his eldest son and heir, Yahya, should take her as a wife, her father had readily agreed. But then, some years later, when the khalifa died, instead of allowing his son-in-law to take the throne as decreed, Qasim decided to take it for himself. The result was many years of bitter fighting, at the end of which Qasim was deposed and imprisoned, allowing Yahya to take his rightful position as Khalifa, and Fatima to become queen. Her father remained in prison throughout Yahya's reign; there was no option. She agreed with her husband that there could be no peace in the kingdom if Qasim was allowed to go free. She never visited her father, but she made sure that he did not go short of food, or any of the other comforts that a man of his rank could expect. But when her beloved Yahya died, everything changed. Not only did her brother-in-law grab the throne for himself and send her and her children into immediate exile, but she received news that her father, who was by then an old man and no threat to anyone, had been poisoned on Idris's orders. It seemed as though Idris was determined to inflict as much damage on her and her family as he could. Was it any wonder that she hated him?

'Mama, have you heard the news?'

'What is it, my child?'

'They say that uncle Idris has been killed in battle,' said Ben Yahya, sitting down beside his mother.

Her heart leapt in her bosom. At last her prayers had been answered. 'That's wonderful news. We must leave for Malaqah immediately,' she said.

'There's no point, Mama. Our cousin Yahya ibn Idris has taken the throne.'

'What? That child is on the throne of Malaqah? I cannot believe Idris would do that.' But the truth was that she could believe it. Idris was capable of anything. And now, even after he was dead he was still depriving her son of his inheritance. Well she wouldn't stand for it. She would go to Malaqah herself and demand that justice be done.

*

Prince Hasan stood on the deck, chewing on the piece of ginger that Razi, his personal slave, had given him to prevent sea-sickness. As soon as he received confirmation that his uncle was indeed dead, slain in battle they said, he had decided to challenge his cousin's claim to the throne. His mother had wanted to come with him, but he said she should stay and keep an eye on Ben Yahya. His brother had been behaving strangely lately; ever since the news had come about Idris's death he had changed. Both he and their mother had wanted to go to Malaqah with him, but he'd persuaded them that it was too dangerous. He promised to send for them both when the time was right. Eventually his mother had agreed, albeit a little reluctantly, but even she could see that there was no point both of her sons walking into a trap. Ben Yahya, on the other hand had been angry, saying he had as much right as Hasan to see what was happening, and that their father hadn't intended that he should remain penniless and dependent on the Barghawatas all his life.

The ship was facing into a breeze that carried the sweet smell of al-Andalus in its arms. Al-Andalus. That fabled land. A paradise on earth, they called it. Many a time, when the light was right and the wind blew from the west, he'd stood on the ramparts of the alcazaba looking at it across the Narrow Straits. Now, as he looked at it through the eyes of an exile returning home, he realised that he had forgotten that the countryside could be so lush and green. No great swathes of desert here. It was indeed the promised land his ancestors had spoken about. The shore was edged with a ribbon of golden sand and indented with small fishing coves, where clusters of flat-roofed houses sat like sun-baked bricks. Well tended groves of olive trees covered the hilly slopes, and herds of goats grazed peacefully. An idyllic scene, but what lay beneath?

'I had forgotten it was so beautiful, Naja,' he said as his former tutor joined him in the prow. 'This land looks rich enough for all of us.'

'Yes, sayyad. This is your birthright. You can't let anyone take it away from you.'

'Do you think it's safe for us to land at al-Jazira?' asked Hasan. He was beginning to wonder if they were sailing into a trap; Muhammad, his cousin, ruled al-Jazira. Would he guess the reason for Hasan's visit to Malaqah? Would he try to stop him?

'Why wouldn't it be? We come lightly armed. We have no army with us. We are not a threat to anyone.'

Somehow Hasan didn't find Naja's words very comforting; they only reinforced his fear that they were being too trusting and would have been better sending an emissary to find out ibn Baqanna's plans—his mother was convinced that the grand vizier was behind this new move to keep Hasan from becoming khalifa. As it was his plan was quite simple and even a little naive; he hoped to appeal to the council of ministers and to the people of Malaqah, who had been shocked and angry when his father had been poisoned. They knew he was the rightful ruler and he prayed they would support him.

The wind that blew constantly through the narrow straits filled the sails of their small ship and propelled it across to the opposite shore. A distance of less than twenty Arab miles and he was in al-Andalus. The port of al-Jazira was busy; Hasan and his entourage pushed their way through the crowd and headed for the alcázar.

Although not heavily armed—their small party consisted of Naja, Razi and eight armed guards—they weren't foolish enough to go without some protection. Naja said that the ten of them would be sufficient to defend themselves in case of attack from bandits on the road to Malaqah but would pose no threat to the new khalifa; it shouldn't look as though Hasan intended to take Malaqah by force. Hasan hoped he was right. But would ten armed men be enough to protect them against an attack from the soldiers of the boy khalifa? He still thought of his cousin as a child, a weak, unambitious boy who used to play with his brother, Ben Yahya, when he was younger. Would he have changed?

*

When Hasan and his retinue arrived at the alcázar in al-Jazira, they were immediately ushered into the sultan's private quarters.

'As-salama alaykum, cousin,' said Muhammad, greeting him warmly despite the fact that they hadn't seen each other since they were both young children. 'Welcome to my home.'

Hasan bowed before the sultan. His cousin was a couple of years older than Hasan but his lack of a proper beard made him look younger.

'Wa alaykum e-salam, Your Excellency. It is good to see you looking so well,' said Hasan. 'We are on our way to Malaqah to offer our congratulations to your brother Yahya, and stopped to wish you well.'

'That is very noble of you. Please stay and eat with me before you finish your journey. It is a full day's ride to Malaqah.'

'We would be delighted to, Your Excellency. Your reputation for generous hospitality is well known.'

'Make sure that my cousin's soldiers are given food and their horses tended to,' Muhammad ordered one of his slaves.

The slave bowed and backed from the room leaving Hasan facing the sultan. His mother had said that they should try to ally themselves with Muhammad—he was the one who could make their task easier—but surely his cousin would be suspicious of them. He must realise that they were not happy that his father had bypassed them and given Malaqah to his young brother.

'Well, cousin, please be seated and I will send for some refreshment,' said Muhammad. He seemed a pleasant young man and gave Hasan an open smile that contained no hint of guile.

He sat on the soft, silk cushions indicated and while Muhammad made polite conversation, enquiring about other family members, Hasan looked about him. The sultan's palace was not large but richly furnished. The multitude of exotic goods that he'd seen in the port on their arrival were on display here, from the brightly coloured Persian carpets to the carefully sculpted statues. Unlike the modest alcázar in Sebta, here was a display of wealth and power.

'I was surprised that you were not at my father's funeral,' said Muhammad. 'It was a splendid affair. I am sure he went to Paradise with a happy heart.'

'We have only just learned of our dear uncle's death,' said Hasan. 'My condolences to you and your family. It is why I am now travelling to Malaqah.'

'Ibn Baqanna took care of everything. He sent word that my father's body was being returned to Malaqah and I set off straight away. Do you know the grand vizier?'

'I do, Your Excellency. How surprising that he never thought to inform me and my brother of our uncle's death. I must admit that I find it strange.' He wasn't sure how to proceed, but he didn't need to worry, because Muhammad came straight to the point.

'He's protecting his own position. You must realise that, cousin. Before he set off for that last battle against Isbiliya, my father signed a document that stated quite clearly that you, Hasan, should succeed him in the event he was killed in battle. It seems that he had some sort of premonition that this victory would come at a cost, and he wanted everything to be set out clearly before he left. He gave that document to ibn Baqanna, so the grand vizier was quite aware of his decision,' said Muhammad.

Hasan stared at him in surprise. So Idris hadn't betrayed him after all. In the end he'd tried to honour his promise to Hasan's father.

'I don't know what the grand vizier did with it. As soon as the news arrived in Malaqah that my father was dead, ibn Baqanna crowned my little brother khalifa. It was ridiculous really, because my brother, Yahya ibn Idris has no wish to be khalifa. He is too young for a start, but not only that, he is a simple soul. Do you remember him?'

'I do. A very quiet child with his nose always in a book.'

'Exactly. Unfortunately he doesn't have the backbone to stand up to someone like ibn Baqanna, which suits the grand vizier very well.'

'I get the impression that you are about to make me an offer,' said Hasan.

'In a way, yes. What ibn Baqanna does not know, is that I also have a copy of the document which names you as my father's successor. You should be Khalifa of Malaqah. It was always your right. My father was only acting as khalifa until you came of age; he told me as much himself.'

Hasan began to feel his heart racing. Which way was this going to go? Was Muhammad suggesting that Hasan should depose his cousin or was he planning to destroy the proof and get rid of Hasan? The latter he could understand, but then why tell him about it? If it were the former, what would his cousin gain from being so charitable?

'So what do you propose, Your Excellency?' asked Hasan, wishing that he had brought more men with him. Even the presence of his brother would help him to feel less threatened.

'It is simple. I propose to give you this document as proof that you are the rightful khalifa of Malaqah, so that you can return to the city and claim your birthright.'

'And what do you want in return?'

Muhammad smiled. 'You are right cousin when you assume that I want something in return, but it is nothing that you will wish to refuse me. I want two things only. No harm must come to my brother. It would please me if he were to join me here in al-Jazira, but that depends on him. He must be free to go wherever he wishes. And secondly, you must give up any claim to the throne of al-Jazira, and ensure that your brother Ben Yahya does the same. We are a small, insignificant taifa and I intend that we remain as such. I have no expansionist ambitions; all I want it to continue to live here, in peace.'

Hasan was astounded. He was so used to the members of his family fighting over who was due what, that he found it surprising that his cousins were totally disinterested in being khalifa, the most important position in all al-Andalus.

'But what of your brother? Does he agree with you? Are you sure he doesn't want to be the khalifa?' asked Hasan.

'I am positive. We had a long talk when I was in Malaqah for the funeral. He is not a man of politics. If anything he is a man of faith and would be happier spending his days reading the Quran than leading campaigns against the Christians. So what do you say, cousin? Do you want to be the new khalifa of Malaqah? Because if you don't then someone else will soon arise to take it for himself. Maybe your little brother, even?' He smiled, as though he were joking, but Hasan felt a chill run down his spine at his words.

'No, my brother is too idle for that. As you say, your terms are very simple to agree to. However, I will have a score to settle with that weasel, ibn Baqanna. I hope you don't object.'

'Do what you will. I have never trusted the man. It wouldn't surprise me if he was behind my father's death. Do you not think that it's very strange that the supreme commander of the army should be killed in battle? After all, the khalifa's role is not to fight but to oversee and direct the campaign. He is never in the front line and there is always a phalanx of soldiers around him. How could anyone penetrate that without help?' He paused and looked at the waiting servants. 'Ah, here is the food. Please relax and enjoy yourself, cousin. Later I will give you the document I have promised you.'

The conversation reverted to pleasantries and discussion of the tuna fishing industry—something which was of great importance to the economy of al-Jazira—leaving the question of who was behind the khalifa's death unresolved. A team of slaves brought in platters of dates, figs, peaches, goat's cheese, vegetable couscous, plates of mojama and baskets of unleavened bread. Hasan could hear his stomach rumbling as the food was placed before him; now that his fears had been allayed he could relax and enjoy his meal.

'Thank you, cousin, but I would like to leave as soon as I have eaten. I don't want to delay my arrival in Malaqah. I will speak to your brother as soon as I get there,' said Hasan.

'Of course. I understand. But be careful. It's best if ibn Baqanna doesn't know that you are coming. I wouldn't want your life to be in danger.' Muhammad then turned to one of his servants and said, 'Make sure our guests' horses are ready to leave within the hour. They have a long ride ahead of them. And send my grand vizier to me.'

CHAPTER 28

When they arrived in the taifa of Dénia, Dirar wanted to go straight to Dragonera but Captain Mustafa refused; first they would complete their business and then they would look for the shipbuilder. This entailed docking in the port of Dénia and loading up with sacks of rice and wheels of cheese; it also meant selling some more of their coveted Malaqah wine and some pottery.

'Can we go now?' asked Dirar. 'Can we do what Avi is paying you to do, look for Bakr and his men?' His frustration was making him bold. He was getting tired of this journey; they had been weeks sailing up the coast, trading at almost every port they came to. He'd have been quicker if he'd borrowed Umar's mare and ridden there. Not that he was much of a horseman; in fact he was rather nervous of horses, if the truth were told.

'We'll go when I'm good and ready,' said Mustafa. 'If you're not happy with that then you can leave right now and find your own way home.' He stared at the boy for a moment then added, in a less strident tone, 'We will make one more call at Medina Mayurqa then we will go to Dragonera.'

'Medina Mayurqa? Where is that?' asked Dirar, feeling even more frustrated.

'It's the large island immediately opposite Dragonera. I thought you could use the time there to find out if anyone had heard of your brother-in-law.'

'Oh. That sounds a good idea,' Dirar replied a little sheepishly. He ought to be careful not to upset the captain or he might really find himself having to make his own way home.

By the evening they were pulling into the beautiful, wide harbour at Medina Mayurqa. Behind the harbour and across the island ran a range of tree covered mountains that sheltered it from the westerly winds. A pod of dolphins playing in the turquoise water, accompanied their ship as they entered the harbour and made for the quay. To Dirar, the island's main port looked very much like the port of Dénia, and all the others they'd visited before it.

'Tomorrow I'll sell the rest of the wine and the olive oil,' said Mustafa, 'and then we will be free to investigate whether your brother-in-law is here or not.'

'Shall I go into the town and see what I can find out?' asked Dirar.

'Yes, but don't get lost. And get back here by midnight.'

'Aye, aye Captain,' Dirar with a grin. By now he was beginning to realise that the captain's bark was, more often than not, much worse than his bite. Although he knew it wouldn't do to push him too far.

*

The first thing Dirar did when he clambered ashore was set off to find a decent eating house. Despite the herbs and spices he'd bought in Qartayannat al-Halfa, the quality of the cook's food had not improved and as usual he was starving. Anyway taverns and inns were good places to chat to local people without arousing suspicion.

He found an ideal place, just off the souk, in a narrow alleyway alongside half a dozen other eating establishments. It wasn't so much the smell of the food coming out of the kitchen that attracted him, as the young serving girl standing in the doorway; she had enormous eyes and the sweetest smile he'd ever seen.

He tried to smile at her, but he felt so tongued-tied in front of such a delightful creature that all he could do was brush past her and sit down at an empty table in the corner.

'What can I get you, sayyad?' she asked, a few moments later, her soft brown eyes rendering him speechless again. 'Fish stew or meat balls and rice?'

Dirar swallowed hard and managed to mutter, 'Fish stew.'

A few minutes later, just as she was serving him his plate of fish stew, and he was summoning up the courage to speak to her, two men, who, from the smell of their clothes, were fishermen, came in and sat down next him.

'None of that fish stew for us, Amal,' one of them called to the serving girl. 'Any meatballs left?'

'The cook kept some by especially for you,' Amal said, flashing him a smile that was as sweet as honey.

Dirar felt his heart melt as he looked at her. Amal. Hope. He sighed. Pity there was no hope for him.

'She's a lovely girl that one,' said one of the fishermen, who had obviously noticed Dirar's appreciative stare.

Dirar felt himself blush and turned his attention back to the fish stew.

'Haven't seen you before,' said the other fisherman. 'You're not from around here, are you?'

'Malaqah,' said Dirar, his mouth full of bread. He chewed hurriedly and added, 'I'm looking for someone. My brother-in-law, to be exact. My sister is beside herself with worry and she wouldn't give me any peace unless I made some attempt to find him.'

'What makes you think he's here?'

Dirar washed the bread down with a long draught of water. 'He was kidnapped by pirates.'

The men stared at him for a moment and then burst out laughing. 'And your sister thinks you're going to find him? You must be mad. And your sister too. With the greatest of respect,' he added.

'Why do you say that? He has to be somewhere,' said Dirar. 'We think he's on one of these islands.'

'Really? Well there certainly are pirates in these waters. but they never come to Medina Mayurqa. In case it had slipped your memory, pirates are criminals; if they landed here and decided to just pop in for a plate of fish stew, they'd be arrested.'

'So why don't they arrest them anyway? There are hundreds of ships in the harbour at Dénia. I saw them when we stopped to sell some wine,' said Dirar. He picked up the remaining hunk of bread and wiped up the remains of the stew.

'Wine? Malaqah wine? Do you still have any?' asked one of the fishermen.

'Yes, there're still a few barrels on the ship. I'm sure the captain will exchange a flagon or two for some information,' said Dirar. 'Perhaps I can buy you a glass of wine now?' By now he didn't have much of the money that his father had given him, but it would be worth spending what was left if it meant that they gave him some news of Bakr. He had seen how easily it loosened a man's tongue when he was in the tavern in Qartayannat al-Halfa.

He beckoned to the barman and asked, 'Do you have any Malaqah wine?'

'It's not cheap,' grunted the portly barman.

'A glass each for my companions,' he said, feeling very important. 'And some mint tea for me.'

'What do you want to know?' asked the fishermen, their eyes gleaming at the thought of the dark sweet wine that tasted of raisins and sunshine.

'Captain al-Awar, have you heard of him?'

They were silent. Then one of the fishermen looked at his companion, who gave an almost imperceptible shake of his head. 'No. Not around here,' he said.

The barman placed two glasses of the ruby wine on the table. 'That's the lot. Did I hear you say your captain has some barrels for sale?' he asked, looking at Dirar.

'Yes, Captain Mustafa.'

'I know him. He's a regular in these parts. I'd better send someone down to the port before he sells it all,' said the barman.

'Yes, he's planning to leave tomorrow morning,' said Dirar.

The fishermen were sipping at the wine as though they were frightened it would evaporate in front of their eyes.

'This is good,' said the smaller of the two, smacking his lips in pleasure.

Dirar tasted his tea; it smelled of fresh mint and was piping hot, just as he liked it.

'Are you sure you haven't heard of Captain al-Awar?' he asked. 'They say he's a very ambitious man. Plans to build a fleet of his own ships.'

'No, never heard of him.'

'We know he was on Dragonera,' said Dirar.

Now the two men looked distinctly frightened. 'No, the pirates around here are just petty thieves. None of them have those sort of ambitions' said the smaller of the two.

Now Dirar was certain they knew more than they were admitting.

'But you're fishermen. I bet there's nothing that goes on around these islands that you don't know about.'

'We told you, we've never heard of this Awar chap,' said the taller fisherman. He was not only tall, but broad and looked as though he would be able to handle himself well in a fight. It wouldn't do to antagonise him.

'And if we had, we'd be mad to tell you. It would be like signing our own death warrants,' said the first one. 'Certainly not for a couple of flagons of wine.' He spat on the floor as if he'd just tasted a glass of vinegar instead of the wine he admired so much.

His companion threw him an angry glance. So they *had* heard of him but it was obvious that they were not going to tell Dirar anything; they were too scared. The best he could do now was to go somewhere else and see what other information he could find out.

'Thanks for the wine,' one of the fishermen called, as Dirar headed for the door.

'Yes, and good luck with your search,' said the other.

Dirar hesitated in the street outside the tavern, wondering which way to go next, when the barman came out.

'Hey you, young fellow. What do you want with this pirate captain?' he asked. He was chewing some sunflower seeds and spitting the husks on the floor.

'I'm looking for my brother-in-law,' Dirar repeated, although he was certain that the barman had listened to every word they'd said inside. 'He's a shipbuilder and we think that the pirates took him to build their ships.'

The barman pulled at his reddish beard and then said, 'He must be a pretty fine shipbuilder if they went all the way to Malaqah to get him.'

'He builds ships for the khalifa,' Dirar said.

'Well, all I can tell you is that they were on Dragonera, but a few days ago they loaded up their ship and sailed out of there. They'd heard that the khalifa had sent a naval ship to look for them.'

'Really?' asked Dirar in astonishment. So his father had managed to persuade the admiral to search for Bakr after all. 'But how did they know?'

'We all knew. News travels fast on these islands. And as soon as the pirates got wind of it, they were off. Like bats out of hell.'

'And you've no idea where they went?'

'None. But they'll be back. Like homing pigeons, they always come back here to roost.'

He was probably right, but the question was 'when?' When would they return? And were Bakr and the others still with them?

He left the barman standing in the doorway, chewing his sunflower seeds, and pushed his way through the colourful crowds milling around in the souk: Arabs in flowing robes and turbans, women in brightly coloured tunics with flimsy scarves around their heads, tailors, cobblers, merchants and sellers of fruit and vegetables, all very similar to the souk in Malaqah but somehow different. In Malaqah there were more Berber faces and dark-skinned slaves from north Africa; here there were Greeks and Sicilians, pale skinned Normans, Tuscans and people from Sardinia. He felt he was in a strange land.

'Ah, there you are, my lad. Well, have you found out anything?' asked Captain Mustafa, catching him by the sleeve.

'Yes, but nothing very useful,' said Dirar. 'There's been a naval ship here looking for Bakr.'

'What the devil? Do you mean the khalifa has sent one of his ships to look for your brother-in-law? That's impossible.'

'It's true. But when they got here the pirates had gone, so it looks like the admiral has left too.'

'So we've come all this way for nothing?' said Mustafa.

'Not for nothing, captain. We know they're alive. That's something.'

'No, lad. We know they were alive. We don't know where they are now or if they are still alive. Now that the pirates realise that the khalifa has sent his navy to look for them they may have decided that it's safer to get rid of them.'

Dirar felt a sinking sensation in his stomach. The captain was right. Somehow it seemed so much worse to know that the men had been alive and that they'd been so close to finding them. Now they were back to square one. 'They wouldn't do that, would they?'

The captain shrugged. 'These are pirates we're talking about. Human life is cheap as far as they're concerned.'

'So what do we do now?'

'We might as well go home,' Captain Mustafa continued. 'No need to go to Dragonera if they're not there. We'll leave first thing in the morning. I've just got a bit more business to do then I'll see you back on the ship.'

'Yes, captain,' Dirar said. 'But couldn't we just have a quick look at Dragonera? The man I spoke to might be mistaken.' He couldn't put into words just how defeated he felt. To have spent weeks getting there only to find they'd gone, only Allah knew where, was more than he could bear. Surely there was something more they could do?

'Look lad, I'm not keen on sailing into pirate waters with a merchant ship heavily laden with a cargo of silver, silk and rice. It would be like a gift for them. Even if this al-Awar isn't there it's likely we'll bump into other pirates. You might not be afraid, but I'm not ready to go to Paradise just yet.'

*

While Captain Mustafa went back to get his ship ready for the journey home, Dirar continued to wander around the town. He stopped at a wayside stall where an old woman was serving glasses of fruit juice.

'Well, young man, what's it to be? Lime and lemon, pomegranate or orange?' she asked.

'I'll have a glass of pomegranate juice, please,' he said.

Standing not far away were two men, talking in rather loud voices about the disappearance of a young woman. One of them appeared to be the father of the girl, and he was very agitated.

'I tell you, When I was in Andrach, I saw your daughter talking to a stranger. They went into your brother's place.'

'The apothecary?'

'Yes, she looked as though she'd been crying.'

'Crying? What does she have to cry about? I'll give her something to cry about, if I ever catch up with her,' shouted her father.

'Excuse me,' said Dirar. 'I couldn't help hearing you mention a stranger. I'm looking for someone and I wondered if it might be him.'

'The town's full of strangers,' spat the father. 'That's the problem. They bring all these fancy ideas with them and the next thing you know, your daughters don't want to settle down and become dutiful wives. They want excitement. I ask you. Excitement. I told her she'd have enough excitement to last a lifetime when she had a brood of children to look after.'

The other man ignored him and asked Dirar, 'Who are you looking for? It's possible it was him, but this wasn't here in Medina Mayurqa; it was in Andrach.'

'Where's that?' asked Dirar.

'Not far from here, just a few miles along the coast. It's a small town and we don't get many foreigners there; that's why I noticed him. What do you want him for?'

'He's my brother-in-law. My sister sent me to look for him. He's about forty and quite well built.' Dirar paused, trying to recall any distinguishing features about Bakr. He realised that he'd never really paid much attention to his appearance. 'He builds ships.'

'No. It definitely wasn't him. This was a young man. About your age. Fair hair. Well spoken. He had a scarf around his face, so I can't tell you much else.'

'What was he doing? Where was he from?'

'No idea where he was from, but I heard him ask the apothecary for some medicine for his friend. Sorry, that's all I can tell you about him.'

'His friend? Did you see him?'

'No. The lad was on his own, well except for Mayy.'

'Mayy?'

'His daughter.' He nodded to the father who was now moaning bitterly to the old woman about the state of today's youth.

Dirar drank his pomegranate juice and handed the glass back to the stall holder. 'I don't suppose you've heard anything about a pirate named Captain al-Awar?' he asked.

'Plenty of pirates in these waters, but we keep well away from them. Why do you want to know?' asked the man.

'We think he may know something about my brother-in-law.'

'Is he the one who's offered a reward for the capture of three men? Says one of them ran off with his wife.'

'Reward?'

'Yes, twenty gold dinars.'

'Did anyone claim it?'

'No. There's been no sign of anyone fitting their descriptions. And there're plenty of people looking for them.'

'Are you?'

'No. I don't trust those pirates. I can't see any pirate paying twenty dinars to get his wife back; more likely to slit your throat for your trouble. As I said, best to keep well away from them all. They're the most untrustworthy, deceitful band of cutthroats you'll find anywhere on the Middle Sea.'

'I'm off to Andrach to have a word with my brother. Maybe he knows where Mayy went,' said the girl's father. 'Ma'a salama. Good luck with finding your brother-in-law, stranger.'

'Thank you. I hope you find your daughter,' said Dirar, although he wasn't sure that he really wanted the father to find her. 'Ma'a salama.'

It was time he headed back to the ship and tell Captain Mustafa what he'd found out. It sounded as though Bakr and his men had escaped and al-Awar was looking for them. Perhaps now he could persuade Captain Mustafa to sail around the island of Dragonera at least once before they left.

CHAPTER 29

The admiral had lain awake all night wondering what he should do. He knew he couldn't go back to Malaqah without proof that Bakr was dead, but how was he going to get it? The khalifa would be displeased if he returned empty-handed. No, not displeased. Furious. It could be the end of his career. What an ignominious way to leave the navy, dismissed for failing to locate a missing person. His years of valiant service would count for nothing. The powerful navy that he had built up under the rule of three khalifas would pass to another commander. The victorious sea battles would be forgotten. No, he had to make at least one more try to find this elusive shipbuilder.

One other thing was bothering Admiral al-Maraghi. The smoke that had been seen yesterday. The more he thought about it, the more he felt that it could have been a beacon. After all, nobody lit bonfires in the middle of summer, not even here in the Balearic Islands; it was too risky. He'd seen wildfires sweep across the countryside before. They devastated the land and reduced everything to ashes: crops, trees, villages. Wild animals and birds died, leaving the land completely barren. Sometimes even domesticated animals perished and, if they weren't quick enough to get to safety, people died too. Some villagers in the remoter parts of the country still liked to use slash and burn techniques to clear their land, but even then it never happened in the full heat of the summer months. No farmer would try it and if he did, his neighbours would soon stop him.

It was just possible that the smoke had been a signal. Why hadn't that sailor spoken up sooner, then they could have checked it our straight away? Maybe Bakr was still alive. Maybe somehow, he had managed to escape to the larger island of Mayurqa.

The horizon paled as dawn approached. He lay under his canopy on the deck and watched the stars gradually fade and disappear. The noise of the sailors wakening and beginning to move about the ship roused him from his lethargy; he could hear the captain's shrill voice giving orders to the sleepy crew. It was just possible that Bakr was here, lying awake and looking at the very same milky sky. Had he seen them? Had he seen their ship on the horizon? It was no good; he had to be sure before he gave up the search. He sat up, throwing his sheet to one side. Very well, he would make one more journey around the island of Mayurqa before heading for home.

*

Eventually Dirar had managed to persuade Mustafa to take him to Dragonera but they had barely left the harbour of Medina Mayurqa when the crewman posted aloft as lookout shouted down to them.

'Captain. I can see a ship coming towards us.'

Dirar felt his stomach contract with fear. Pirates? Was he leading them all into an ambush? Allah protect him. If the pirates didn't kill him then Mustafa surely would.

'What sort of ship is it?' shouted the captain. 'Can you see its pennant? Is it a pirate ship?'

'It's still too dark to make out the colours, Captain.'

'Do you want us to turn around, Captain?' asked the first mate. 'If it is the pirates, we can probably make it back into port before they reach us.'

'How fast is it approaching?' asked Mustafa.

'It's travelling faster than us. It looks like a naval vessel to me,' said the first mate, peering into the gloom. 'Hard to tell until the sky gets brighter.'

'It could be the admiral's ship,' said Dirar. 'Maybe they haven't left yet. Maybe they're still patrolling the islands. It looks as though the ship could have come from Dragonera.' The excitement was making him gabble like a child.

'Ever the optimist, young man. Well I don't think we have much option but to trust in Allah. If they are pirates there's no hope in hell that we can outrun them. Let's hope you're right, my young fisherman and that it is the admiral.' He turned to the first mate, and shouted, 'Alert the deck crew that they may be needed to fight.'

'You'll fight the pirates?' asked Dirar, surprised. He had imagined that the captain would just turn tail and run back to port.

'You don't think I'd give up my cargo without a fight, do you? Nobody would ever trust me to carry their goods again if I did that,' said Mustafa. 'Now find yourself a sword and get over there in case you're needed.'

Dirar knew that the rowers were not trained fighters, but they were at least fit and strong. But would they be any match for the pirates?

'They're getting closer, Captain,' the man on the forecastle called.

The rowers had shipped their oars and now stood, armed and ready to repel boarders. Dirar stood behind them, his knees quaking.

'I don't think it's a pirate ship, Captain,' shouted the lookout man. 'It's a naval ship, all right. And I think the flag is green and white. Praise Allah. It's from Malaqah.'

Dirar let out an enormous sigh of relief, only now becoming aware that he had been holding his breath for the last few minutes. He sheathed his sword and swaggered over to the captain. 'I told you it would be the admiral,' he said. 'I knew he wouldn't leave without Bakr.'

'Not so cocky, young man. We still don't know if they're pirates or not. It wouldn't be the first time pirates have captured a naval vessel and masqueraded as sailors just to lure a merchant ship closer. Let's wait until we're sure.'

The crew remained standing in position as they watched the naval ship approach. As the sun burst over the horizon it became clear to all of them that this was definitely one of the khalifa's ships and it appeared to be manned by the khalifa's marines.

'Right, Dirar. Get into that tub and row across to see what you can find out. Here you, go with him, just in case there's any trouble,' said Mustafa.

Trouble? What did he mean? Dirar felt his stomach tighten once more but there was no time to question the captain. One of the crew had already lowered the tub into the water and jumped in.

'Come on,' he shouted to Dirar, who was left with no option but to leap over the side and into the flat-bottomed boat.

It took only a few minutes for the rower to reach the admiral's ship and pull alongside. It was less imposing than Dirar had expected and a slight feeling of disappointment came over him. Was this the best the khalifa's navy could send?

'Ahoy there. I have someone here who wants to come aboard,' shouted the rower. 'He needs to speak to your captain.'

Dirar could feel his knees trembling. He'd never spoken to an admiral before. What was he going to say to him? He didn't even have any worthwhile news about Bakr. The admiral would think he was a complete simpleton.

'Come aboard,' shouted one of the crew and threw a rope over the side so that Dirar could clamber onto the deck.

Two men stood waiting and watching Dirar as he scrambled aboard; one was obviously the captain and the other, dressed in a fine white djubbah edged with gold over green pantaloons, had to be the admiral. His beard was white and neatly trimmed and, as might be expected for a sea-faring man, his face was deeply tanned from the ravages of the sun and wind. Although the lines on his face said that he was now past middle-age, he still stood tall and erect, an imposing figure.

'Well lad, what is it you want?' asked the captain, his right hand resting lightly on the sword in his belt.

'As-salama alaykum, Captain. Actually it's Admiral al-Maraghi I'd like to speak to,' said Dirar boldly looking at the admiral.

'Indeed. Well speak up,' said the admiral.

'I am the son of Makoud, the apothecary who came to speak to you, sayyad, about my brother-in-law. Bakr the shipbuilder.'

'Are you? Well I hope you have some good news for me, because I am tired of searching for your bloody relative. You would think the khalifa's navy had better things to do than search for kidnapped shipbuilders, wouldn't you. So spit it out. What do you want?' asked the admiral.

'We have found out that the pirates have left Dragonera,' said Dirar.

'Is that all? Have you come all this way to tell me that? That's old news, lad,' he said. 'Who's that with you?' He nodded in the direction of Mustafa's ship. 'What's a merchant ship doing in pirate waters? Either he's insane or this is some sort of a trick.'

'It's no trick, admiral, I assure you,' said Dirar, looking anxiously at the captain, who had unsheathed his sword. 'Captain Mustafa took a lot of persuading but he's taking me to Dragonera to see if the kidnapped men are there.'

'Well, you're wasting your time. There's no-one on that island. It's deserted. But I can tell you that they were there, that at least is true. The pirates are planning to increase their fleet. We found evidence to prove it.'

'So where are they now?' asked Dirar.

Admiral al-Maraghi stared at him for a while and then said, 'So you're Makoud's son are you? Are you an apothecary too?'

'No, sayyad. I'm a fisherman by trade.'

'I see you take after your father. Is everyone in your family as outspoken?'

'My apologies, Admiral. I did not mean to be rude. I'm just concerned about my brother-in-law.'

'I can see that. But what do you hope to achieve young man? There is little that can be done now.'

'Can't we search the other islands? They wouldn't have taken them far. I've heard that they've been using these islands for years. It wouldn't make sense to suddenly move to somewhere miles away,' said Dirar.

'We have no jurisdiction here. The sultan has given us permission to patrol these waters but not to land anywhere; I can't go against those orders. The khalifa would have my head if I caused an international incident over a few shipbuilders.'

'But I could go?' said Dirar. 'Let me go with you and I'll swim ashore and search the islands. As I said I'm just a fisherman. If I get caught I can say my fishing boat was wrecked and I managed to make my way to land.' He grinned at the admiral. 'But don't worry. I won't get caught.'

For a while Admiral al-Maraghi said nothing. He stood there stroking his white beard and staring at the horizon. The sun glinted on the large emerald set in the handle of his scimitar. What was he thinking? It was impossible to tell from his expression. Had Dirar overstepped the mark?

'Captain. A moment,' the admiral said at last and motioned for the captain to follow him.

Dirar could see them talking and from time to time they looked across in his direction. Did they still think this could be a trap? His initial exhilaration was dying down and all he could feel now was nervousness. Had he said too much? His mother was always telling him he talked too much. Had his boldness offended the admiral?

At last the men returned. 'Very well, fisherman. We will sail as close as we can to the beach and that man who's with you will row you ashore. But if you get into any trouble, we won't be able to help you. Is that understood?' said the admiral.

'Yes, sayyad. But can you send some men to protect the merchant ship? Captain Mustafa won't wait for me otherwise.'

'Captain?'

'Yes, Admiral, I'll see to that,' said the captain.

'Right, then we will get going. The sooner we check these islands the sooner we can set sail for Malaqah.'

*

Dirar watched the merchant ship sail back towards the port of Medina Mayurqa, with six marines on board; he hoped that Captain Mustafa would still be there when he returned. If he did return. All he could think about now was that this was probably the last opportunity to find Bakr. If he and the others were not somewhere on these islands then they would never find them. He would have to go home and tell his sister that all was lost. He couldn't bear the thought of that; he'd always been very fond of his sister.

Suddenly, to Dirar's surprise, the captain began to steer the ship away from Dragonera and the mainland, and head back towards Mayurqa.

'What's happening, Admiral?' he asked. 'I thought we were going to search the island.'

'Come here, lad. I need to tell you all that we have discovered. First of all, there is no-one on Dragonera. My men searched the island thoroughly—but do not repeat that to anyone. The pirates have left. Secondly there are dozens of islands in this archipelago; you can't search them all.'

'But I can. At least let me try,' Dirar cried.

'Calm down, lad and listen to me. We are going to try Mayurqa first.'

'But the pirates won't go there. I know. Everyone says that the pirates never go to Mayurqa. That's part of their agreement with the governor,' Dirar interrupted again.

'If you don't keep quiet and listen to me, I shall have you thrown into the hold until you calm down. Is that understood?'

'Yes, Admiral.'

'If your brother-in-law is as clever as everyone says he is, then it's possible he has found a way of escaping from the pirates.'

Dirar was about to tell him about the reward but thought better of it. He didn't want the admiral to carry out his threat.

'When we were sailing back from Dragonera a few days ago, one of the crew saw some smoke. Unfortunately he didn't think anything of it, and didn't mention it until much later. Apparently it was coming from a small cove on the opposite side of Mayurqa, facing the mainland and out of sight of the town of Medina Mayurqa. I believe it's worth investigating before we do anything else,' continued the admiral. 'Of course, the sailor might be right, and it's nothing to do with the shipbuilders.'

'So…?' Dirar hesitated.

'Yes, what is it?'

'So you think they might be on the island of Mayurqa? You think it was a signal?'

'I'm just saying that it's worth checking out. I don't believe in jumping to conclusions,' he said, scowling at Dirar.

'May I speak?' Dirar asked.

'Go ahead.'

'When I was in the port I overheard some men talking about a stranger, a young, fair-haired man who was buying medicine from the apothecary. Bakr's apprentice fits that description.'

'Maybe he does, but that doesn't mean anything. Medina Mayurqa is a busy port; the place is always full of strangers.'

'But I also heard one of them say that the pirates are offering a reward for three men, one who is supposed to have run off with his wife.'

'Is that so?' The admiral tugged at his beard. 'Doesn't mean it's our men though. Can't see them complicating their lives by taking one of the pirates' women. Can you? Is that something your brother-in-law would do?'

Dirar shook his head. No it definitely wasn't something Bakr would do.

'So what if they're not on Mayurqa?' he asked.

'Then we look elsewhere.'

'Yes, Admiral.'

'You can take two marines with you for protection. However if you find that there are pirates on the island, don't try to rescue the prisoners on your own. Come back to the ship and we will plan how to make our attack. I don't want any harm coming to them, or you for that matter. That's an order. Is that clear?'

'Yes, Admiral,' said Dirar. His heart was pounding with excitement.

CHAPTER 30

They were all exhausted. Bakr had been driving them hard to get the ship finished. They'd had to abandon the fire because it was using up too much of their valuable wood, and he had given up any possibility of someone coming to rescue them. Ever. It was a lovely idea that a ship might sail over the horizon and release them from their torment but it wasn't going to happen. It was the sort of thing that only happened in romantic stories; the kind that his sisters liked to listen to. In his heart he knew that. Bakr had always been someone who relied on his own resources; he wasn't going to let that change now.

'Sayyad, the oars are finished,' said Kamil.

The boy's hands were chafed and bleeding from the hours he'd spent planing the oars to a smooth finish. If only they had brought more tools with them. He thought of the bag of tools he'd left behind with the pirates; how useful they would be now.

'Well done, Kamil. We need to create a mast for the sails. See if you can get that useless old man to help you with rigging up some kind of sail. Use that bit of sailcloth we brought with us.'

'It's not very big, sayyad.'

'I know, but it's all we've got. Do the best you can.'

'Sayyad, sayyad. Come and look at this,' called Asim. His health was improving but he still wasn't able to do much heavy work, so Bakr had him spend most of his time as a lookout and guarding Wassil.

'What is it?'

'There's that ship again. Or one like it. It seems to be anchored off shore. What do you make of it?'

Bakr looked to where Asim was pointing. It certainly looked like the same ship, but it was too far away to identify.

'Pirates?' asked Asim.

'Maybe. We'd better take cover just in case. Tell Mayy, and take Wassil into the cave with you. And keep him quiet. I'll let Kamil know.'

'I've got the sailcloth,' said Kamil as Bakr approached. 'I think I can do something with it.'

'Into the cave, quickly. There's a ship.'

'Shouldn't we be waving at it? Letting them know we're here?'

'I'm not so sure. We don't know who they are. It could be the pirates,' said Bakr. 'We'll hide and see what happens. Don't leave anything out in the open. And hurry.'

It didn't take them long to remove all their possessions from the beach and take cover in the cave. Anyone landing on the beach would think the place was deserted. Kamil brushed their footprints carefully with a branch from one of the palm trees which he kept ready for that purpose, and backed into the cave. All they had to do now was sit tight and wait to see who they were.

'I still think we should let them know we're here,' whispered Kamil.

'No. It could be someone looking for Mayy,' said Asim.

'Anyway, do you really think they're going to send a ship all this way to look for us?' asked Bakr. 'We're not that important. There are plenty of other shipbuilders. Why go to all that bother for three men?'

'My father wouldn't send a ship to look for me,' said Mayy. 'He's far too mean to do that.'

'Maybe they're looking for you, Wassil?' said Kamil, with a laugh. 'Who have you upset?'

'Hush. I can hear voices,' whispered Bakr. The sound of men talking floated in through the narrow entrance of the cave. He picked up his cudgel and, indicating for them all to move back further into the gloom, he crept outside, closely followed by Asim.

The ship hadn't come any closer to the shore, but a rowing boat was now heading for the beach. Bakr could make out three men, two of them rowing and the other sitting in the bow, staring ahead of him.

'Who are they?' whispered Asim. 'Could it be the pirates?'

'I don't know. We'll have to wait until they get closer; from this distance they could be anyone.'

Bakr pulled his gaze away from the approaching boat and looked at the beach. Had they left anything out in the open? Anything to give their presence away? His heart sank; there was the piece of sail that they'd been about to stitch.

Asim saw it at the same time and started to edge forward, 'I'll get it, sayyad.'

'No, leave it. You'll never get there in time.'

'But I can see footprints too. They will know straight away that someone is here.'

Before Bakr could protest, his foreman had run over to the sailcloth and grabbed it. He bent double and backed away as quickly as he could, wiping his prints from the sand, but instead of backing towards the cave, he took the shorter distance and made for the trees on the opposite site of the beach.

'What the hell are you doing, Asim?' Bakr muttered.

Asim dived under cover of the trees just as the rowing boat veered off and disappeared behind the rocks; the men were heading for the adjacent cove. What should they do? Take their chances and stay hidden in the cave, and hope the men didn't find them, or climb up the path and hide in the woods until they knew who they were?

He could see a movement in the trees; Asim was trying to make his way back to the cave.

'They've gone to the other cove, sayyad,' he gasped, as he joined him. 'Do you know who they are yet?'

Bakr shook his head. Asim was struggling to breathe. He would never be able to get to the top of the path before the men returned. And then there was Wassil; could he be trusted to keep quiet? There was nothing for it, they would have to stay in the cave.

'Let's get back to the others,' he said. 'Here, tie that scarf over Wassil's mouth. I don't want him suddenly calling out to his friends.'

'Don't have any friends,' Wassil muttered.

*

Dirar jumped out of the boat as soon as the men beached the boat. It didn't take them long to realise that there was nobody there and never had been; there was no sign of any fire or anything else that suggested that anyone had lived there. The rocky inlet was surrounded by steep limestone cliffs that offered no way of venturing inland.

'This is no good,' Dirar said to his companions. 'Let's move on to the next one.'

They clambered back into the boat and rowed around the headland into what seemed to be a much more hospitable cove. Its golden beach was surrounded by palm trees and stone pines that provided shade and led up to what looked like a dense forest above. Dirar could see a small stream cascading down the steep hillside and into the sea.

'This looks a more likely place,' he said. 'Let's try this one.'

The rower took them in close but there was no sign of any movement on the island.

'There's no-one here,' said one of the marines. 'It's deserted.'

One by one they jumped out of the boat and pulled it up onto the beach.

'What are we looking for?' asked the marine.

'Signs of a bonfire. Or anything that says that someone has been here recently,' said Dirar. 'Spread out and try to cover the whole beach. If there's nothing here, we'll move further down the coast.'

It was a sheltered spot, completely out of sight of Dragonera and the farthest end of the island from the port. Dirar could see the admiral's ship anchored off the island and, behind it, a hazy outline which he knew was the mainland.

'Maybe they're hiding up there, in the woods,' said one of the marines. 'That's good cover. That's what I would do if I didn't want to be found.'

'Over here,' shouted the other marine. 'Someone's had a fire here. They've tried to cover it up but the tide has washed away some of the sand. Look.' He pulled out a charred piece of timber and held it up for them to see.

Dirar raced across to where the marine was squatting on the beach. He was right. There was no doubt that someone had built a fire here, and quite recently. A big fire. The question was, had it been the pirates or Bakr? And where were they now?

*

They huddled together in the cave, hardly daring to breathe. The tension was making them all nervous. Who was out there? And were they looking for them? Was it someone who'd come to rescue them? Bakr doubted it; it was more likely pirates sent by Captain al-Awar to find them and take them back. The captain wasn't going to forgive Bakr for making a fool of him; of that much he was certain. Ever since he'd heard about the reward he'd expected someone to come looking for them. It was a lot of money; many men would be tempted by it.

At first the voices were indistinguishable from the screeches of the seagulls and the lapping of the waves on the shore, then gradually he could make out not just sounds but words. Was that his name?

'Bakr. Bakr,' he heard someone calling. 'Are you here, Bakr?'

He placed his finger on his lip. There was not a sound in the cave; you couldn't hear a single breath. Even Kamil was quiet.

'Bakr.'

'Bakr,' a different voice had joined in. Then another one. 'Bakr where are you?'

Still he didn't move.

'Bakr, Aisha is waiting for you. Bakr. Are you here?'

'What did he say?' asked Asim. 'Did he say Aisha?'

Bakr's heart began to race. The pirates didn't know anything about Aisha, certainly not her name. Had someone actually come to rescue them? He couldn't believe it.

'Wait here. I'll go and see who it is. Don't move until I call for you. All right?' he said, gripping the cudgel tightly and edging his way closer to the entrance to the cave.

'Bakr. Aisha is waiting for you,' the voice said again. It sounded familiar. Who was there? Was that Dirar's voice? Impossible.

He bent down and crawled out into the open, blinking in the bright sunlight and stopped in astonishment. He couldn't believe his eyes. There, standing in the middle of the beach, was his brother-in-law, Dirar. It was incredible. Somehow Dirar had come all that way and found them. They were going home. He would see his beloved Aisha again.

CHAPTER 31

It was dusk by the time they arrived at the gates of the alcazaba. Hasan felt a surge of emotion as they trotted up the ramp towards the main entrance; he was home at last. He stopped by the guard at the Boveda Gate, reining in his horse and dismounting.

'Prince Hasan. As-salama alaykum and welcome to Malaqah. Have you come for the coronation?' the guard asked, bowing politely to the young prince.

Hasan recognised him immediately; he had been a palace guard, and one of his duties had been to keep an eye on the young princes when they lived in the alcázar.

'Wa alaykum e-salam, soldier. Yes indeed. This is my tutor, Naja al-Siqlabi. You may remember him?'

'Yes, Your Highness, I do. And are these all the men you have with you?'

'Yes. There didn't seem any reason to bring more. I merely wish to speak to my cousin and give him my congratulations.' He looked around him. 'It is good to be back in Malaqah again.'

'Please enter. I will send someone to take you to the khalifa, so that you may proceed unhindered,' said the guard, indicating to the young soldier next to him that he should accompany Hasan and his party.

It all seemed unreal, but it wasn't without trepidation that Hasan made his way into the fortress that surrounded the royal palace. His conversation with his cousin

Muhammad had surprised him but now that he'd had time to think about it, his cousin's proposal made perfect sense. The sultan of al-Jazira understood that his brother would never be able to hold onto the wealthy taifa of Malaqah, and that whoever deposed him would sooner or later turn his attention to al-Jazira; he didn't want to take that risk. Fortunately for Hasan, his cousins had already discussed the dangers that faced Yahya and agreed to make a deal with him. Now there was no need to involve the Barghawata, a strategy which would carry its own dangers for Hasan and probably Muhammad too.

They walked their horses up the cobbled paths, through various arches and into the inner citadel. Hasan remembered running through the arches as a boy when he and his brother played at soldiers; how long ago that seemed now. A cold breeze was blowing from the sea and Hasan pulled his djellaba closer around his shoulders.

'One moment,' Hasan said to the guard who was accompanying them. 'I must speak to my servant before we go any further.'

He beckoned to Naja and whispered, 'You know what to do. I will talk to my cousin now and in the morning I expect to hear from you that all has been accomplished as we agreed. Then you must return to Sebta to look after my mother and my brother. Is that understood?'

'Yes, Your Highness. But wouldn't I be more useful here, with you?'

'No. I want you in Sebta; if anything goes wrong with our plan, you will be safer there. Besides, I want you to keep an eye on my brother.'

'Very well, Your Highness. But what about the Barghawata?'

'If Muhammad is right about his brother, then we won't need to ask for their help. I don't trust them anyway.'

'I agree, Your Highness.'

'Razi and two of the soldiers will come with me. You take the rest of the men and the horses and see that they are all fed and watered. If all goes well, then you can take them back to Sebta with you. I will send for you later. But remember what I have asked you to do. I am relying on you.'

'Thank you, Your Highness,' said Naja and bowed.

Hasan waited until his former tutor and the handful of soldiers had headed for the stables. For a moment he felt naked without his personal guard around him, and his hand went subconsciously to his sword. Now was the time to meet his cousin. He wondered if the boy had changed much in the last four years.

*

His cousin, Yahya, had, as promised, made no resistance when Hasan told him that he had come to claim his inheritance. It was exactly as Muhammad had described; the lad was grateful to be relieved of the responsibility.

'We must inform the grand vizier and the council of ministers,' Yahya said. 'Ibn Baqanna has been making plans for my coronation. He will need to know that things have changed.'

He seemed to believe that there would be no opposition from any of his minsters, not even the grand vizier. Hasan smiled to himself; Muhammad had been right, Yahya would not have lasted six months on the throne before someone would have ousted him. And probably killed him.

He made his way to the throne room. A meeting had been arranged with all the viziers and the acting Supreme

Commander, General Rashad. The only men he had to worry about were ibn Baqanna and Rashad. If Naja had done as he promised then ibn Baqanna would be no trouble, but what of the general? Hasan remembered him as a grizzly warrior who was always by his father's side. Would he support Hasan's claim to the throne or had his allegiance changed? Well he would know soon enough.

Most of the council of ministers were already in the throne room when Hasan arrived. His cousin was standing, talking to one of the viziers and turned at once to welcome him. The throne was empty and there was no sign of ibn Baqanna or General Rashad.

'Welcome, dear cousin,' said Yahya I. 'We are just waiting for a few more to arrive and then we will tell them the news.'

Hasan bowed respectfully and stood beside him. His eyes kept returning to the empty throne. Soon that would be his.

The viziers were puzzled at Yahya's behaviour and began to whisper among themselves. Something was not right. Why was the khalifa not sitting on his throne as usual? What news did he have to impart? And where was ibn Baqanna?

The heavy double doors swung open and General Rashad marched in, followed by two of the palace guards.

'My apologies, Your Majesty. I have been looking for your grand vizier. It seems that nobody has seen him since last night. Not his servants, nor his wives and family. Everyone thought he was in the Dar al Wuzara but when I went there they said there had been no sign of him since yesterday. I'm sorry, Your Majesty, I thought I had better let you know. My men are still looking for him,' he added.

'Thank you, General Rashad. We will investigate the whereabouts of our grand vizier later, now I have some news for you all,' said Yahya I. He stretched out his hand and touched Hasan lightly on the shoulder. 'You may remember my cousin, Hasan ibn Yahya ibn Ali. He has grown a lot since he was last in our beautiful city. And that is why he is here. He is now a man. And as the rightful heir to the throne of Malaqah he has come to claim his inheritance.'

A gasp echoed around the room. If anyone had guessed what was about to happen, they had kept it well hidden.

'My father, Khalifa Idris I, always intended that his nephew Hasan should one day take up his birthright. He even drew up a document to that effect some days before he left for Écija.' Yahya held up the document that Hasan had given him and waited for his ministers to stop muttering to each other. 'My father was a shrewd man. He made two copies of the document, in which he clearly states that in the event of his death, his nephew, Hasan ibn Yahya ibn Ali, would succeed him. One copy he left with his grand vizier, ibn Baqanna and the other he sent to my brother, Muhammad.'

'But why have we never seen this document before?' asked one of the viziers.

'That is a good question. Why have I, the acting khalifa of Malaqah, not seen it? Because the copy given to ibn Baqanna was destroyed. And I can only assume that it was ibn Baqanna who destroyed it, as he was one of only three people who knew of its existence.'

'Where is he?' asked another vizier.

'Yes. He must explain himself. Where is he?'

'I would guess that if our previous grand vizier has heard of the arrival of my cousin Hasan, then he has left the city,' said Yahya.

'We must find him and deal with this,' shouted an irate minister. 'He destroyed vital information. This could have led to war.'

'Yes, we must find him. He must answer for his behaviour,' said another.

'Indeed he must. As you say this situation could have ended badly, my friend. However, thanks to the common sense of both my brother and my cousin, we have come to an amicable solution, with no need for bloodshed.' Yahya I stopped and surveyed his ministers. 'Tomorrow, the coronation will still take place but it will be Hasan ibn Yahya ibn Ali who will be crowned khalifa of Malaqah, not I. I am going to abdicate in favour of the true heir to the throne. And after the coronation, my family and I will join my brother in al-Jazira for a while.'

The babble of chatter from the ministers sounded like the souk on its busiest day; everyone was stunned at the news, as Hasan knew they would be. But no-one questioned it and no-one was in disagreement, or if they were, then they kept it to themselves. Even General Rashad had nothing to say against it.

Yahya led Hasan to the throne so that he could sit and accept the homage of his minsters. And the first to bow before him was his own cousin. After that, it was easy, everyone took it in turn to bow before the second new khalifa that they'd had in as many months.

Already he could feel his heart racing with excitement. Tomorrow he would be officially crowned Khalifa of Malaqah. This was what his father wanted for him, wealth, power and position, but it didn't come without its dangers. Of this he was well aware. Ben Yahya, for example, would he be happy to remain in the shadow of his older brother? Or would a time come when he'd want more for himself?

CHAPTER 32

The khalifa of Malaqah, Hasan ibn Yahya ibn Ali al-Mustansir, wandered through the Patio de los Naranjos, his new grand vizier and General Rashad trailing behind him. Six weeks had passed since he had left Sebta and become the new ruler. It had all gone as planned, even the people of Malaqah—many of whom remembered his father and the suspicious circumstances of his death— had welcomed him as their khalifa. To consolidate his position he had immediately taken a wife, the sister of his cousin Yahya.

'Your Majesty, we need to discuss the continuing threat from Isbiliya,' General Rashad said, tentatively.

Hasan stopped and turned to look at his most experienced general. 'Has my brother arrived yet?' he asked.

'His ship has just moored in the harbour, Your Majesty,' the grand vizier interrupted. 'I have sent some of the Palace Guard to escort him here, to the alcázar.'

'Indeed. And did I ask you to do that?'

'Well, no, Your Majesty. But I thought you would like him to be greeted in an appropriate fashion and brought straight here to the royal palace. He is your brother, after all. And a prince.'

'Exactly.' Hasan turned to the general once again. 'Send a troop of your best men to the ship at once and arrest my brother. Take him straight to the dungeons on the north wall of the alcazaba.'

'Your Majesty?' the grand vizier looked lost for words. 'Is that wise? What will people think? Your own brother.'

'It is extremely wise, Labib. You do not know my little brother. I do. Already he is dreaming of sitting on my throne. That I cannot have. For all we know he may already have the backing of the Barghawata; we cannot risk it. The country needs peace and stability and I intend to see that it has it. Now do as I say, General Rashad.'

'As you command, Your Majesty.'

The general hurriedly left the throne room, calling for some of the palace guards to accompany him. He and his men had never found ibn Baqanna; the man had disappeared off the face of the earth as if he'd never existed. Naja had kept his word when he swore to get rid of him. But still Hasan didn't feel safe. Now that he was the khalifa, the world looked a different place; there was danger around every corner, betrayal and treason, plot and counter-plot. He heard hidden meanings in every word, threats in every action. It was impossible to sleep easy at night. There was his brother, for example; until Hasan had any sons, he was next in line for the throne. For all his easy-going ways, Ben Yahya lusted for power as much as anyone else. Well Hasan would make sure that he didn't get the opportunity to take it from him.

'And make haste. That brother of mine is a slippery as an eel,' he added.

*

As the ship entered the harbour, the dolphins turned and swam away, their smooth grey bodies glistening as they jumped through the waves. Ben Yahya strained his eyes to see if his brother was among the crowd of people waiting on the quayside, but all he could make out were a few fishermen selling their catch and some merchants disembarking from their ship, closely followed by a train of slaves weighed down with heavy sacks and rolled up carpets, which they proceeded to load onto the backs of some waiting camels. The rest was a sea of colourful but indistinguishable faces.

'I don't see your brother,' said Naja, pointing to a group of soldiers who were pushing their way through the crowd towards the harbour's edge.

'No. I don't see him, either.' His brother was tall with a thick black beard, not easy to miss. 'Perhaps he's too busy to meet me, himself.' Ben Yahya felt disappointed.

The ship edged closer and closer to the land until one of the crewmen was able to jump onto the quay and make it fast. They had arrived. He was in Malaqah. A thrill of excitement ran through him. But where was Hasan? Surely his brother would come to greet him.

'Well, it looks as though he's sent his soldiers to escort you to the palace,' said Naja, looking perplexed.

'Why couldn't he come himself?' grumbled Ben Yahya. He'd been looking forward to walking into the alcazaba by the side of the khalifa himself. Maybe it was much more formal here than in Sebta. Perhaps it wasn't how the khalifa should behave. He was probably waiting for him in the throne room, wanting to impress him. The prince walked slowly down the gangplank to meet the palace guards who were lined up, patiently waiting to greet him.

'As-salama alaykum, Sayyad. Are you Prince Idris ibn Yahya ibn Ali?' one of the soldiers asked. He wore the insignia of a quaid and was clearly in charge.

'Wa alaykum e-salam, soldier. Yes, I am Idris ibn Yahya ibn Ali, brother of the khalifa.'

'Your brother sends you greetings, Sayyad, and says you are to come with us,' the quaid said, standing aside to let Ben Yahya walk ahead. 'I am to escort you to the alcazaba.'

'My brother?'

'He will see you presently, Sayyad. He is occupied with matters of state.'

'You are to address Prince Idris as Your Highness,' Naja rebuked the quaid. 'He is, after all, the khalifa's brother and heir to the throne.'

The quaid smirked and turning to Ben Yahya said, 'My apologies, Your Highness.'

'No matter. Naja, make sure my luggage and my servants are taken to the alcazaba and I will see you there, later.'

'Very well, Your Highness.'

'Did you have a calm crossing?' the quaid asked, politely. 'There had been talk of storms today.'

'It was uneventful,' Ben Yahya replied, frowning. Something was not quite right. Was this how things were done in Malaqah? Was a soldier allowed to speak to a prince in such a casual way? In Sebta, nobody spoke to him unless he gave them permission, except Naja. His tutor took advantage of his position occasionally, but even he was wary of the prince. He knew when he could speak out and when to hold his tongue.

The quaid led Ben Yahya away from the quayside, past the fisherman selling their catch and the merchants directing their servants where to take their goods, past the men labouring in the ship yards, under a magnificent tiled arch and through the Puerta del Mar into the walled city. People were heading for the fish market—its smell was strong and pungent in the rising heat of the morning— and beyond the market he could make out the dome of a mosque. He was home again. A thrill of excitement ran down his spine. Life was going to change now that Hasan was Khalifa.

'This way, Your Highness,' said the quaid, turning right along a narrow cobbled street lined with small shops. They passed women sitting in doorways weaving baskets and mats, past salt factories; they took a sharp left to avoid the rancid smell from the abattoir and then carried on past the Customs House until they arrived at the entrance to the alcazaba, a fortified tower, flanked by thick stone walls.

Despite his initial delight at being back in his home town, Ben Yahya was feeling more and more irritated with his reception. This wasn't a royal welcome; it was almost as if he were being arrested, marched through the streets like a common criminal. He wished that Naja was there, and some of his own men. Instead of feeling safe with the palace guards, he began to feel threatened by their attitude but he had no option but to continue following the quaid as he led him into the tower and out onto a wide cobbled incline on the other side that led to a huge horseshoe arch. It was a familiar sight and memories of childhood came flashing back.

Once through the arch, he stopped and turned to the quaid. 'Where is my brother?' he asked but the officer didn't bother to reply, just indicated that he should keep walking. Well, he'd had enough of the man's insolence; he would report his lack of respect to Hasan, as soon as he saw him.

The alcazaba was a veritable fortress. Any invader would be slowed down by the constant twists and turns in the entrance and lose any advantage of surprise. Once inside, the walls were as thick as he remembered and even taller; the towers stood, well built and strategically placed to see their enemy from a great distance. As they continued walking, through another huge gateway and all the time heading uphill, he could hear the sea slapping against the castle's walls.

'Through here,' the quaid said, rather brusquely. Ben Yahya noticed he had ceased to address him as Your Highness, not even Sayyad. What on earth was going on?

They entered an open parade ground, the Patio de Armas, and marched through the Dar al-Jund, past soldiers who leapt to attention when they saw their superior officer and busied themselves with cleaning their weapons, past the stables with the stink of horse manure and the grooms waxing saddles, past the armoury, past the soldiers' barracks and the smell of cooking and finally down a narrow passageway.

Was this the normal way to receive a royal visitor? He doubted it. Even in Sebta, visitors were treated with more respect.

'Where are you taking me?' demanded Ben Yahya, stopping and staring around him. 'I cannot believe my brother asked you to give me a tour of the alcazaba. Take me to him at once. Take me to his royal apartments. Immediately.' He could feel the danger around him and his hand slid down onto the dagger in his belt.

'You won't need that,' the quaid said and before the prince could stop him, he'd grabbed the bejewelled dagger and handed it to the guard following behind them. 'Use it, if you have to,' he told him.

'What are you doing? Give me back my dagger. Do you hear me. Give it to me at once. The khalifa shall hear of this. I promise you. You will regret the day you crossed my path. My brother will not tolerate your insolence to me. I am his brother. I am the heir to the throne.' Ben Yahya began to panic; unarmed and without his usual bodyguard, he felt vulnerable and confused.

'Fighting words, Your Highness, but the khalifa doesn't like his visitors to be armed,' the quaid said.

'Visitor. I am his brother. Don't you understand Arabic?' The quaid ignored him.

'Where is the royal residence? Take me there. My brother will be waiting for me. Do you hear me? Enough of this tomfoolery.' He pulled himself up to his full height and said, rather pompously, 'I don't think you understand who I am. I am Prince Idris ibn Yahya ibn Ali, the son of Khalifa Yahya I—may Allah protect his soul—and the brother of your new khalifa Hasan al-Mustansir.'

The quaid still said nothing and resumed walking down the passageway.

'I'm not going any further until you tell me what is happening. Where is my brother?' The prince tried to shout, but all he could muster was a squeaky whimper. He was angry and frightened and it showed in his voice.

Where was the discipline? Why was this soldier so insubordinate? He began to fear that something had happened to Hasan already. Maybe Yahya had not been deposed after all and Hasan was dead. Had it all been a trick to get him here? His mind was spinning with what was and was not.

One of the soldiers pushed him in the back. 'Move along,' he grunted.

'What is this? How dare you speak to me like that?'

The soldier just laughed and waved Ben Yahya's curved dagger under his nose. 'Keep walking unless you want this up your arse,' he said. 'Stabbed by your own weapon. That would be something.' He looked at the dagger in his hand and laughed—even in that gloomy light the precious jewels set in the handle gleamed and glittered, seeming to taunt the young prince.

Ben Yahya knew he had no alternative. They had taken so many twists and turns that he had no idea how to get out of this wretched place, even if he could escape the soldiers. He would just have to wait and see what they were going to do with him.

At last they came to a dark, dingy building that smelled of damp and something else, the unmistakable stench of death and despair. Despite the fact that they had never been allowed to enter this area when they were children, he immediately recognised it for what it was—the alcazaba's dungeons. He was to be a prisoner. But whose prisoner? His cousin's or his brother's? Or some other usurper? He began to tremble; fear was already draining the strength from his limbs.

The quaid unlocked the heavy wooden door and spoke to the gaoler. 'He is to be treated well. Make sure he has water to wash every day and I will arrange for his food to be sent from the kitchens. But no visitors. Is that clear? No visitors.'

'Clear as day. Who is he anyway? Looks a bit full of himself. Some sort of prince is he?' asked the gaoler, a man whose skin had grown grey and ashen from the hours he spent in that dark hole.

'I am Prince...' began Ben Yahya but before he could finish, the quaid had shoved him through the door, saying in a gentler voice than hitherto, 'The less you say, the longer you'll live. Remember that.'

Then the door slammed shut with a deafening bang. For a moment Ben Yahya was blinded. He was too frightened to move.

'Come on with you. It's not as bad as all that. You heard him. You'll get a good meal every day and clean water. That's more than most of them get in here. Just follow me.'

It was all a bad dream. How could this have happened to him? How had he walked into this trap so easily? He should have listened to his gut; he knew something was wrong when Hasan wasn't at the quay to meet him. He should have stayed on the ship and returned to Sebta. Now what could he do? Nobody even knew where he was. Not even Naja.

He breathed deeply, instantly regretting it as he inhaled the rank odours of the prison. He must try to keep calm. There had been a mistake. They had confused him with someone else. When Hasan found out what had happened to him, he would have that quaid's head.

'Here we are. Home sweet home,' said the gaoler, opening a door at the end of the passage. 'You have the best room in the place. Look, you even have a view and fresh air,' he said, pointing to a tiny slit in the wall high above Ben Yahya's head. 'You just make yourself at home and I'll be along later with your supper.'

The door slammed shut and instantly Ben Yahya felt the walls closing in on him. There was barely any light, only a glimmer that forced itself through the slit in the wall. Soon that would go and he'd be in complete darkness. He sat down on a sack of straw in the corner and looked about him. His cell was even smaller than the room where his servant Qusay slept. Qusay. Where was he now? And Naja? Had they been locked up too? Or worse, had they been killed and their bodies thrown in the sea? If that was the case, then he'd never get out of here. Salty tears ran down his cheeks as he contemplated his fate.

CHAPTER 33

When the ship taking Bakr and his men home to Malaqah had pulled into the harbour, he could hardly believe it was all over. Against all the odds they had escaped from the pirates and now they would be reunited with their families. Aisha. How he longed to see her again. And his children. His poor children. Having already lost their mother, they must have been terrified he would never return. But return he did, and now he stood in the prow of a ship flying the admiral's pennant, alongside Asim and Kamil, watching as the quayside grew closer and closer. His apprentice was crying, and his foreman too was trying to hold back the tears. The only person unmoved by all this was Mayy; for her this was an adventure. Bakr had promised Kamil that he would be happy to act as Mayy's guardian until they were ready to be married—because this is what Kamil had confessed the couple wanted to do. Although, if he were honest, it wasn't much of a surprise; they'd been bickering like an old married couple from day one. They were eminently suited to each other. It had certainly solved the problem of what to do with this rather headstrong young woman. He just hoped Kamil's father would be so pleased to have his son back that he would agree to their rather unconventional plans.

'There's my father,' said Kamil. 'He's come to meet us.'

He began waving at an elderly man, standing with a group of smiling people. Bakr lifted his hand to shade his eyes from the sun. Was she among them? Was Aisha there, waiting for him?

'My wife. I can see her,' shouted Asim. 'And my daughters. They're all here.'

People were crowding closer and closer to the edge of the quay, eager to see the new arrivals, but still he couldn't locate her. Everyone was happy, waving and shouting; some were crying tears of joy. It looked as though all of Malaqah had come out to welcome them home. Then he saw his father-in-law, standing there alone. Where were the others? Had something happened to his beautiful wife while he'd been away? He tried to work out how long it was since they'd been kidnapped but the months merged together in a blur of loneliness that he wanted to forget. Where was she? Oh, why hadn't they managed to escape sooner?

The ship bumped against the quay and he felt the juddering of the anchor as it was dropped into the sea. They had arrived. It was chaotic; people were desperate to welcome the rescued men, to hear their stories, to see for themselves the shipbuilders who'd escaped from the pirates. He saw Asim whisked away in a swirl of colourful skirts as his wife and four daughters enveloped him in their arms. Kamil's father was hugging his son as if his heart would break with joy, while his mother stood patiently by waiting to kiss her only son. Of his own family there was no sign. Had pirates taken them as well? Had his family been sold as slaves? Were they dead? His sisters? His mother? His children? Where were they? He had always assumed that they were safe but he had no way of really knowing. Dirar had said everything was fine at home, but was he telling the truth? Had he been trying to shield him from what had really happened? Or had something arisen since Dirar had left? Bakr's imagination was racing ahead of him. He felt the pounding of his heart beneath his djubbah. His mouth was suddenly dry as he watched Makoud push his way through the excited crowd towards him, fearful of the news he carried.

'Bakr, my son. Welcome home. Ahlan. Ahlan,' his father-in-law cried, tears running down his cheeks, as he gave him an enormous hug.

'Where is she? Where are Aisha and my children?' Bakr asked, his voice cracking with fear.

'She couldn't come. None of the women could come. You have arrived home just in time to see your new child; it is entering the world as we speak. Praise be to Allah. Aisha is convinced it's a boy. Maybe by the time we get home we will know. My, it's good to see you, Bakr. I had almost given you up for dead, but Aisha wouldn't even consider it. She knew you would come back. And to be honest, it was her and that determination of hers that made it come true.'

His father-in-law was babbling on, but all that Bakr could think about was getting home to see Aisha. Another baby. Boy or girl, he didn't care. He felt as though he were walking on air.

Only one cloud lay on the horizon; Captain al-Awar knew exactly where to find him. It wasn't over yet. The pirate was a proud and vengeful man and Bakr knew he would never give up until he had found him and taken his revenge for the humiliation they had caused him.

*

Aisha lifted the new baby out of his cot and rocked him in her arms. Happiness spread through her body like a warm oil, easing away the months of tension and fear that had held her in its grip. Now, at last, she could relax and be herself. Bakr had been so surprised, delighted in fact, to find that he had another son. His homecoming had been quite an event; his mother calling the imam to arrange special prayers of thanksgiving to Allah, and her daughters contacting all the relatives to invite them to a huge feast. Aisha, having just given birth, would have preferred to have been alone with her husband and their children, but she couldn't deny her mother-in-law the chance to demonstrate both her love for her son and her happiness at his return.

It was early but Bakr had already gone to the yard to supervise the work. How amazed he had been when he saw that she had kept the shipyard going while he was away, and as she recounted how she, her father and the men in the yard had not only completed the half-finished ship, but taken on orders for more, he had stared at her open-mouthed. Then he had taken her in his arms and hugged her. Later she overheard her mother-in-law telling Bakr that Aisha had worked night and day to hold the family together, and even admitted that her son had done the right thing in marrying her. High praise indeed from her.

'Mama, can I hold the baby?' asked Maryam.

'Yes, but take care. Put your hand behind his head to support it; he is still very fragile.'

'I know, Mama. You've had babies before. We know what to do, don't we Naila?' Her daughter turned to her half-sister and smiled. The two were such good friends now. Bakr's return had brought all the family closer together; even his sisters treated Aisha with more respect and even affection.

The baby began to cry loudly, his little wrinkled face turning red in annoyance.

'He's hungry, Mama,' said Maryam, hurriedly returning the squirming child to his mother.

'It's time you two were off to school,' Aisha said, taking the baby from her daughter and allowing him to latch his little mouth onto her breast. 'And take the boys with you.'

How peaceful it was, just the two of them. Mother and baby. She closed her eyes and leaned back on the sofa; she was going to make the most of these tranquil moments because experience told her they would not last. Soon her mother-in-law would come in and ask what should she buy in the market, and remind her for the tenth time that her brother Umar was joining them for lunch today—his recovery was remarkable but it had left him weak and unable to return to work yet. Then Rayya would come and insist that she bathe the new baby and Rudaba, who'd just had a child herself, would come to ask her advice about some trivial matter: a sore on the baby's bottom, a cough that was keeping her awake, whether she thought the child was slightly cross-eyed. Without doubt her father—who seemed to have an endless list of excuses for calling at their house—would come to see how his new grandchild was doing. This was her extended family and although she loved them all, she longed for the moment when Bakr returned home and they could be alone. Her heart which for so long had seemed unable to heal was now whole again. Her love for Daud was still there—it would always be part of her—but now it was Bakr's love that made her the woman she was.

GLOSSARY

Aleichem shalom peace be upon you (Jewish greeting)
Ahlan welcome
Ahlan wa sahlan. the reply to welcome
Alla ysalmak response to goodbye
ammu uncle
Arab mile between 1.8 and 2 kilometres
As-salama alaykum hello
Baba father
Calendula used as a disinfectant
Churros a sweet fried batter
Dar al-Jund soldiers' quarters
Dar al Wuzara house of the viziers
dirhams silver units of currency
dinars gold units of currency
Djubbah a simple tunic
Djellaba a hooded cloak
Hama mother-in-law
Hammudid dynasty rulers in al-Andalus 1016 - 1056 AD
Iddah period of mourning: four months and ten days
Imam holy man
insha'Allah God willing
Jinete horseman
Ma'a salama goodbye
Medina a town
Mojama dried tuna
Muhtasib officer in charge of municipal police
nazir sergeant in charge of a squad of 16 men
Omayyads the rulers of al-Andalus 970 AD - 1031 AD
Qarib a wooden ship, strong enough to go out into the ocean but also close inland

Quaid officer in charge of a corps of 10,000 men
Quran the central religious holy book of Islam
Puerta   gate
Saqaliba a slave from northern and eastern Europe
Sayyad master or sir
Sayeda madam
Sayyida queen, queen mother or mistress
Sayyida al-Malika, mother of the khalifa
Shatrang check-board banner
Souk market
Taifa an independent Muslim-ruled principality
Teta nickname for grandmother
Tisbah ala-kheir goodnight
Wa alaykum e-salam Peace be upon you
Zenana the innermost apartments where the women in the
harem live

* 9 7 8 8 4 0 9 1 2 4 5 0 3 *